The
WAR OF THE WORLDS MURDER

Max Allan Collins

BERKLEY PRIME CRIME, NEW YORK

THE BERKLEY PUBLISHING GROUP
Published by the Penguin Group
Penguin Group (USA) Inc.
375 Hudson Street, New York, New York 10014, USA
Penguin Group (Canada), 10 Alcorn Avenue, Toronto, Ontario M4V 3B2, Canada
(a division of Pearson Penguin Canada Inc.)
Penguin Books Ltd., 80 Strand, London WC2R 0RL, England
Penguin Group Ireland, 25 St. Stephen's Green, Dublin 2, Ireland (a division of Penguin Books Ltd.)
Penguin Group (Australia), 250 Camberwell Road, Camberwell, Victoria 3124, Australia
(a division of Pearson Australia Group Pty. Ltd.)
Penguin Books India Pvt. Ltd., 11 Community Centre, Panchsheel Park, New Delhi—110 017, India
Penguin Group (NZ), Cnr. Airborne and Rosedale Roads, Albany, Auckland 1310, New Zealand
(a division of Pearson New Zealand Ltd.)
Penguin Books (South Africa) (Pty.) Ltd., 24 Sturdee Avenue, Rosebank, Johannesburg 2196, South
Africa

Penguin Books Ltd., Registered Offices: 80 Strand, London WC2R 0RL, England

This is a work of fiction. Names, characters, places, and incidents either are the product of the author's
imagination or are used fictitiously, and any resemblance to actual persons, living or dead, business
establishments, events, or locales is entirely coincidental. The publisher does not have any control over
and does not assume any responsibility for author or third-party websites or their content.

THE WAR OF THE WORLDS MURDER

A Berkley Prime Crime Book / published by arrangement with the author

PRINTING HISTORY
Berkley Prime Crime mass-market edition / July 2005

Copyright © 2005 by Max Allan Collins.
Cover design by Steven Ferlauto.
Cover art by Ben Perini.

ISBN: 0-425-20401-4

BERKLEY® PRIME CRIME
Berkley Prime Crime Books are published by The Berkley Publishing Group,
a division of Penguin Group (USA) Inc.,
375 Hudson Street, New York, New York 10014.
The name BERKLEY PRIME CRIME and the BERKLEY PRIME CRIME design are trademarks
belonging to Penguin Group (USA) Inc.

PRINTED IN THE UNITED STATES OF AMERICA

10 9 8 7 6 5 4 3 2 1

For Leonard Maltin—
my brother
in twentieth-century pop culture

Though this is a work of fiction, an underpinning of history supports the events depicted in these pages. Still, the reader is cautioned to keep in mind what Orson Welles said in his 1973 film *F for Fake*: "Any story is almost some kind of lie." In any case, the author intends no disrespect for the real people who were caught up in the so-called "Panic Broadcast" of 1938.

•

You don't play murder in soft words.

—Orson Welles,
press conference after
"The War of the Worlds" broadcast

It is my intention to introduce legislation
against such Hallowe'en bogeymen.

—Iowa State Senator Clyde Herring

Everything seemed unimportant in the face of death.

—A radio listener,
the day after the broadcast

Prologue

A Hallowe'en Shadow Play

Suddenly 1975 seems like a long time ago.

Not as long ago as 1938—when the bulk of this story takes place (and long before I was born)—but nonetheless distant, right out on the edges of my memory.

I graduated MFA from the Writers Workshop in Iowa City in 1972, right after selling my first mystery novel, and promptly took a job teaching Freshman English at the small-town community college where I'd been attending a few years before. I was just a kid, really, though I'd been married since 1968.

By '75 I'd already sold half a dozen mystery novels. But only two of them had been published when I decided to attend my first Bouchercon, which was in Chicago, a city my wife Barb and I both felt comfortable in.

My childhood sweetheart and I had honeymooned for a week in Chicago, going to movies, dining in wonderful restaurants, checking out the sights, as well as the usual things newlyweds do . . . plus some they don't, specifically risking my bride's life during those turbulent times by having her help me chase down old used paperbacks I needed for my mystery collection, in some of the roughest parts of town. Toward the end of that week, Robert Kennedy was assassinated—we were RFK supporters and anti-Vietnam War—and the event . . . in the context of celebrating our marriage . . . brought home just how fragile happiness can be. On the other hand, we're still together.

On this return visit to Chicago, Barb did not attend the convention: she shopped at Marshall Field's and along Michigan Avenue, though in those days it was mostly window-shopping. I, for the first time, mingled with mystery fans and my fellow writers, awkwardly straddling the two factions. That it was the weekend before Hallowe'en seemed appropriate for such benignly criminal doings, and Chicago was its chilly windy city self, the Palmer House hotel in the El's shadow (the Wabash-side entrance, anyway); I felt almost like a grown-up.

My generation of mystery writers was perhaps the first to emerge largely from "fandom"—we had not only read the fiction of our writer-heroes, we had written and published "fanzines" celebrating that fiction and those creators, much like the world of comics, where I was also a fan (but not yet a writer).

Had I not already attended two or three comic book conventions, I would have been much more intimidated at Bouchercon Six, with its bustling dealers' room that seemed so large (though by today's convention standards was minuscule) and its panel discussions bracketed by informal conversations (in hallways and bars and dealers'-room aisles) between strangers with mutual interests. Many of us were what is now called geeks and even then were known as nerds—lonely oddballs pleased to encounter their own kind.

Patterned after similar events that had grown up in science fiction, the Bouchercon—named after celebrated *New York Times* critic/mystery-author Anthony Boucher—is the World

Mystery Convention. Fans, authors, editors, literary agents, publicists and of course booksellers attend these fan-run gatherings, and as I write this in the early twenty-first century, the events—held in cities from London to New York, from Toronto to San Francisco—are attended by thousands, unlike the hundred or so who came to Chicago in 1975.

I was a barely published author—two paperback-original novels, *Bait Money* and *Blood Money,* had seen print—and certainly not a "name" fan, that is, a fan who'd published a fanzine. I'd contributed a few articles to such self-published publications, mostly defending and celebrating my favorite mystery writer, Mickey Spillane; but mine was definitely not a name that would resonate with the average attendee of Bouchercon Six.

I prowled the dealers' room, wearing a name badge of course, and before long, a small miracle happened. A dark-haired, mustached kid stood grinning at me, his eyes large behind horn-rim glasses; he wore a light-blue dress shirt with the sleeves rolled up, and chinos, and seemed to be only mildly insane.

"You're *Max Collins!*" he said.

I frowned. "That's right . . ."

I checked the name badge of this guy: *Robert J. Randisi.* His home was identified as "Brooklyn," a legendary city known only vaguely to Iowans such as myself.

"I can't believe it!" this Randisi creature blurted.

Did I owe him money? I sometimes bought comic books and old paperbacks through the mail. Maybe he was a dealer I'd shorted on the purchase of Jim Thompson or Richard Stark paperbacks. He seemed harmless enough, if over-enthusiastic—of medium size, solidly put together, but not a threat.

"*You* wrote the *Nolan* books!" he said, pointing a pleasantly accusing finger.

Nolan was the thief anti-hero of my two published novels.

"Right," I said, waiting for a shoe to drop.

"Those are *great*! I love those books!"

My eyes tightened. "Really?"

He reared back and laughed, once. "Why? Don't you believe me?"

"Well . . . it's just that I never met anybody before who's read my books . . . at least, that I wasn't related to."

"Well, I'm a fan. Big fan."

This was a first for me; and a moment I'll never forget.

"Muscatine, Iowa," he said, reading my name badge further. "Is that 'Port City'?"

Port City was the fictionalized version of my hometown that I used in the books.

"Sort of," I admitted.

"Where is it?"

"On the Mississippi—between Iowa City and the Quad Cities."

"Like in your books!"

"Like in my books."

We shook hands and fell in alongside each other, walking and talking.

"What do you think of this place?" Randisi gestured around a dealers' room rife with rare books and vintage paperbacks.

"It's heaven," I said. "Also, hell. . . . I can't afford any of this stuff."

"I know the feeling. . . . Y'know, there are some big writers here. The Guest of Honor wrote the book that Steve McQueen movie came from—with the car chase? But the *really* cool thing is . . . Walter Gibson is here."

"Really? The guy who created the Shadow?"

" 'Maxwell Grant' himself—pretty spry for an old boy, too."

"How old is he?"

"Late seventies, I think. Still writing. Still doing magic

tricks. He knew Houdini and Blackstone and all those guys, y'know."

Robert J. Randisi and I continued to walk and talk, and so began a friendship that endures to this day. In ensuing years, Bob would found the Private Eye Writers of America, and become a bestselling writer of Western fiction, as well as authoring many fine mystery and suspense novels.

That evening, we wound up having dinner together—meeting up with Barb—at the now-defunct George Diamond's Steak House, where the fillets were the size of a football and the salads were half a head of crisp cold lettuce slathered in three dressings that mixed so well I'm salivating now. My lovely blonde wife lived up to Bob's high expectations of the standards of a "successful" hardboiled mystery writer.

And I was impressed to learn he'd sold a story to *Mike Shayne Mystery Magazine;* I'd never been able to crack the short story market (ironically, the first short story I would publish was sold to Bob, editing a PWA anthology, about ten years later).

After dinner, Barb headed to our room at the Palmer House to "play with" the things she'd bought, while Bob and I retired to a corner of the hotel bar. We talked for several hours about our respective dreams—many of them now realized—and he paid me the huge compliment of asking me to describe, in some detail, the three Nolan novels that were as yet unpublished, and at the time languishing in a publisher's inventory, fated not to see print till the early '80s.

Bob, it turned out, was a civilian employee of the Brooklyn P.D., taking what are now 911 calls, and I was further complimented that a guy who worked in a world where he encountered real crime and criminals could be impressed by my imaginary ones. I told him I thought his writing future was bright—he was damn near a cop, and that was useful in lots of ways, from background info to PR possibilities.

A handsome, sharply dressed young black guy swung by the table—Percy Spurlock Parker, a mystery writer who was also just starting out—and informed us about a cocktail party in a hotel suite, where the con's Guest of Honor . . . who I'll call Lawrence R. Trout . . . was holding court.

I was not particularly a fan of the Guest of Honor. Under his real name, he remains held in high esteem by a lot of writers and fans, particularly those in the New York area who have long been active with the Mystery Writers of America; a major mystery award in his honor is given by the MWA. Among his crowd, Trout must have been a nice enough guy, and no writer has a long career without talent and ability. But at the time I found his work dull and unremarkable. (Truth be told, I still do.)

Still, he was a pro, and I'd met precious few of those— a real-life successful mystery writer. He'd even had a Steve McQueen movie made out of one of his novels—what would that be like, I wondered, having a major movie star bring one of your characters to life! So I eagerly followed Bob and Percy onto an elevator and up to a small suite, where lots of mystery writers and fans were crowded in.

Cigarette and cigar smoke hung thick, but it wasn't really a *noir*-ish atmosphere (particularly since nobody was using the *noir* term yet in these circles); it reminded me of the bars my rock band played in (I'd turned down a booking to attend the con) and, while not a smoker myself, I was used to such a smokehouse stench. A few women were among this group, but it was predominantly male. In future years, that ratio would reverse, but the mood (and for that matter reality) of that suite on that evening was strictly Boys' Club.

Booze was flowing fairly freely, its blow softened by chips and pretzels. I'm no teetotaler, but I've never particularly been a drinker either, so I stayed with Coca-Cola.

I engaged in several conversations with people who no doubt would become my friends in future years, though I frankly don't recall any of them specifically, with the notable exception of Chris Steinbrunner.

Chris was one of the sweetest, kindest, most articulate and knowledgeable men in the world of mystery. Heavyset, his clothes (suit and tie) an unmade bed, his comb-over dark hair disheveled, his eyes constantly on the move behind heavy-rimmed glasses, moonfaced Chris was as focused mentally as his appearance was a blur.

"I know you," Chris said, taking in my name tag, gesturing with mixed drink in hand. "You're the Mickey Spillane defender!"

"Guilty as charged," I said with a grin.

One of the oddest things about my career, for that matter about my life, is that I have become the premiere defender of one of the world's best-selling writers. Heavily exposed to the wave of private-eye TV shows in the late '50s and early '60s, as a junior high kid I inhaled private-eye novels, starting with twenty-five- and thirty-five-cent paperbacks featuring the wild likes of Richard S. Prather's Shell Scott and G.G. Fickling's Honey West, then discovering Dashiell Hammett, Raymond Chandler and Mickey Spillane, and loving all three, particularly Spillane, whose fever-dream sex-and-violence writing style set my adolescent brain on fire.

Imagine my surprise, growing older, when I learned that many mystery writers and even some snooty fans considered the incredibly popular Spillane to be beneath contempt—they adored Hammett and Chandler (as did I), but Spillane was a boorish, right-wing lout. I happened to be a boorish, left-wing lout, but I took offense nonetheless, and my contributions to fanzines were spirited defenses of Spillane, with scholarship about his comic-book work and his "lost" stories that had appeared in pulpy men's adventure magazines.

At another Bouchercon, in Milwaukee in 1981, I would be the con's contact man with Spillane, the Guest of Honor, and the creator of Mike Hammer and I would become great friends. He is my son Nathan's godfather, has been my collaborator on numerous projects, and the subject of an Edgar-nominated critical biography I cowrote with fellow Spillane buff Jim Traylor, as well as a documentary film I made a few years ago, which was screened to much acclaim in Italy, England and (for the Mystery Writers of America) in New York.

Back in '75, however, most mystery writers—major and minor—were saying disparaging things about Mickey. Not only had he never been nominated for the MWA's prestigious Edgar Allan Poe Award, he was the only published author ever refused membership in the organization . . . a shameful occurrence.

So in that smoky suite, Chris Steinbrunner—who with mystery-world maven Otto Penzler had written one of the first and best books on the history of mystery—looked me in my young eyes and said, "God bless you, my son."

"Really? What did I do?"

"Merely defended a great writer."

I worked up my most boyish smile—and they were pretty boyish back then. "You and Otto Penzler defended him, too. I got tears in my eyes reading the nice things you said about Mickey."

Though I hadn't yet met Mickey, I already loved the man; he was my literary father.

"He's the most influential mystery writer alive," Chris said. "No contest."

Randisi, who was at my side, said, "I've always loved Spillane. I pretty much love all private-eye books. But Spillane, he's one of the biggies."

"He's *the* biggie," I said.

Still intimidated by my incredible two-published-novels

career, Randisi merely nodded, respecting my every word (this would soon change).

"You must let me introduce you to Walter Gibson," Chris said, his round head swivelling to take in the landscape of the crowded room. Then his eyes returned to mine. "Are you a 'Shadow' fan?"

"When I was a little kid," I said, "I used to listen to him on the radio."

"Oh, but the pulp novels were far superior to the broadcast version! And Walter turned out hundreds of those. Typing till his fingers bled."

"I read that 'Shadow' paperback he wrote a few years ago," I said. "A lotta fun."

"You need to tell *him* that . . ."

But Gibson was holed up in a corner of the room doing card tricks for a clutch of wide-eyed fans, children of ages ranging from twenty to fifty. Gibson himself was a tall, somewhat heavyset gentleman in a dark suit with a crisp tie; his hair was starkly white and fairly long, though neatly combed—his wire-rim glasses and beaming smile reminded me of the science-fiction author, Ray Bradbury.

I don't believe I've ever used the word *avuncular* in a book before, but it applied to him, perfectly: he was your favorite uncle. Right now he was getting as big a kick out of doing his card tricks as his little audience was watching them.

"Let's not bother him," I said. "Maybe later?"

"If you wait till Walter's not busy talking to somebody, it'll be a very long wait—he loves people, loves to make conversation."

"I can see that. Seems like a real sweetheart."

"And when you do talk to him, get him going about the old days. I've never seen anybody with a memory like his—he can pull up something that happened to him in childhood with photographic detail, and make it as colorful as a Shadow yarn."

"I promise to find the right moment, Chris."

"Well, then," Chris said, taking me by the arm, "in the meantime, you should meet the Guest of Honor."

Lawrence R. Trout was in his early sixties, tall with salt-and-pepper hair, dressed in a professorly manner, and a little drunk. He seemed affable enough, if full of himself. Hard to hold him to account for that: he was the Guest of Honor, after all.

Chris introduced me, and said, "Max has published two novels. He's from Iowa."

There was some (relatively) good-natured disparagement from Trout about my Tall Corn roots (he was from Connecticut), and then Chris made the mistake.

The big mistake.

"Max is quite the Mickey Spillane fan," Chris said, cheerful as Santa's top elf. "He's written some very nice articles supporting Spillane."

Trout snorted distastefully over his cocktail. "Spillane? He's a damn hack. Everybody knows it."

"Actually," I said, "it's my dream that one day Mickey will receive a Grand Master Award from the Mystery Writers of America. I hope to do everything I can to make that happen."

Trout, I later learned, was very active with the MWA.

"Over my dead body," Trout said. "He's the only published writer we ever rejected from the membership! He churns out pulp dreck—ridiculous trash."

"Hammett and Chandler were pulp writers, too," I said tersely.

"Spillane was even *worse* than a pulp hack—he was a *comic-book writer,* you know."

"So what?"

He eyed me over the drink with orbs that suited his name. "What, are you going to defend *comic books* now?"

"Chester Gould created the most famous American detective," I said.

Chris put in, " 'Dick Tracy.' Wonderful stuff."

Trout put a condescending hand on my shoulder. "Let me put the period on this sentence. . . . I have no respect for any writer who poses on his book covers with guns."

Mickey, a former WWII fighter pilot and very much a blue-collar writer, had sometimes posed as his famous detective, Mike Hammer, for publicity shots, with Hammer's trademark .45 in his fist.

"Ian Fleming did the same thing," I said.

"Please!" the Guest of Honor said, removing his hand from my shoulder before I had to. "*He* was a hack, too."

I felt the red climbing into my face; and I could hear the quiver in my voice, as I said: "Let me tell you something, Mr. Trout—everybody in this room, including yourself, has a career *because* of Mickey Spillane. It was his enormous success in the early '50s that made crime fiction, and paperbacks, explode. You don't have to like his work to show a little gratitude and have some common respect for the man who gave all of us . . . yourself included . . . a career."

Quite a few people were listening now. The moment could not have been more awkward. An upstart, barely published brat from Iowa had verbally assaulted their honored guest. On the other hand, a few heads were nodding. Here and there. Less than vindication, but nice.

"Mickey Spillane will never receive a Grand Master Award from the MWA," Trout said. "He . . . poses . . . with . . . guns . . . on . . . his . . . dust jackets."

Then the Guest of Honor moved unsteadily away for another drink.

But when he'd passed across my vision, Trout revealed someone else . . .

. . . Walter Gibson.

The creator of the Shadow was smiling at me as if he'd just spotted his long-lost nephew.

He approached me with the grace of the trained stage

performer he was. His blue eyes holding eye contact with me, he said to Steinbrunner, "Chris, why don't you introduce me to this young man?"

But Gibson's hand was already outstretched.

I shook it; the grasp was firm. "Mr. Gibson," I said, "it's an honor. I'm a big fan."

That might have been overstating it: I was not a collector of the valuable old pulp magazines, but I'd read some of the reprints, as well as that recent Shadow paperback I'd mentioned to Chris.

And this was the man who created one of the most famous characters in popular fiction: the Shadow, the sometimes-invisible crimefighter who clouded men's minds, and knew what evil lurked in their hearts.

Chris made the introductions, and then Gibson said, "I admire you for standing up to that pompous fool."

"Really? Are you a Spillane fan?"

He shrugged. "Not particularly. He's done very well updating the *Black Mask* pulp technique—Carroll John Daly originated that kind of thing with Race Williams, of course. And there's some of the Shadow in Mike Hammer, too, don't you think?"

"Well, yes."

"The old idea of an avenging figure is just as good today as it ever was—the best mysteries always center around one character. Look at Sherlock Holmes, and Dracula."

"But if you're not a Spillane fan—"

He patted my shoulder. "You were absolutely right to defend a writer you admire. Writers shouldn't go around bad-mouthing other writers. And I don't much like hearing disrespect to pulp writers, either. That was my world, you know."

I nodded; sipped my Coke. "How much work did you do for the radio *Shadow* show?"

"Not much—conceptual stuff in the beginning. Sort of helped map it out." He shrugged. "I like my stuff better."

Spoken like a true writer!

Gibson's face creased with amusement. "But you don't look *old* enough to've heard the Shadow on the radio."

"It was still on in the mid-fifties," I said. "I was five or six . . . I'd listen to it, and *Yours Truly, Johnny Dollar,* and *Dragnet.* In bed at night." I gave a mock shiver. "The Shadow was the first *good* guy who ever scared my little behind."

Gibson gave a grudging nod. "Well, that sinister laugh was a good touch. I'll give 'em that. But you *are* too young for the pulps."

"I read your Shadow paperback. Really liked it. And the reprints. A lot of fun."

"Good—that's what they were meant to be. . . . That 'Shadow' laugh, you know, it wasn't Orson Welles."

"Really?"

"Everybody thinks it was, and Orson always claimed it as his . . . but it was a fella called Readick, Frank Readick. He was the first 'Shadow,' when the character was just a spooky narrator, not active in the stories. They used Readick's opening till the end, I think. But Orson got the credit—typically."

"Did you *know* Orson Welles?"

The *Citizen Kane* wunderkind had famously played the Shadow on the radio in the '30s, barely out of his teens.

"Oh, I knew him all right," Gibson said.

Chris's owlish countenance brightened. "Really? You never mentioned you met Welles."

Gibson's shrug was as grand as it was casual. "I don't believe you ever asked, Chris."

"You have me there, Walter. But I knew you didn't have much to do with the radio version, so I never *thought* to ask."

Gibson smiled in a way that said he had nothing more to add to this subject.

The conversation turned to Gibson's enduring penchant for magic, and how he could still do a mean card trick. He showed us a couple, and they were suitably mystifying—cards appearing in one of Gibson's pockets, the apparent mind reading of a card I'd selected. Finally, Chris—who'd seen this magic many times—wandered off and got involved in another conversation; and by now Bob Randisi had disappeared somewhere.

Suddenly it was the Shadow creator and the kid from Iowa, alone in the crowded suite.

"I've always loved Orson Welles," I said, returning gingerly to the topic. "What were the circumstances of you knowing him, if you weren't very involved with the radio program?"

"Well . . ." Gibson, who was nursing a beer, glanced about the smoky room, as if to make sure no one was around; of course, thirty or thirty-five people were around. . . .

"If I'm overstepping . . ."

Gibson studied me; something about him seemed at once ancient and childlike. "It *is* a hell of a story."

"And you're a hell of a storyteller, Mr. Gibson."

He let out a single laugh. "And don't think I wouldn't get a kick out of sharing it with somebody. It's just . . . well, a lot of the people are still alive."

"I'm afraid I don't understand . . ."

"People could still get in trouble—at the very least, be embarrassed, badly so." He leaned in conspiratorially. "Suppose we went down to the bar, and found a quiet corner . . ."

"I know just the corner."

"Would you promise not to tell anyone? At least, not until the players have . . . shuffled off this mortal coil? As Orson might put it."

"I won't betray your confidence, Mr. Gibson."

"When a magician shares a magic trick with a student, he must do so in full confidence that the student will guard the secret of that trick."

"You're killin' me, Mr. Gibson. . . . I *have* to hear this story. . . ."

He grinned his uncle's grin. "You deserve a reward, young man. For sticking up for your hero. For sticking up for pulp writers everywhere. . . . Let's go down and have a few more beers. Who knows how good this story might get?"

The two us eased out of the suite, unseen shadows slipping into the night—or at least, the hallway.

Soon we had settled into our corner of the little bar off the lobby, and I'd bought a pitcher of beer, though over the next hour and a half, we barely dented it. The tale Walter Gibson told provided all the intoxication either of us needed.

His eyes narrowed in thought in the pleasant, jowly face. "It was just about   let me do the computation . . . thirty-seven years ago. Almost exactly thirty-seven years ago. I was older than you, but not by much."

"Thirty-seven years . . . what, 1938 then? Was Welles still doing the Shadow?"

"He'd just quit. The show was on Sunday afternoons, done live, and young Orson had a new program . . . *The Mercury Theatre on the Air*. . . ."

"Wait a minute. . . . this weekend—Hallowe'en's just days away."

"Yes it is."

"Isn't Hallowe'en when . . . ?"

"Yes it was."

I was sitting forward. "'The War of the Worlds' . . . most famous radio show of all time. And you were *there*?"

"Yes," Gibson said, eyes twinkling. "I was." He was staring at me with mischievous delight over his folded hands, those fingers that had pounded out so many pulp yarns, one of them wearing an impressive gold ring that I realized was a replica of the Shadow's famous fire opal. "And I've never told a soul about it . . . not even any of my wives."

A chill of excitement went up my spine; I hadn't felt anything like it since my bedroom was dark and I was six and the Shadow was laughing his deep, sinister laugh. . . .

"But you're going to tell me, aren't you, Mr. Gibson?"

"Call me 'Walter.' . . . And yes, I am. I am indeed going to tell you. I'm going to tell you about the murder that happened thirty-seven years ago, right in the CBS studios—the day, the night, that Orson Welles sent America into a panic. A murder that even the *Martians* didn't know about. . . ."

And he began to speak, in a mellow voice that was not as commanding as that of Orson Welles, but commanding enough, stage magician that Walter Gibson had been, and still was. His was a voice in the near darkness, and I sat enthralled by it, much as so many in the mid-twentieth century had crowded around their radio consoles in their own homes in Depression-era America.

Now another thirty years have passed.

And I've never told anybody the story. Not my wife. Not even Bob Randisi.

Walter Gibson is gone; so is Chris Steinbrunner, and Lawrence R. Trout, too. A few years ago I was Guest of Honor at a Bouchercon, and I'm pleased to report that no one treated me as badly as I treated the esteemed Mr. Trout. Mickey Spillane, at 87, is still with us; and a few years back, I was among a handful of mystery writers who saw to it that Mike Hammer's creator did indeed receive a Grand Master Edgar® Award from the Mystery Writers of America.

But just about everyone who was at CBS the day and night of "The War of the Worlds" broadcast is long since gone—among them, Howard Koch, the scriptwriter, and Welles's partner and future nemesis, John Houseman. Paul Stewart (so memorable a bad guy in the film of Spillane's *Kiss Me, Deadly*) has left the earthly studio, as has the musical genius Bernard Herrmann, who lives on in such film scores as *Vertigo, North by Northwest* and *Taxi Driver.*

Welles himself, of course, has also departed, though leaving behind a handful of classic films and a certain unforgettable, history-making radio broadcast.

No one can be hurt now, or even embarrassed, by my revealing what *really* occurred at CBS, on the eve of Hallowe'en in 1938.

I have added to the account Walter shared with me in that Palmer House bar in Chicago in 1975 a good deal of research into the other events of October 30, 1938—the ones that occurred outside the CBS studios. So the picture I will paint, in the theater of your mind, will flesh out somewhat the story the Shadow's creator shared with me.

And I must admit that nothing in my research confirmed what Walter said, in our dark corner of the hotel bar at Bouchercon Six; but nothing contradicted it, either. . . .

I leave it to you to decide, and remain obediently yours,

Max Allan Collins
October 31, 2004
Muscatine, Iowa

THURSDAY

October 27, 1938

By 1938, that experimental novelty known as radio had become mass communication, informing and entertaining listeners from (as announcers of the era so loved to point out) coast to coast.

In 1920 the first public broadcast told the United States that President Harding had been elected; now President Roosevelt was using the medium for "fireside chats" . . . and when November rolled around, FDR (and all American politicians) would listen with rapt attention to election returns, courtesy of this most immediate of mediums.

The first radio entertainment emanated from a garage in Pittsburgh—station KDKA—serving thousands; now ventriloquist Edgar Bergen with his dummy Charlie McCarthy brought laughter to over thirty million every Sunday night on their Chase and Sanborn Hour. *The drawing power of the young medium could hardly be denied, even if the popularity of a ventriloquist act unseen by its audience did raise certain questions about the willingness of these listeners to buy just about anything, and not just what the sponsors were selling. . . .*

If the diversions radio provided were less sophisticated than those of a concert hall, the Broadway theater or even your neighborhood moviehouse, Amos 'n' Andy, Major Bowes and Fibber McGee and Molly didn't cost a dime, and were accessible at the flip of a switch and the turn of a dial. After all, just about everybody had a radio—ten million were sold per year, most homes having at least one, with car radios and portable sets making broadcasting a mobile member of the family. Radio was seriously undermining newspapers as the nation's preferred news source (ironically, many stations were owned by those same papers), even while providing—in a country still reeling from the Depression—a cheap alternative to movies.

Popular music over the air also helped fight those Depression blues, with remote broadcasts from ballrooms and nightclubs in major cities bringing big bands and that new fad, swing, into living rooms. And of course if a news story broke, an announcer could always interrupt to keep Americans "coast to coast" instantaneously informed.

Which meant the average person felt more a part of things these days—even in the smallest American hamlet a listener could witness the marriage of the Duke of Windsor to Mrs. Simpson, and attend the Braddock-Louis heavyweight fight; or get firsthand reports on the great flood of the Mississippi Valley, and have the dirigible Hindenburg *explode before their very ears.*

It was a world where listeners were quite used to hearing from the president and comedian W.C. Fields within the same half hour—a world that happened to be on the brink of war, a populace waiting by the radio console for news of a first attack. . . .

In the meantime, between this steady diet of comedy, music and news, a hardy handful of creators attempted to bring quality drama to the networks. Arch Oboler, with his pioneering, Twilight Zone–*like* Lights Out *used innovative sound effects to project his movies of the mind, while radio's "poet laureate" Norman Corwin trusted well-chosen words to grant his fantasies and satires literary qualities rare in a medium that already seemed crass.*

At age twenty-two, Orson Welles—acclaimed and controversial as the boy genius of Broadway, a radio veteran thanks to a rich deep voice beyond his years—brought his skills and his talented associates to a project called First-Person Singular, *soon to be renamed* The Mercury Theatre on the Air. *He was the star, narrator, writer, producer and director—at least according to the press releases—and a more ambitious slate of radio adaptations would be difficult to imagine: the first season (1937) began with an outstanding version of Bram Stoker's* Dracula, *and was followed in short order by* Treasure Island, A Tale of Two Cities, Oliver Twist, Around the World in 80 Days *and* Julius Caesar, *among others.*

But the 1938 season found the celebrated, acclaimed new series up against the most popular radio show in the nation—Edgar Bergen and Charlie McCarthy's aforementioned Chase & Sanborn Hour, *which pulled in about 35 percent of the radio audience. After seven broadcasts in its new Sunday-night slot against America's most popular puppet,* The Mercury Theatre on the Air *was drawing less than four percent.*

Something would have to be done.

CHAPTER ONE

Radio Daze

Walter Gibson had never been on an expense account before.

Not even in the earliest days of his writing career, when he'd been a reporter on the *North American* in Philly, and then the *Evening Ledger*—never.

Of course, even then his work out in the field had been limited, once the editor learned of the Gibson facility for puzzles and quizzes. Turning out "brain tests" and crossword puzzles—not to mention articles on magic and bunco games—Gibson had spent more time in an office in front of a typewriter than out news gathering.

The irony was, Walter Gibson had the soul of an adventurer—his mind, since earliest childhood, had brimmed with magic and mysticism and men of action. He enjoyed the great out-of-doors; and he craved the companionship and conversation of lively, intelligent people—as fetching as his wife Jewel was, her ability to stand toe-to-toe with him intellectually, on any number of esoteric topics, had attracted him most.

From his teens on, he'd performed in semi-professional

magic acts and had sought, successfully, the scintillating company of stage magicians, including some of the most eminent—Thurston, Blackstone, Dunninger, even Houdini.

And yet Walter Gibson's talent for storytelling, his ease with words, had condemned him to this jail cell of a career. Not that this was a sentence he minded serving: self-expression was his overriding obsession; and the challenge of a writing assignment energized him, though each one consigned him further to a solitary life in a small room with his only company a typewriter and his imagination. Even his association with those illustrious magicians had led primarily to ghostwriting articles and books for them.

Under his nom de plume Maxwell Grant, Gibson had learned to be content with the adventures of his famous character, the Shadow, playing out in the theater of his mind; and the conversations in which he found himself most often engaged were between characters of his own creation, speaking to each other with sharp, pointed intelligence, courtesy of his flying fingers.

Right now those famous fingertips ("1,440,000 WORDS WERE WRITTEN BY MAXWELL GRANT IN LESS THAN 10 MONTHS ON A CORONA TYPEWRITER," went one national ad) were bandaged; well, all but his thumbs. He looked like someone who had ill-advisedly placed his fingertips on a stove's burner; instead, he was a professional writer of pulp magazines who had yesterday completed his twenty-fourth 50,000-word "Shadow" novel of the year, opening up the remaining months of 1938 for other assignments.

Though he was not by nature a greedy man, Gibson wrote for money; despite his pen name's fame, and his popular character's prominence, his pay rate for pulp publisher Street and Smith did not compare to those of writers in the slick magazines like *The Saturday Evening Post* and *Collier's*, much less authors of hardcover books—pulsters like Dash Hammett and Erle Stanley Gardner had made the switch, but Gibson had never had room enough in his schedule to give it a try. These were hard times, and the $500 per novel was good money only if he kept up his output.

After all, a writer couldn't sell a story he hadn't written. So Gibson's motto was: *Write till it hurts; then write some more.*

As he rode through Manhattan in the back of a Yellow Cab, wraithed in his own cigarette smoke, Gibson sat with a small valise on the floor and his portable Corona typewriter on the seat next to him, a rider as important as himself—at least.

With his salt-and-pepper hair neatly combed back, his round-lensed wire-frame spectacles, his oval face with the regular, intelligent features, he looked more like a lawyer or a businessman than the master of intrigue who dispatched the cloaked avenger known as the Shadow to take on campaigns against crime (any time he visited New York, he only half-consciously scouted locations for such gangster tales), and to bring down world-domination-minded masterminds like the Voodoo Master and Shiwan Khan.

He'd come down this morning by train from Maine—his home was in Philly, but he and Jewel had a cabin up north, on Little Sebago Lake, where they were spending more and more of their time. No stranger to Manhattan, he and his wife had lived in an apartment on West 46th for about a year, so he could be closer to the editorial offices of Street and Smith.

But he'd found the city distracting, too many plays and movies and restaurants to tempt a writer away from work; plus he was spending not nearly enough time with his son Robert (who lived with first wife Charlotte). Returning to Philadelphia and then building the cabin in Maine had made seeing Bobby more practical; the boy had been summering with his father and stepmother these past several years.

The cabin provided a kind of knotty-pine womb for Gibson's ideas to grow within. He would sit at a large pinewood desk in a corner of the central room with its vaulted ceilings, chain-smoking (cigarettes his chief stress reliever) and dreaming up yarns. No phone was allowed (calls came in to the cabin next door, where his cousin Eaton lived) with the silence punctuated only by the calls of loons and other birds out on the lake.

Not that silence was required for him to create: he'd written one Shadow novel while the carpenters built his office around him. He'd written much of another at a party in New York, with other guests reading the yarn over his shoulder—the experience had only exhilarated him.

Trips to New York were commonplace to Gibson, who enjoyed delivering plot synopses in person to editor John Nanovic, who'd become a good friend. Nanovic made useful suggestions, and Gibson felt the editor had come to know the Shadow as well as his creator.

Unlike a lot of editors, Nanovic did not stint on the compliments. He frequently told Gibson (in varying words), "You've got the newspaperman's knack for giving me just enough facts to take me into the next paragraph . . . and the magician's flare to intrigue me with hints of what's to come."

Later this afternoon, he would meet with Nanovic. Right now (it was just after one-thirty) he had his first stop to make—at the Columbia Broadcasting Building at Madison Avenue and 45th Street. The Shadow had been born in this building, and yet the father of the character had never visited the birthsite before.

Technically, of course, Gibson was the character's *step*-father. In 1930 a radio show had been introduced at CBS, *Detective Story*, that based its episodes on stories from the Street and Smith pulp magazine of the same name; a sinister-voiced narrator—dubbed the Shadow—presented the tales. A voice actor named Frank Readick gave the narrator a haunting laugh and a spooky presence that had made something of a national sensation.

Instead of serving to promote *Detective Story Magazine* as intended, however, the show inspired listeners to request at their newsstands "that Shadow detective magazine."

Which was where Walter Gibson came in. Frank Blackwell, then the Street and Smith editor, challenged Gibson to come up with a character to go with the memorable name and the spooky voice.

Already Gibson had been toying with the idea of doing a mystery-story hero who was himself mysterious, and a little nasty, unlike the straightforward goody-two-shoes heroes of other mystery series—an avenger who would wear not a white hat, but a black one. He reflected upon his magician friends and came up with a character who combined the hypnotic power of Thurston and Blackstone with Houdini's penchant for escapes. By early 1931, "Maxwell Grant" had begun his punishing, profitable run, charting the adventures of this tall, black-cloaked figure with the broad-brim *black* felt hat tucked over a hawkish countenance.

And by 1937, the radio show had dropped its narrator-version of the Shadow to adapt Gibson's avenging hero—embodied by a new young actor with a magical second-baritone: Orson Welles.

Though Gibson had helped develop the radio version of the Shadow with scriptwriter Edward Hale Bierstadt (it had been gratifying to hear Ed say how much he loved Gibson's yarns), the creator of the character was contractually tied up with Street and Smith to produce those twenty-four novels a year. So the radio Shadow had gone its own way, deviating somewhat from Gibson's vision—rather over-emphasizing the character's rich-man-about-town secret identity, Lamont Cranston (admittedly a perfect fit for Welles)—but staying mostly on course . . . and becoming a household word among radio listeners.

Which meant—everybody in America.

The Columbia Broadcasting Building was no longer

home to the Shadow show—it was a Mutual program now, and broadcast out of New York's powerhouse WOR—but the skyscraper remained home to Orson Welles, whose amazingly resonant voice and ironic delivery had much to do with the radio Shadow's success.

Welles had just finished his two-season run as the Shadow to take on a more ambititous project—*The Mercury Theatre on the Air*, an extension of the wunderkind's acclaimed Broadway theater company—and so Gibson had been surprised to be contacted by the showman himself, to discuss a Shadow project.

Not as surprised as Jewel, however, when she came rushing breathlessly into the cabin with news that a phone call from the famous young radio actor awaited next door . . .

. . . where Gibson gave both his wife and his message-screening cousin a long cool look that told them this was business and that they were dismissed, and the two were reluctantly taking their leave when the writer brought the receiver to his ear.

"Do I have the honor of speaking to my illustrious father?"

The deep voice on the other end of the line, filtered through long-distance, had the processed sound of the Shadow on the air, attempting to frighten that week's evildoer.

Gibson, however, neither frightened nor impressed easily.

"Hello, Mr. Welles," he said.

The two men had met exactly once, at a Society of Magicians gathering in Manhattan where the radio actor had performed as a perfectly respectable amateur magician—respectable for a celebrity, at least.

"This is a much overdue call," Welles said, amusement and something like chagrin in his formidable voice. "I have been told that . . . in the beginning . . ." The latter had proper Biblical weight. ". . . you personally recommended me to the Shadow's sponsor."

Gibson had indeed pointed the way toward Welles as an ideal radio Shadow—he had been impressed with Welles's stagecraft (even if his magic was merely competent) and by his rich, worldly voice. Also, Welles had done work on *The March of Time* radio show that had bowled both Gibson and Jewel over; so when the Shadow creator's counsel was sought in matters of casting, he'd thought immediately of Welles.

In fact he had said, "There's only one actor on the face of the earth who, using only his voice, can do justice to the Shadow."

Nonetheless, this was Gibson's first direct contact (since that Society of Magic gathering, where they'd been introduced and shared a few words) with the actor who had brought his character to life, and to radio fame.

"I may have played a small role in getting you that part, Mr. Welles," Gibson admitted. "But you've more than made up for it by boosting the circulation of *The Shadow Magazine* with your fine work."

"Very kind of you, Walter—may I call you 'Walter'?"

"If I might risk 'Orson,' certainly."

"Please!" Welles's warm laugh had nothing to do with the Shadow's sinister one. "Walter, I know we're going to be great friends."

Gibson shook his head—actors. "The last time I saw you . . . Orson . . . was on the cover of *Time*. What's the occasion?"

Welles dove right in: "Walter, I have an interesting offer from Hollywood. They've made several lousy pictures out there about our character, as I'm sure you know."

Our character apparently meant the Shadow. Gibson smiled to himself at this presumption, but kept this reaction out of his voice as he replied: "You're telling me? The wife and I walked out on both of 'em."

Welles chuckled. "Frankly, I didn't bother going. People I trusted warned me off. I mean, honestly, Walter, with a character as wonderful and famous as ours, how *could* they? I mean, *Rod LaRocque*! Didn't he single-handedly kill off silent pictures?"

"I don't know about that, Orson—but he made a good stab at killing off talkies with those two crummy Shadow pictures."

"Agreed! Warners Brothers agrees, as well. They are prepared to make up for those B-movie embarrassments, if we can come up with a worthy scenario."

"A top-budget affair this time? With a first-rate director, and a real star, you mean?"

"Precisely!"

"What director?"

"Why me, of course."

"And the star?"

"You're speaking to him!"

". . . Have you ever directed before, Orson? I mean, a moving picture?"

Welles did not miss a beat: "Actually, my dear fellow, I *have* taken a few experimental steps—I made a short film as a student, and recently I dabbled in the art for a stage production we did of Gillette's farce, *Too Much Johnson*, with the Mercury players."

"Ah," Gibson said noncomittally.

"But the point is I have been staging plays with a cinema director's eye from the beginning—you've heard of my voodoo *Macbeth*, and my Nazi-ified *Julius Caesar*, no doubt?"

Gibson had; he followed the radio Shadow's career with a certain proprietary interest . . . and anyway, the *Time* magazine article had covered all of that and more.

"Where would I come in?" Gibson asked.

"I'm told there's nothing you can't write."

Smiling to himself again, Gibson thought: *he knows this*

*secondhand; he doesn't read the magazine featuring "our"
character, apparently. . . .*

"Well, that's true," Gibson said. Welles wasn't the only
one who could afford to be immodest. "But where did you
hear it, Orson?"

"Our mutual friends among the magic community, of
course."

"Ah," Gibson said again. Nothing noncommital about it,
this time.

"I believe," Welles said, with the richness of voice and
surety of a revival-tent preacher, "that only the creator of
my famous character can help me properly conceive it . . .
*re*conceive it . . . for the screen. Are you willing to try?"

"I'm . . . interested."

"And your schedule, Walter?"

"I'll be done for the year, with my Shadow work, within
days."

"How is next week, then?"

"Feasible."

"I would of course be paying for first-class travel and
hotel accomodations—you'll be here at the St. Regis,
where I'm living currently. Full expense account. How . . .
'feasible' is that, Walter?"

"Entirely."

Hanging up the phone, Gibson had the feeling that he'd
just spoken to a man of wisdom and experience far beyond
the author's own. And yet he knew that Orson Welles was
almost ten years younger than himself. . . .

The cab drew up to 485 Madison Avenue, and Gibson—
typewriter handle in one bandaged hand, valise in the
other—was deposited (for an outrageous fifty cents including tip) (he mentally noted that for his expense account) on
the sidewalk above which loomed the massive overhang of
the marquee that boldly stated CBS RADIO THEATRE. The
Welles program, though, received no boost, as the side panels touted:

**THE CHRYSLER CORPORATION
PRESENTS
MAJOR BOWES ORIGINAL
AMATEUR HOUR.**

By craning his neck like any other rube of a tourist, he could see the vertical sign stretching nine or ten stories above:

C
B
S

R
A
D
I
O

T
H
E
A
T
R
E

but he could also see that lower floors of the impressive building had windows bearing less grandoise imprimaturs, such as CARLOS TAP AND BALLET and MIDTOWN TAX SERVICE.

The uniformed guard in the lobby found Gibson's name on a list, had him sign in, and sent him over to an elevator, where he and the elevator operator rode up to the twentieth floor. Mildly disappointed by the lack of show biz trappings—he might have been inside any nameless office

building, to get a tooth drilled or have a wife followed—
Gibson found nothing to get excited about at his destina-
tion, either: the twentieth-floor lobby was an unimpressive,
sterile world of walls covered in a light-green industrial
paint broken up by the occasional potted plant and some
art-moderne chairs and sofas out of the latest *Sears and
Roebuck* catalogue.

Next to a bulletin board—covered in schedules and lists
that might just as easily have referred to bus-station not
radio-station timetables—sat an attractive strawberry-
blonde receptionist of perhaps twenty-five. In her smart
white blouse with navy buttons and a navy scarf with white
polka dots knotted at her throat, and with her heart-shaped
face and light-blue eyes and fair lightly freckled complex-
ion, she was a heart-stopper, even to a married man. Or was
that, especially to a married man? Candy-apple red lipstick
made her guardedly professional smile as dazzling as one
you might see in a Sunday supplement toothpaste ad.

"Walter Gibson to see Mr. Welles."

She checked a clipboard and said, "Your name is here,
Mr. Gibson . . . but I'm afraid Mr. Welles isn't."

"He said to meet him in Studio One at one-thirty. I'm a
tad early."

"Ah. Well, it's right through there." With a tapering finger whose scarlet nail polish matched the lush lipstick, she
pointed toward a doorless doorway just to Gibson's left.
"Studio One is the first door down. . . . If the 'On the Air'
light is on, don't go in."

Gibson frowned. "My understanding is the show isn't
broadcast till Sunday night."

"It isn't—but every week, Mr. Welles makes an acetate
recording of the Thursday afternoon rehearsal. To review
the week's program."

"Is everyone around here as knowledgeable as you,
miss?"

"It's Miss Donovan, Mr. Gibson. Probably not—but like

every receptionist or secretary you're likely to meet in this building, I'm an aspiring actress."

"Ah. Any luck?"

"I fill in on several of the soaps, as needed, and I've had some bits with the *The Mercury Theatre,* too, and even *The Columbia Workshop.* Guess you'd say I'm kind of an understudy."

"An understudy in radio. That's a new one on me."

"Well, you have to understand that the voice actors in this town have to bicycle all over the place—NBC's over at Sixth Avenue and Fiftieth, and Mutual's on the other side of the world—Broadway and Fortieth. You know, Orson . . . Mr. Welles . . . he sometimes travels by ambulance."

Gibson grinned. "Sounds like Mr. Welles is as big a character as they say?"

"Oh, he's wonderful. You'll fall in love with him."

Something in the girl's expression made Gibson wonder if she might be speaking from experience.

Miss Donovan allowed the author to leave his valise and typewriter with her, behind her desk, and was kind enough to inquire about how he'd hurt his "poor fingers." To prevent this from dominating every other conversation of the day, Gibson ducked into the men's room and removed the bandages from his fingertips, which looked reddish but nearly healed.

The ON THE AIR sign over the Studio One door was not alighted, so Gibson moved on through a vestibule that separated the hallway from the studio, apparently for sound-proofing purposes. He pushed open a door whose window was round, like a porthole, and found himself on a small landing, with a chrome banister, five steps above the floor of a large noisy chamber bustling with men who mostly had their suitcoats off—a sea of suspenders, rolled-up sleeves and puffing cigarettes.

Gibson was no stranger to radio: well over ten years ago, the writer had appeared on station WIP in Philly, presenting puzzles and their solutions. And he'd written and helped produce a series for magician Howard Thurston early in the decade.

But an operation of this scale was beyond his experience, and he felt a bit like Dorothy having her first look at Oz.

The walls of the big, high-ceilinged room were light gray, and the few doors sky-blue with those porthole-style windows. The far left wall and the facing one alternated dark drapes with sound-baffling panels the color of caramel. To Gibson's left was a plywood, carpeted podium a little larger than a cardtable with a microphone and a music stand. The podium faced the short end of a twelve-foot by twenty-four-foot space marked off with white words on the dark-painted cement floor saying, on all four sides, MICRO-PHONE AREA. Within this carpeted rectangle resided four well-spaced microphones on stands (every mike in the room wore either a little metal CBS hat or dickey).

Just outside the microphone rectangle a couple of tables were home to coffee and sandwiches, or the aftermath thereof, along with scripts, magazines, newspapers, and ashtrays. Cigarettes bobbling, half a dozen actors wandered with folded-open script in hand, fingers pressed to an ear, reading aloud, and adding to the general chaos.

To Gibson's left, beyond the podium, a small orchestra was arrayed, seven pieces plus a grand piano; their leader, a bespectacled, rather odd-looking man, sat at the piano, frowning as he made notes on his score, paying no heed to the musicians filing in and taking their seats and going through little practice scales and other warm-ups.

Across the room, beyond and behind the carpeted MI-CROPHONE AREA, lurked a sound-effects station, including a table with two turntables for Victrola records, a wooden door on a heavy frame (for opening or closing as a script demanded), a bench with an odd assortment of items (saw and hammer, milk-bottle rack, coconut shells, etc.), a flat box of sand on the floor, and a rack of electronic gizmos. A statuesque middle-aged woman, who in her floral-print frock might have been a housewife, sorted through the inventory of this area, assembling things in order—cellophane for the crackle of fire, a bundle of straw for noises in underbrush, a large potato with a knife stuck in it—her pleasant face mildly contorted with intensity.

Though this was a fairly massive studio, it lacked audience seating. Gibson knew elsewhere in this building, the ground floor most likely, would be at least one theater-style studio, for programs like tonight's *Major Bowes Amateur Hour.* Game shows and comedies benefitted from spectators: those presenting the dramatic fare *The Mercury Theatre on the Air* specialized in might find that a distraction.

A door adjacent to the one he'd come in opened suddenly, and Gibson—mildly startled—whirled to see a small, dark man with salt-and-pepper hair lean out, his striped tie hanging like the flag on a football play. Indeed, the entire manner of this fellow was that of a referee, calling foul at this stranger's interference.

"Can I help you?" Though diminutive, the man had an intimidating bearing—including an actor's strong baritone, and eyes that bored into you.

"I'm Walter Gibson—I had an appointment with Mr. Welles."

The man—like so many here, in suspenders and rolled-up shirtsleeves—stepped onto the landing and his features softened but his eyes remained skeptical, a maitre d' not convinced you should be seated.

"Mr. Gibson, I don't doubt what you say . . . Orson is fairly cavalier about not keeping me informed about guests he's invited . . . but we're about to rehearse and record Sunday's show."

"I take it Orson isn't here."

The man twitched a smile. "No. He always says he's

going to participate in these recorded rehearsals, and we always wait half an hour past the time he sets, before starting without him."

"How often does he actually show up?"

"So far, never." Gibson's reluctant host frowned, the cacophony of musicians, actors and sound effects making it hard to converse. "Step in here, would you? . . . I'm Paul Stewart, by the way."

The two men shook hands as they pushed through a portholed door. They entered a cubicle adjacent to the control booth, where a desk faced a window out onto the studio; this, Gibson knew, was where the network rep would likely sit.

With no rep present, however, this cubicle made a good place to talk.

Through a doorless doorway was the actual control booth, with its bank of slanted panels with switches and dials against a generous horizontal window onto the studio. An engineer in earphones was already seated there, ready to "mix" the show, i.e., bring voices and sound effects up or down. A chair next to the engineer, with a microphone and headset waiting, would be the director's post, Gibson knew.

But what, then, was that podium out there for? And where was their famous "child" director? As if reading his guest's mind, Stewart spoke.

"Mr. Gibson, I'm the program director, and my hands are going to be very full. Maybe you'd like to sit here and watch—there's always an off chance Orson might stop by."

"I wouldn't mind at that. I'm a writer, by the way—you may know me better as Maxwell Grant."

Stewart's eyes narrowed. He sighed, shook his head, his expression softening with chagrin. "My apologies—Orson *did* mention you—the Shadow author. He's planning a project with you, I'm told."

"That's right."

Friendly now, Stewart put a hand on his guest's shoulder. "You've made me a few pennies, Mr. Grant."

"Gibson. How so?"

"I've played half a dozen villains on your Shadow show."

"Ah."

Stewart raised an eyebrow. "If this mug of mine ever gets in front of a camera, maybe I better get used to that. Gable doesn't have anything to worry about."

The ice broken, Gibson said, "Uh, I can either sit and be an eavesdropper for a few minutes . . . this is my first time at a major network setup like this . . . or I can head over to the St. Regis. Whatever's you pleasure, Mr. Stewart."

"Call me 'Paul,' and I really would love to have you join us. Might even trouble you for an opinion or two—we're having some real problems with this one."

"This week's program, you mean? Why, what piece are you doing?"

Gibson knew the Mercury usually adapted a famous literary work.

Stewart was lighting up a cigarette. "One by that *other* Wells . . . H.G. 'War of the Worlds.' " He waved his match out, made a face. "I'm sure it seemed fresh and frightening at the turn of the century, but we're having no little tough time making it something a modern audience can appreciate."

"It's a great story, Paul . . . and you people always do a fine job. I'm sure it'll be a real crowd pleaser."

"Let's hope." Stewart snapped his fingers. "You know, there's a couple people who'll want to meet you! We're a good fifteen minutes away from starting this thing. . . . Mind if I send 'em up?"

"Not at all."

Stewart disappeared out the door, and Gibson sat at the network rep's desk and looked out the window where his host was approaching one of those actors milling around.

The director pointed to Gibson's window and did some explaining, and the actor—a mustached fellow with slicked-back black hair, who looked like he might specialize in slightly gone-to-seed gigolos—was nodding and smiling.

Then the actor—one of the few not in shirtsleeves, tie not even loosened—came Gibson's way, heading up the small flight of steps, and within seconds the author was on his feet shaking hands with the man.

"At last we meet!" the actor said, in a silky baritone.

Gibson smiled a little. "I'm afraid you have the advantage on me, sir. . . ."

"I'm the Shadow! . . . The *first* Shadow, that is."

After a single laugh, the author said, "Frank Readick! The man who put me on the map. That voice and delivery of yours got me the Shadow assignment in the first place."

Readick chuckled. "Small world, huh? Two Shadows on the same show? And me, the original, working for my replacement, yet! . . . Ah, but I was just a glorified announcer, until you made a character of the guy, and then of course Orson brought *him* to life."

"But they're still using your laugh and your opening: 'Who knows what evil lurks in the hearts of men!' "

"Well, the Shadow may know," Readick said, head tilted, "but don't bring that up with Orson. It's a sore point."

The two men sat, Gibson at the desk.

"What's your role in 'War of the Worlds,' Frank?"

"Mostly I'm a reporter on the scene of the alien landing. I have a couple roles, actually, which is typical for voice actors on an ensemble show like this. But it's a good part, the Carl Phillips reporter one, I mean. I'm the one describing the monsters, plus I get to be burned alive on the air!"

"What fun," Gibson said, appreciatively. "Not just your ordinary death scene. But Mr. Stewart doesn't seem as enthusiastic about the piece."

"Well, Paul's a tough taskmaster. But the thing is a little . . . I don't know, it's missing something. Just kinda lays there. You know, when Orson did 'Dracula,' that vampire came alive . . . or as alive as the living dead can come. But these monsters just aren't making the grade. What the hell—it's early yet."

"Early? You broadcast on Sunday!"

Readick shook his head, grinned. "Oh, Welles and his buddy Jack Houseman, *and* Paul . . . and for that matter Howard, their writer . . . they're maniacs, polishing and goosing these things up till the last second." He pointed out the window to the podium. "Hell, Orson rewrites and cuts and shapes *while* he's on the air. He's a madman! A wonderful madman, but a madman."

"Frank, one thing I don't get— isn't Orson the director? Paul introduced himself as that, and as far as I can see, he's the one running things."

"Paul directs the rehearsals—he does the casting, gets these things on their feet. You see, Orson is busy with this latest play the Mercury is putting on—it opens in about a week—and anyway, the boy wonder is always involved in multiple things. But on Sunday, believe me, it'll be Orson's show, all right. Top to bottom."

"Then Orson *is* the director."

Readick's eyes tightened. "I'd say more . . . conductor. He stands up there on that podium like Toscanini and wrings the 'music' outa these scripts."

"So it's not an 'in-name-only' thing."

"You mean like Cecil B. DeMille on the *Lux Radio Theatre*? Not at all—ol' C.B. just plays the director on that show. Strictly an actor. Orson . . . he's a *real* DeMille around this place."

The author and actor chatted a few more minutes, then the latter took his leave. And his place in the mike-area rectangle.

A few minutes later, while Gibson sat smoking a Camel and watching through the window—as Stewart moved around the room giving instructions to actors, sound-effects technicians and even the orchestra conductor—another figure slipped into the cubicle.

An Ichabod Crane of a spindly six-two or -three, in his early thirties, with a spade-shaped face and unruly blond hair, in a rumpled tan suit and dark-brown tie, the fellow had the abashed manner of someone reluctantly knocking on your door for charity. He also had hollow, tired eyes and the pallor of one who rarely got outside.

In other words, a writer.

"Mr. Gibson?" The voice was earnest and even a little timid, which was almost a relief after all these sonorous radio tones.

"Yes?" Gibson got to his feet.

"I'm Howard Koch—the one-man Mercury writing staff." He extended his hand, which Gibson promptly shook. "I've been turning these sixty-page shows out at a rate of one a week, all season so far. And you must be the only man on the planet who thinks I'm a piker."

With a burst of a laugh, Gibson sat back down, gesturing for Koch to pull up a chair and join him. "We pulp writers do make you hardworking radio writers look like you're loafin' . . . but then, *I* don't have to put up with the endless meetings and rewrites."

Koch rolled his eyes. "It does get a little hairy around here. Welles and Houseman consider sleep a luxury—their saving grace is they deny themselves, too."

"Even I don't envy you your time schedule, Howard . . . considering you're adapting and carving up huge novels, most of the time, to fill a little old hour."

Koch chuckled wryly. "It's either that or pad out a short story to the same purpose. Butchered or bloated, those are the options."

"Say what you will, but my wife and I would never miss your show."

With half a smile, Koch said, "Even when you're on deadline?"

"Howard, I'm like you—*always* on deadline."

With a sigh, the radio writer said, "I just wish I had something better this afternoon, to share with you. This one's kind of a . . . a mess, I'm afraid."

"Don't know why. Destroying the world ought to fill an hour perfectly well. And hell, you've got Martians doing it!"

"That's the problem. It's so goddamn unbelievable. With what's going on in the world right now, fantasy has its appeal, all right . . . but it can be a hard sell to people beaten down by horrific realities."

"Maybe the fact that it takes place forty years ago will make the fantasy go down smoother."

Koch shifted in his seat. "Walter, tell ya the truth, that was the first change I made: I thought that hurt the reality of it—radio has an immediacy. Sure, we can go back to the foggy London of Sherlock Holmes and lose ourselves there; or to Treasure Island with Long John Silver and Jim Hawkins. But to do science fiction, something futuristic, that's set forty years back? I don't think so."

"So, then, you've modernized it?"

"Yes—it's happening today, and it's happening in America, not London."

"Ah!" Gibson stubbed out his Camel in a glass ashtray, with CBS in it. "So where do the Martians land, now? Times Square?"

"Actually, I thought somewhere out in the obscure countryside would be better. Something rural, where the contrast would be great . . . and where an invading army might logically deploy itself."

Nodding, Gibson said, "I like that. You've thought about this, really thought it through. Sounds to me you're doing fine—where exactly then did you have them land?"

"Grovers Mill, New Jersey."

"Where?"

The radio writer patted the air with both hands, his tone apologetic. "Let me explain—Monday's my only day off.

I was making a quick trip up the Hudson, to see my family, and I was on Route Nine West—"

"Which took you through New Jersey."

"Exactly. Anyway, I stopped at a gas station and picked up a road map of the state, knowing the next day, at work, I'd have to be figuring out my . . . or I should say the *Martians'* . . . battle plan. So back in my office in New York, getting down to it, I spread the map out on the floor, closed my eyes . . . and dropped a pencil."

"On Grovers Mill."

"Right. I liked the ring of it—sounded like the real place it was. Plus, it's near Princeton, and I have this astronomer character in the show, called Professor Pierson, who works out of the Princeton Observatory."

"Luck was on your side."

"We'll see." He spread his hands out in the air, his eyes gleaming, suddenly. "I can tell you that that map became my best friend. There I was, deploying the opposing forces over an ever-widening area, wreaking havoc like a drunken general . . . making moves and countermoves between invaders and defenders."

"It's good to be God."

"You'll have to check with Orson for the answer to that one! But . . . I *did* enjoy destroying New Jersey."

"Who wouldn't?"

He chuckled, like a kid about to share a terrible, wonderful secret. "If you hang around to listen, Walter, you'll find I also demolish the very Columbia Broadcasting Building we're seated in."

"Wishful thinking, no doubt. Howard, why are you recording this rehearsal?"

"Well, *I'm* not doing anything—I'm just the writer. I'm somewhere about ten rungs in importance below Ora Nichols, the sound-effects gal. Why record it in advance? Timing, for one thing—Paul will be sitting by his script in the booth next to us, stopwatch in hand, to see if we're long or short. But mostly it's so Orson can attend without attending—so he can listen to the acetate tonight and make his notes for me to do revisions, and to make production demands of Paul, even music suggestions to Benny—Benny Herrmann, that is, our in-house maestro."

With Koch seated at his side, Gibson listened to the rehearsal and went through several more Camels; because they were recording, no stops could be made—the invasion from Mars went forward even with flubs.

The adaptation of the Wells novella began imaginatively enough with a news bulletin interrupting a remote broadcast of a dance band. Then a second bulletin took reporter Carl Phillips (former Shadow, Frank Readick) to the Princeton Observatory to interview Professor Pierson, played by a small man with a big voice. Soon the two men were at the scene, and a more or less conventional fantasy melodrama played out.

When it was finished, director Stewart emerged from the adjacent control booth to speak to Koch, with Gibson still at the radio writer's side.

"Well?" Stewart asked.

"It wasn't terrible," Koch said.

"No," Stewart admitted. "It was worse than terrible: it wasn't good," The director pulled a chair up. He looked to his guest. "What do you think, Walter?"

"I don't know that my opinion matters."

"I'd like to hear it."

"Well, you don't have the sound effects perfected yet. . . ."

"No," Stewart granted. "We'll be doing that on Saturday. Ora's the best—the effects'll be first-rate by air."

"Good. And that one actor was obviously filling in for Orson."

"Yes. Bill Alland. He always sits in for Orson on these rehearsals."

"He's not bad, but Orson's a star, with the greatest voice in radio. He'll sell this."

Stewart nodded. "What works for you? What doesn't?"

Gibson shrugged. "It starts out great. Those news bulletins are compelling. I like the bit, after the holocaust, where the ham radio fella is wondering if he's the last person on earth, alive." He glanced at Koch. "All that plays into the immediacy of the medium that you were talking about."

Stewart grunted. "More bulletins, you think?" He seemed to be asking Gibson as much as Koch.

Koch threw up his hands. "We better wait for Orson on this. He'll have an opinion."

Stewart arched a dark eyebrow. "*An* opinion?"

Everyone stood, and after some small talk, Gibson was about to take his leave when Stewart was called to the phone. Since good-byes hadn't been exchanged yet, Gibson waited politely. Stewart returned a few minutes later.

"That was Orson," the director said. "He's tied up at the theater working on *Danton's Death*—the new play. I told him you sat through the rehearsal, Walter, and he'd like you to join us when we listen to the acetate, and help us brainstorm over how to fix this thing."

"Well . . . I'd be glad to. It's an honor."

Koch smirked. "Not really. Orson loves to charm free help out of professionals."

Gibson lifted one shoulder in a shrug. "I'm on expense account. What time?"

Stewart sighed. "That's the bad part—can you make five A.M. over at the Mercury Theatre?"

"Sure." Gibson shook his head, and chortled, "But I didn't figure a theater-type like Orson Welles for such an early hour."

"More like late," Stewart said. "He'll probably still be rehearsing the cast when we get there. . . ."

FRIDAY

October 28, 1938

On May 6, 1915, Orson Welles was born in Kenosha, Wisconsin, not far from Chicago, Illinois. His family was well-off, even well-to-do, his father an inventor and a hotelier, his mother a renowned pianist. From early childhood, he was surrounded by friends of the family who were intellectuals and artists—musicians, writers, actors, painters, and the occasional industrialist. He was welcomed as a prodigy, a child genius, and Orson lived up to the challenge. Before long a headline in a Madison newspaper was proclaiming him: "Cartoonist, Actor, Poet—and Only Ten!"

"My father," he once said, "was a gentle, sensitive soul whose kindness, generosity and tolerance made him much beloved. . . . From him I inherited the love of travel, which has become ingrained within me. From my mother I inherited a real and lasting love of music and the spoken word, without which no human being is really a complete and satisfactory person."

His father, however, often travelled without him; and his mother died within days of the boy's ninth birthday. His *guardian, Dr. Maurice Bernstein (a former lover of Orson's mother), shared with the parents a belief in the boy's genius—Bernstein gave the child a conductor's baton at age three. The guardian ("Dadda," Orson called him) also introduced young Orson to magic tricks, and gave him a puppet theater where the precocious one could concoct his own shows.*

He was fifteen when his father died, and his youth thereafter was spent in a series of progressive schools; by high school he was an old hand at producing Shakespeare, coming up with a version of Julius Caesar *that won top prize from the Chicago Drama League for a student production (once the jury had been shown proof that the young actors were not professionals).*

At sixteen, he set out from the latest of these schools for Europe with five hundred dollars and a dream of becoming an artist—he had painted and drawn since age two. He wound up in Dublin, broke—travelling by donkey cart, paying his way with his artwork after the money ran out—and presented himself to the prestigious Gate Theatre company as an American broadway star, "the sensation of the New York Theatre Guild."

His confidence was credible, if not his story, and soon in this old city with its rich theatrical tradition, the young actor was on stage, winning good notices—playing a Duke, the ghost in Hamlet, *and even the King of Persia. Soon offers came from England, but when the boy tried to follow up on these opportunities, the Ministry of Labor refused a work permit, and Orson Welles returned to America, a seasoned veteran of the Dublin stage.*

But Broadway was—initially—unimpressed, and young Welles sought theatrical satisfaction offstage, creating an annotated stage edition of Shakespeare's works (The Mercury Shakespeare) *and returning to the pursuit of painting, first in Morocco, then Spain. When playwright Thornton Wilder rec-*

ommended him to Katharine Cornell, the celebrated actress hired him to appear in touring productions of The Barretts of Wimpole Street *and* Romeo and Juliet.

Operating out of Chicago, Welles further dabbled in theater in nearby rural Woodstock, organizing a festival through the Todd School, one of the progressive institutions he'd attended as a child. In addition to attracting attention, and making his first short film, Welles won a wife, a lovely and privileged eighteen-year-old actress, Virginia Nicholson.

His touring for Katharine Cornell finally led to Broadway, where a struggling producer—John Houseman—saw the teenager's performance as Tybalt in Romeo and Juliet, *and knew at once his own destiny would be bound up with that of this "monstrous boy—flatfooted and graceless, yet swift and agile . . . from which issued a voice of such clarity and power that it tore like a high wind through the genteel, modulated voices of the well-trained professionals around him."*

At thirty-three, the balding, stocky former Jacques Haussmann—born in Bucharest to an English mother and French father, a successful grain merchant turned Broadway writer/producer/director—was at a personal crossroads. Despite an intimidating bearing, including the accent of a cultured English gentleman, Houseman had little confidence in himself—"My shame and fear were almost unbearable, my ineptitude so glaring"—and in the nineteen-year-old Welles, Houseman saw in full bloom the qualities he himself lacked.

A partnership began with Houseman hiring the teenager to play a sixty-year-old failed industrialist in the prophetically titled Archibald MacLeish play, Panic. *The show ran only three performances, but Welles was praised, and a partnership was forged, Houseman as business adminstrator, Welles as artistic director. Together they mounted New*

York's most compelling theatrical productions of the mid-1930s. For the Federal Theatre, a WPA project designed to create work for actors, they staged an innovative, all-black-cast Macbeth in a striking Haitian voodoo setting designed by Welles himself. Then, with barely two nickels to rub together, the two men created their own repertory company, the Mercury Theatre.

Their first production, Julius Caesar, was performed in modern dress in a stark, startling setting—actors in business suits and facist military uniforms against a blood-red background. Their most famous production, Marc Blitzstein's opera The Cradle Will Rock, found the dynamic duo thumbing their noses at the WPA shutting them down, and skirting union demands despite the play's (and their own) left-wing stance, by staging the show from the audience, actors standing and performing their lines in the aisles amid dazzled theatergoers.

During this same period, Welles had become a popular radio actor—a brilliant serialization in 1937 of Les Miserables had paved the way for future glories, and by 1938 The March of Time and Shadow star was making a thousand dollars a week . . . even before he brought his and Jack Houseman's repertory company, the Mercury Theatre, to CBS.

In October 1938, Orson Welles was twenty-three years old.

CHAPTER TWO

Broadway Malady of 1938

Through the early morning fog came the brooding bray of a great liner—the *Queen Mary*—steaming through the Narrows, turning north toward the slender island of Manhattan. Elsewhere, chugging through darkness still shrouding New Jersey, a train carried sightseeing familes (115,000 daily, even in this Depression) as well as hopeful youths seeking fortune and fame, while in the city, night workers were just starting home (some of them anyway), their steps as sharp as a tap dancer's, though considerably less regular, on sidewalks otherwise uncharacteristically quiet. Nearby, the occasional automobile and water wagon haunted empty streets, and in perhaps half a dozen night-clubs around the big town, bands played on, mostly after-hours improv sessions by musicians seeking to use up the last shreds of a night long since turned to morning. In the next half hour, alarm clocks would begin to trill across the Upper East and Upper West Side alike, and in Hell's Kitchen and the Gashouse, too, as well as Greenwich

Village and Chelsea, their ringing ricocheting off mostly vacant streets.

And in a taxi, moving through skyscraper canyons that were still sporadically lit by neon, Walter Gibson was making his way from the St. Regis—an absurdly posh hotel at which the writer would never have stayed, off expense account—to a theater at 41st and Broadway that had once been called the Comedy. Now, as its still-burning neon insisted, visible from Sixth Avenue to Broadway, it was the

**M
E
R
C
U
R
Y**

after the theater company that inhabited it.

Like the St. Regis, the Mercury had an Edwardian façade, though the former seemed to have frozen spectacularly in time around the turn of the century, while the latter with its glittering green-and-gold woodwork had a freshly painted, facelifted feel, more out of last week.

This impression continued as Gibson moved through a small lobby, quietly classy with its pearl-gray walls and crystal chandelier. A pretty, plump blonde of perhaps fifteen in a fuzzy pink sweater could be seen through the box office window, where she was sleeping on her arms, like a schoolgirl taking a teacher-enforced nap.

Careful not to wake her, Gibson crept into the theater itself—no one, at 4:32 A.M., was taking tickets.

For Broadway, the auditorium was rather intimate, a rococo affair with two balconies and perhaps seven hundred seats. The licks of paint and the fancy touches (the gilt feathering on the façade, the chandelier in the lobby) appeared to represent the Mercury's major investment in refurbishing the old house—the red aisle carpeting and the wine-color frayed seats had been sewn, though not with thread precisely matching the originals, and the walls and proscenium had the patchy look of plaster repairs and selective painting that were practical first, and cosmetic a distant second.

A showman of sorts himself, Gibson knew that the Mercury putting its money in the outside and outer lobby made sense: these imperfections would disappear in the dark, and anyway, the productions on stage would consume the eyes and dazzle the imaginations of playgoers.

This Gibson knew at a glance, as he took in the stunning, almost mind-boggling stage set of the Welles production about to open: *Danton's Death*.

The play, while hardly a household word, happened to be one with which Gibson was familiar—he'd seen an elaborate Broadway production of it, about ten years before, directed by the legendary showman Max Reinhardt, who had filled the stage with mob scenes and grandeur. Written by Georg Buechner, a political activist who died at twenty-four in 1837, the play centered on a brief though pivotal episode in the French Revolution. Set in the spring of 1794, *Danton's Death* reflected the full social and political upheaval of the Reign of Terror.

By ironic coincidence, Gibson had spent Thursday evening (on the Welles expense account) taking in a picture at the Astor starring Norma Shearer—*Marie Antoinette*. But the Mercury version of the French Revolution did not seem to have much in common with the MGM take on the same subject matter . . . though Gibson could see how the movie company currently courting the boy director, Warner Bros.—who after all gave birth to *Little Caesar*—might well be attracted to Welles's expressionistic, melodramatic approach. . . .

A dress rehearsal was in full swing, but it was the set that commanded Gibson's immediate attention.

Dominating was a massive curved backdrop arrayed with hundreds of blank masks that, through shifting dramatic lighting (blood-red, steel-gray, garish purple) now might suggest the murderous mob, later invoke the skulls of the mob's victims, or even the tribunal deciding life or death for the play's characters.

In front of that wall of faces, just behind the forestage, rose a four-sided tower with steps on either side, so that actors could emerge from beneath—a pit had been carved out of the stage itself—and if that weren't enough, the structure contained a working elevator that climbed a good twelve feet. The platform that rode the elevator was used in many ways—a rostrum, garret, salon, prison cell and, finally, at its full height, the scaffold of a guillotine.

Gibson watched, impressed but not quite getting the point of any of it, despite having seen that earlier production. Lighting effects seemed to shoot from every direction, performers appearing or disappearing as if from thin air, this lone actor orating to an unseen shouting multitude, that small group emerging from the darkness to discuss the effect of the Revolution on their lives and potential deaths. Occasionally music interrupted the drama, a revolutionary hymn, a macabre celebratory chorus chanting "Carmagnole," with the actor playing Danton obviously speaking English as a second language, as he expressed his opposition to "pipple in welwet gowns."

Welles and the Mercury had a reputation, from their informal *Cradle Will Rock* to their street-dress *Julius Caesar,* for making Highbrow Thea-tah accessible to the masses. But right now the resolutely middlebrow Walter Gibson was feeling pretty lowbrow. . . .

One of the actors was not in costume, and after a while, Gibson recognized him: Bill Alland, the little big-voice guy who had sat in for Welles at the radio-show rehearsal yesterday afternoon. He seemed to be filling in for Welles again, so that the director did not have to be distracted by his own acting.

In fact, early on, Gibson—who'd tucked himself in a seat toward the back of the house—spotted Welles up in the seventh row, on the aisle, with his feet up on the seat in front of him. Now and then, in rolled-up shirtsleeves and suspenders and dark baggy trousers, the great man-boy would rise and pace that aisle—although on his return, that pacing would be backward, his eyes always on the stage.

During the forty or so minutes that Gibson watched, Welles at first was eating ice cream—pistachio?—with a spoon from a quart container, and then was smoking a cigar large enough for a relay-race baton, its sweetly fragrant smoke wafting all the way back to Gibson.

Though mostly the writer was viewing the director from the rear, Gibson did get glimpses of that famous baby face, always frowning, and could strongly sense that Welles was restraining himself. Gibson could not just sense that Welles wanted to interrupt; waves of that desire seemed to roll up the aisle.

However, as Howard Koch had told Gibson, *Danton's Death* had been in previews already—with previews for last night and tonight and tomorrow night cancelled to make way for more rehearsal—and now the next preview loomed on Monday with *real* opening night on the following Wednesday.

According to both Paul Stewart and Koch, Welles was having fits with this play, and disaster had courted it: not long ago, the elevator had collapsed, hurling an actor into the basement, where the man had broken his leg (he had been replaced, and Stewart had wryly commented that the other actors considered him "the lucky one").

Needing to function smoothly on a stage littered with perils, the actors—navigating a stage strewn with gaping holes, catwalks and scaffolding—had lobbied for several uninterrupted run-throughs (Orson normally did not wait till the end to give notes, but constantly called the proceedings to a halt, to provide a running commentary).

When the guillotine finally fell, Welles rose grandly from his aisle seat and roared, "All right, children—we've killed this thing! The question is, do we put it out of its misery, or try for resurrection?"

The cast had lined itself up as if waiting for a firing squad. They hung their heads; they looked bleary-eyed and exhausted.

Their condition did not appear wholly lost on Welles, whose voice modulated into a gruff warmth, though the volume continued to rumble the house seats.

"Here at the Mercury," he said, "we are compelled to work under pressure—that is because we must make up in intensity and creativity what we lack in money! We can't afford to take a show out on the road to whip it into shape. We have finally mastered the technical aspects of this production. Now, my children . . ."

Virtually every one of the haggard "children" on stage was older than Welles, some by a decade or two.

". . . we must attempt to breathe life into this corpse."

A hand tapped on Gibson's shoulder, and he practically jumped from his seat. He looked back and up at the heart-shaped face of the sweetly pretty blonde in the fuzzy pink sweater who'd been slumbering in the box office booth. Her hair was a tumble of curls atop her head, and her blue eyes had an apologetic cast.

"Are you Mr. Gibson?" she asked, in a squeaky little voice that was at once comic and appealing. She had a womanly shape for a kid. "If you are, Mr. Houseman would like to see you . . ." Her voice lowered an octave. ". . . upstairs."

Whether intended or not, the effect was comic and Gibson, standing in the aisle facing the girl, said, "That sounds almost as ominous as the French Revolution."

"More ominous than that," she squeaked, rolling her eyes.

Soon he was following her through the lobby—not an unpleasant task, as the movement of her backside beneath the tight dark woolen dress had a hypnotic effect—and then up several flights of stairs to the upper balcony. Welles's booming voice, alternately furious at incompetence and lavish with praise, filled the house.

After a long, complicated climb, the shapely teenager led him to yet more steps, iron ones up into what had clearly been an electrician's booth.

The girl stepped inside the narrow, stuffy room, Gibson poised in the doorway behind her. Welles's voice, muffled, going over tiny details, leached through the twin holes in the wall that had once been used, presumably, for follow spots in the Comedy Theatre's musical days.

"Mr. Gibson is here, Mr. Houseman," the girl said, rather timidly.

Gibson took in the office with a few glances: an exposed paint-peeling radiator, hot enough to fry an egg on; a bulletin board with a much-annotated 1938 calendar courtesy of some bank, various reviews with sections underlined, and a sheet boldly labelled MERCURY THEATRE 1937–38 SUBSCRIBERS LIST; 8-by-10s of actors and production sketches taped haphazardly to the walls; and a couple battered secondhand-looking bookcases brimming with scripts and books and boxes of Mercury letterhead and envelopes, in stylish brown ink.

Nothing unexpected, really, with a single exception: on the wall, riding some nails, was a large sharp-looking hunting knife with a gleaming blade and a light-brown wooden handle bearing a bold ORSON WELLES autograph.

The space itself had been divided by a beaverboard partition into two even smaller offices—the nearer was a secretarial area, with a small gray metal desk and typewriter, unattended, a row of filing cabinets behind; the other side had a glorified card table with a chair behind it and several chairs in front of it, a daybed hugging the left wall. On the table were two telephones, and a small portable Victrola, and seated behind the table, hands folded like a school teacher patiently waiting to reprimand a wayward student, was a formidable fellow who projected various contradictory messages.

His yellow-and-black checkered sportcoat said casual, his black bow tie said formal; his dark slashes of eyebrow on an egg-shaped noggin (well on its way to being completely bald), sent signals of strength, while a languid weakness was implied by a feminine, sensuous-lipped mouth that seemed permanently formed in a mild condescending smile. Or was it a sneer?

And his eyes seemed at once drowsy and keenly alert.

"Thank you, Judy," their host said, in a British-tinged voice—was the tone kind, or patronizing?—and rose, extending a soft hand across the table. "John Houseman, Mr. Gibson. Please call me Jack."

"And I'm Walter," the writer said, Houseman's soft hand providing a firm handshake.

The stocky study in contrasts sat and gestured to the chair opposite for Gibson. In the background, Welles's voice droned on and on about a hundred details, while Miss Holliday was frozen in the doorway, like Lot's wife.

"Is that all, Mr. Houseman?" she quavered.

"It is not." Houseman lifted his arm, slid back a sleeve, and gave a royal look to his wristwatch. "My sense is that our resident genius is winding down, and we're expecting both Mr. Stewart and Mr. Koch within the next ten minutes. Would you be so kind, Miss Holliday, as to go next door to Longchamps and order Mr. Welles's usual repast, and . . . is standard eggs and bacon and potatoes suitable, Mr. Gibson?"

"Sure."

Houseman twitched a polite smile the writer's way, and to Miss Holliday intoned, "Three standard breakfasts plus my usual lox, onion and scrambled eggs. Only a *single* baked potato for Mr. Welles—he informs us that he's dieting."

Miss Holliday was moving from shoe to shoe. Her hands were fig-leafed before her and she seemed clearly distraught. "But Mr. Houseman . . . I told you before—Longchamps won't give us credit anymore. I had to pay cash myself for his ice cream tonight."

"For which you will be reimbursed."

Her eyes widened. "Mr. Houseman—Mr. Welles owes them over two hundred dollars."

"Shit!" The word exploded from Houseman, as if trying to escape from the prissy prison of the man. "You tell those fucking people that I will personally vouch for Mr. Welles."

Tears were flowing down the girl's apple cheeks. "But Mr. Houseman . . ."

"God-*damn*-it!" Houseman stood, fished a billfold from inside his jacket, and handed Gibson a twenty-dollar bill, which the stunned writer passed to the girl, who padded over for it.

Arm outstretched like the pope blessing the masses, Houseman said, "Pay the bastards in cash, and don't mention Mr. Welles by name!"

"But Mr. Houseman," she sobbed, "they'll know it's for him. . . ."

"Order the steaks separately, my dear—as if for two people—and if they ask if the two meals are for Mr. Welles, lie through your delightful pretty teeth."

"Oh, Mr. Houseman . . ."

"*Do* it."

She swallowed, nodded, and disappeared, her footsteps on the metal stairs ringing like gunshots punctuating Welles's ongoing harangue.

Gibson nodded toward where she'd stood. "Does she *always* cry like that?"

"Only when I swear."

"Ah."

"I do it for her own good—swear at her, that is."

"Is that so?"

Houseman nodded sagely. "She's a nice girl, from a respectable family, but . . . sad to say . . . she wants to be in show business. So I'm breaking her in, so to speak. If she wants to make it in this trade, she'll need to acclimate herself to coarseness."

Gibson was shaking his head. "A kid that nervous? You really think she could make it in show biz?"

"Don't underestimate Judy, Walter. She's smarter than either of us . . . and her sense of finance is admirable." Houseman shifted in his chair. "That is, frankly, why I asked to see you, prior to our little *Mercury on the Air* staff meeting. Which I understand you've agreed to attend?"

"I have. I figure I'm on Orson's dime, no matter how you look at it."

An eyebrow arched. "Actually—you're on the Mercury Theatre's dime . . . which is how *I* look at it."

"Not sure I understand, Jack."

The permanent sneer twitched, and Houseman folded his hands on the table again. His head tilted to one side, and his eyes were hooded as he said, "My young partner has no sense of money. He throws it to the wind. You've seen the production he's mounting, currently?"

"I have. It's . . ."

"Impressive. And a bewildering exercise in pretention, as well . . . but he is the artistic director, not I. This theater, this old warhorse, needed renovation—one of the first things, first expenses, we undertook was to put in a new stage."

"Ah. And Mr. Welles ripped much of that stage out, for this production, for that fancy tower he rigged."

The drowsy eyes flared; the sneer took on a tinge of pleasure. "You are bright man, Mr. Gibson, and perceptive."

"And you have called me here to request that I not abuse my expense account."

Houseman nodded once; he exuded the wisdom of Buddha. Also the stature.

"Jack, it's not in my nature to take advantage. Mr. Welles made the St. Regis reservation . . ."

Another nod. "For his own convenience, since he's living there, more or less."

"More or less?"

"He's a married man, you know—with a baby girl, as well as a wife. They live on Sneden's Landing, well out of the city. But Orson, while he's working, has decided to stay mostly in town."

"And he's always working."

"You already have a grasp of the situation, Walter."

Gibson shrugged. "Don't worry yourself, Jack—I am not by nature extravagant. I need to take cabs, because I don't have my car here in the city; and I have to eat. But I won't be running up any elaborate bills to stiff the Mercury."

Houseman's tiny smile seemed somehow huge. "You are a gentleman. And I understand Orson owes you much."

"All I did was recommend him to the producers of the Shadow show, once upon a time."

"Yes, but that was the Welles watershed—without his success as the Shadow, we'd have no radio program. I know he is very grateful to you."

Gibson did not point out that Welles had waited until just a few days ago to thank him. For some reason, he glanced at the hunting knife, displayed on the wall, just to his left.

"You've noticed our little memento from *Julius Caesar,* I see," Houseman said with a smile as sly as it was slight. "That's our eternal reminder to our enthusiastic leader that even a genius must contain his enthusiasm."

"How's that?" Gibson asked.

"Well, all of the other conspirators in our production were satisfied with heavy rubber daggers, with aluminum-painted blades. Not good enough for Brutus, that is, Orson, who felt the final confrontation with the tyrant required the reality of a gleaming blade."

Houseman gestured casually to the mounted hunting knife.

"For more than one hundred performances, Brutus held that sharp point against our Caesar's chest; then as, actor Joe Holland clung to Orson, in beautifully performed death agonies, Brutus would make the final thrust, with a turn of his body."

The producer tented his fingertips and continued.

"One spring night—without either Orson or Mr. Holland being aware of it—the blade went through the cloth and slipped . . . quite painlessly . . . into Joe Holland's chest, and through an artery in the region of his heart. No one realized anything had gone awry, until Orson himself slipped in the blood. . . . In the blackout following Antony exclaiming, 'Cry havoc and let slip the dogs of war,' we were able to cart Joe's inert form from the stage. As the show continued, he was taken by taxi to the nearest hospital."

"My God, but he surived?"

"After several days . . . and several transfusions. Orson initially experienced a brief spasm of guilt, but soon managed to convince himself it was Joe's fault, for turning incorrectly and impaling himself."

"You're lucky you weren't sued."

"We paid Joe Holland's bills. Our Caesar even wound up apologizing to Brutus . . . but I never saw it that way. So I mounted that dagger in an attempt to provide our gifted boy with a conscience of sorts."

"How's that working out?"

Houseman twitched a wry smile. "Not terribly well, so far. As you can see, his response was merely to *sign* the weapon. . . ."

Footsteps on the iron stairs announced a new arrival—and it couldn't be Welles, because his alternate scolding and praise continued from below—and then Paul Stewart, looking mournful and tired, his sunken cheeks blue with beard, stepped inside. An acetate recording in a brown-paper sleeve was tucked under his arm. His gray suit looked rumpled, his blue tie already loose at his collar.

"Mr. Gibson," Stewart said with a nod, as the writer rose briefly, returning the nod. Stewart handed the shellac disc across to Houseman. "Here it is, Jack. Any chance Orson will finish that harangue by Sunday?"

Placing the disc neatly next to the record player on the table, Houseman said, "I believe he'll release his prisoners, any moment now."

Stewart deposited himself on the daybed, nearer Houseman than Gibson. "Breakfast on the way?"

With a nod that took about three seconds, Houseman replied, "Breakfast is indeed on the way. The mission is Miss Holliday's."

"We oughta put that kid on the Mercury program," Stewart said. "I think she's a natural comedienne."

"Despite her constant tears," Houseman said, "I tend to agree . . . ah. Here's Howard."

Koch had clanged up the stairs and was in the cubbyhole's doorway. He, too, looked haggard and unshaven, his tan suit and yellow tie like clothes he'd removed from a hamper, after wadding.

The two writers exchanged warm greetings, and Koch dropped himself on the daybed next to Stewart. He eyed the transcription disc grimly.

"So," Koch said to Stewart. "You've brought the evidence."

Stewart smirked humorlessly. "Some is found at the scene of every crime."

Welles's voice had ceased. The sound of movement below indicated the cast had finally been dismissed. Everyone in the electrician's booth office lighted up a cigarette and a swirl of blue smoke was waiting when Welles's heavy trod could finally be heard coming up those iron stairs.

Gibson didn't know what to expect—an exhausted tyrant, most likely.

And yet the figure framed in the doorway appeared energetic and strangely cherubic. His big body, both tall and bordering on heavyset, his arms limp at his sides, his head rather large for even this formidable frame, with a small mouth in the round face no less a baby's for the cheeks needing a shave.

Most amazing were the vaguely Asian eyes which seemed to light with delight upon the sight of Gibson.

"My dear Walter," he said, moving quickly to the writer, who got quickly to his feet. Welles's expression might have been that of a man reunited with his oldest friend after a painful separation. "How kind of you to sit in with us on this postmortem."

"Glad to help," was all Gibson could think to say. The charm, the charisma of this twenty-three-year-old seemed to consume Gibson's very air, his ability to think clearly.

Welles strode to the vacant chair next to Gibson, opposite the seated Houseman—whose expression seemed to define boredom—and said to everyone but Gibson, "Our poor friend has already put up with far too many indignities from me."

Seeking out one face at a time, Welles continued his tale.

"I bring Walter in yesterday, out of his own busy schedule, and then have the wretched rudeness not even to show up at our rehearsal, much less seek him out at our mutual hotel!"

He deposited his weight on the chair next to Gibson, motioning for the writer to sit. Now Welles's gaze was back on Gibson, and his tone was intimate as he said, "I'm afraid it was unavoidable. My current stage production is a train wreck, and my first responsibilty was to be the engineer who got it back up on the tracks."

Gibson swallowed, nodded.

Welles turned toward Houseman. "Now, Housey . . . please tell me that breakfast has been ordered."

Houseman nodded once, a quicker one than before. "But Miss Holliday informs me that you have run up a personal tab at Longchamps in the sum of two hundred dollars."

Welles waved that off. "I assume, after she stopped crying, that you gave her some money and sent her off like a good little girl."

Again Houseman nodded. He was leaning back now, the hands folded over his belly.

Welles sighed grandly. "I suppose we must listen to this thing. . . . Does anyone have anything to say, first? How did it go in the studio?"

Stewart shrugged. "It's not our finest hour, but I think it's shaped up—thanks to Howard, here."

Koch said, "Maybe we should have done 'Lorna Doone,' after all."

Welles shook his head. "No, this will work. I know it will. The potential here is for our most important broadcast."

This opinion seemed to amaze Stewart, whose eyes were unblinking marbles under the dark slashes of eyebrow. "Really? . . . Well, I was just hoping to get through the thing without any of our reputations suffering. . . . Now, of course, Orson, I won't be refining the sound effects until Saturday. Ora has specifically requested that I tell you she will do her best to bring Mars to Earth, effectively . . . not to judge her by these preliminary, perfunctory efforts."

"Dear Ora," Welles said wistfully, looking ceilingward, as if contemplating his first love, "she is a wonder. The best sound man we could ever hope for, despite a lack of cock and balls."

Gibson wondered if he'd actually heard that. . . .

From the doorway, Judy Holliday said, "Oh Mr. Welles, that's terrible," and burst into tears.

Welles went to her, put an arm around her shoulder, and said, "There, there . . . you mustn't let such boy talk upset you so. I had no idea a gentle flower had planted itself in this doorway."

"Can I . . . can I have the food sent up?"

"I'll fire your little ass if you don't!"

She disappeared, her feet travelling down the iron steps sounding like a barrage of bullets, punctuating Welles's roar of hearty laughter.

The other men were smiling and chuckling, except for Gibson, an Alice still trying to get used to Wonderland.

Within minutes, a skinny, put-upon waiter in a white shirt and dark pants brought up a picnic basket, and left without waiting for a tip that he seemed to already know wasn't going to come. Houseman played host and opened the basket on his card-table desk, lifting the metal hats covering each plate, passing out the food to its intended recipient. Miss Holliday reappeared with a coffeepot and cups, and distributed those as well. Welles disappeared with his two plates—two large steaks, one in the company of a single sour-cream-and-butter-slathered baked potato—behind the partition, to sit at the secretary's desk there and eat unobserved.

The table was a good height for both Houseman and Gibson to eat their breakfasts, while Koch and Stewart—still seated on the daybed—seemed at ease eating off the plates in their laps, old hands at this.

Welles did call over a complaint about the single potato, until Houseman reminded him: "Your diet—remember?" To which Welles mumbled an unintelligble answer, a pouting child responding to a firm parent.

Then Welles, from behind the partition, ordered: "Well, play the goddamned thing, Housey!"

And Houseman placed the record on the record player, turned up the volume and they all ate while they listened to the rehearsal recording.

Minus the excitement of the studio, Koch's "War of the Worlds" adapation played even less excitingly, seeming terribly flat and uncompelling to Gibson. They finished their breakfast about halfway through—Martians were killing people at Grovers Mill—and suddenly Miss Holliday materialized again, to gather the plates and put them into the picnic basket, and vanish once more.

Gibson hardly noticed that Welles had taken the chair next to him again. The boy genius showed no emotion as he listened, sitting with arms folded, his expression as distant as it was blank.

When the recording reached its conclusion, and Bill Alland was signing off pretending to be Welles, the listener's "obedient servant," Houseman lifted the tone arm and the needle scratched just a bit. Then their host returned the acetate to its sleeve and looked at Welles, arching an eyebrow as if to say, "Well?"

"It stinks," Welles said.

From the corner of his eye, Gibson saw Koch essentially collapse into himself; and Stewart closed his eyes, as if he'd chosen to respond by going to sleep.

"It's corny," Welles went on, shrugging grandly. His voice was soft, no longer filling the room, making Koch and Stewart listen carefully to hear their work dismissed. "Unbelievable. Dull as dishwater. Also ghastly—no one's going to believe a word of it. . . . Paul, what does the cast think?"

Stewart swallowed. "They think it's pretty thin."

"And John Dietz? He's been a good judge."

"Our esteemed sound engineer thinks it's weak. One of our worst shows."

Welles turned to Gibson. "What's your opinion, Walter?"

"It starts well," Gibson managed.

Welles exploded off the chair. "Exactly right! Precisely right!"

Then the big man somehow managed to move around the little area, waving his arms, his eyes wild.

"Goddamnit, Howard, how you could blow this opportunity! I give you the key to this thing, and you throw it away! Threw it out the window!"

"Orson," Koch said, "I don't know what you mean—"

"And you, Paul," Welles said to the man who was doing his directing for him, "how you could betray me like this?"

Stewart didn't seem hurt or impressed, merely asked, "How so?"

Welles's tone shifted entirely, became genteel as he said to Gibson, "Walter, would you mind moving over for me?"

Gibson did.

"There's a dear." With a huge arm, Welles violently swept the chair Gibson had been sitting in and it clattered against the wall. Welles then filled the space the chair had inhabited, and loomed over the two men seated on the daybed, as if he were parent and they wayward children.

Voice booming, he said, "How many times have I told the two of you that the Mercury's responsibility is to bring experimental techniques to this untapped medium. . . . *Not* to just treat our material like a 'play'—the less a radio drama resembles a play, the better it's going to be!"

Welles thrust a finger at Gibson, who jumped in his chair a bit. "*This man,* who does *not* work in our medium on a daily basis . . . though I might point out his instincts about that medium only gave me the *part* that put us *all* on the map . . . *immediately* honed in on what will separate this show from all the rest."

Houseman, sitting back, hands folded on his belly, said in a voice that tried too hard to be nonchalant, "And what would that be, Orson?"

For the first time, Gibson realized that behind Houseman's mask was something else—insecurity, even fear. . . .

With a weight-of-the-world sigh, Orson Welles picked up the chair he'd tossed aside, righted it and sat, shaking his head slowly, a man devastated by disappointment.

"I suggested that we use news bulletins," Welles said quietly . . . too quietly, "and eyewitness accounts."

"We *did,*" Koch said, pain in his voice.

"You did . . . at the start—exactly twice."

Koch nodded. "Right. To get us into the piece."

Again Welles exploded, exasperated. "Howard—it *is* the piece! We need newscast simulations, absolutely believable. . . . We need that dance-band remote broadcast not to be interrupted once, like our recent 'Sherlock Holmes' broadcast was, but again and again. . . . We need *real* names, details, we need the illusion of up-to-the-second reality. Why do you think I had you change it from London to New Jersey? Why did I insist you do it modern day, not in turn-of-the-century London?"

"Actually," Koch said, raising a timid forefinger, "that was my idea . . ."

"Does it matter whose idea it is? Good God man, this is a collaboration! And the goal of this collaboration is to execute my vision! . . . Flash news bulletins, eyewitness accounts, as the Mars invasion is happening. Keep that going throughout the entire hour!"

Stewart said, "That's impossible—the story covers months. It has to be resolved."

"Fine, but keep it immediate as long as possible—for the first half of the thing, at the very least."

Houseman sat forward. "Orson—don't you realize that if . we present . . . fake newscasts, for a half hour or more . . ."

"Up until the station break midway, precisely."

Houseman swallowed and tried again. "Don't you realize, Orson, that listeners are apt to misunderstand."

Stewart snorted a laugh. "What, and think Martians are really invading?"

Welles was sitting with his arms folded now, his expression that of a pixie—a damn big pixie, but a pixie.

"And why not?" he asked.

Everyone sat forward, except Welles.

Houseman said, "Surely, you don't mean to fool our listeners into . . ."

"If that's all the more intelligent they are, why in hell not? Let me tell you where I got this idea. Back in 1926, a BBC broadcast out of Edinburgh, Scotland, presented a false news report about an unemployed mob in London sacking the National Gallery, blowing up Big Ben, hanging the Minister of Traffic to a tramway post, and blowing up the Houses of Parliament."

Everyone but Welles sat open-mouthed.

Welles, eyes twinkling, continued, "The 'newscast' concluded with the destruction of the BBC's flagship station. . . . After the broadcast, the BBC—and the police and the newspapers—were besieged with frantic citizens calling to see what was happening, and to find out what they could do in this terrible crisis."

Then he laughed and laughed, patting his knees like a department-store Santa Claus.

"You see it was a period of unusual labor strife—days before a general strike—and . . . what's wrong? You all look as if your best friend died."

Houseman held out a hand in the fashion of a traffic cop. "Orson, you surely can't be suggesting—"

"Oh, Housey, if a few loonies buy what we're doing, what's the harm? It'll make a wonderful Hallowe'en prank, and we'll have terrific publicity."

Koch, thinking aloud, said, "Well, we certainly can't go on the air cold. . . ."

"No, of course not!" Welles blurted. "We'll have a standard opening. And is it *our* fault . . ." Welles smiled with infinite innocence. ". . . if after Charle McCarthy's opening monologue, listeners just happen to check around their dial for something more lively than Chase and Sanborn's weekly guest singer, and happen upon our little charade?"

Stewart was starting to smile. "Well, I don't think it will

work—I don't think anyone will fall for this. But it's a hell of a good way to bring some extra punch to this yarn."

Koch was nodding. "It would be easy enough to rework it that way, too."

But Houseman was shaking his head, gloomily. "I don't approve. I do think people might well be fooled, just as those British listeners were. It's irresponsible, and it's cruel, not to mention a risky venture for the Mercury—I can envision lawsuits, and—"

"Ah, Housey," Welles said, "don't be a little girl!"

Houseman looked daggers across the desk. "Orson, you need to take more care. Or one day your comeuppance will come, and it will not be a pleasant thing to behold."

Welles waved that off. "It's the medium of radio that needs the comeuppance, that needs to get the starch taken out of it. It's *the* voice of authority, nowadays—too much so. And maybe we'll just give a little kick to the seat of the voice of authority's pants. Anyway, what's your alternative—any of you? To go on the air with this boring hour of hokum?"

Leaning forward, as if taking everyone into his confidence, which he was, Welles said, "My little hoax notion will save this show . . . but in case you're right, Housey, and things do get a little out of hand, like in England that time—let's just keep this to ourselves. After all, it's like a magic trick—a prank only works if the pranksters don't let anybody else in on the joke. . . ."

SATURDAY

October 29, 1938

Broadway began as a cowpath, only to be transformed by neon—chiefly red with dabs of yellow—into the blazing nighttime main stem of the world's largest frontier town. But as garish as it was by night, Broadway by day was drab and even dreary. Around Times Square, a score of dance halls thrived (ten cents per "beautiful hostess"), and all along the Great White Way, sidewalk spielers offered health soap, hand-painted ties, reducing belts, hot buttery ears of corn, and Get Rich Quick real-estate booklets. Good-looking gals shilled bus rides to Chinatown, and a haberdashery shouted "Going Out of Business Sale" (in its tenth year). Bus terminals, with their foul-smelling, lumbering coaches, offered cheaper fare than train, and adventurous tourists and locals alike were invited to partake of an array of theaters, movie palaces, hotels and cafes—also flea circuses, chop-suey parlors, burlesque houses, sideshows and clip joints. Millionaires mingled with panhandlers, youthful new stage stars brushed shoulders with aging burlesque comics, and current heavyweight champs bumped into derelicts who'd once been contenders or even champs themselves.

The current shabby state of Broadway could be traced to Prohibition—later aided and abetted by the Depression—when "nightclubs" first came into vogue. From the turn of the century, upper and middle-class Americans had sought European-style amusement in the form of exhibitions and expositions, rooftop gardens and crystal palaces, while the working class sought out the sawdust-under-foot fun provided by beer halls and carnivals. But Prohibition had sent American nightlife down its own quirky, particular path. . . .

A "nightclub" sought to circumvent the liquor laws by presenting itself as private, with members who dropped by for fine food, top entertainment, good conversation and, of course, their favorite soft drinks. That anyone who knocked three times might enter, and that the drinks were invariably hard, was the reality behind a fantasy kept alive by a casually law-breaking populace and their on-the-take law enforcement agencies.

By the time Prohibition was winding down, with the Depression kicking in, nightclub life was an American social tradition like baseball, circuses and the picture show. But the glittery clubs of the speakeasy era were an endangered species, saved from extinction by, as Fortune magazine put it, the "recent success of what is commonly known as the big Broadway joint, the gaudy bargain offer of fifty hot babies and a five-course dinner for $1.50 and no cover charge."

Take the French Casino, a swooping, curving artmoderne exercise in scarlet and silver, their terraced rows of tables comfortably seating fifteen hundred. The same number of patrons could be welcomed by the International Casino (not a casino at all), in the heart of Times Square, a red and gold wonder with "curtains" that were mirrors riding on electric tracks, and a flooded, frozen stage accommodating the Ice Frolics. Billy Rose's Casino de Paree—the remodeled New Yorker Theater on Broadway—offered a *five-buck meal, gorgeous chorus girls, headliner Gypsy Rose Lee (America's most famous striptease artiste) and the Benny Goodman orchestra.*

An impressive new arrival—perched on the top floor of a building at Broadway and 48th Street—was actually an old standby, a relocated Cotton Club, the famed Harlem landmark that had (in 1936) found its white clientele increasingly reluctant to travel to a Depression-ravaged ghetto for their entertainment.

The Cotton Club began in the fall of 1923 in an old theater on 142nd Street and Lenox Avenue, its primary owner one Owney Madden, who'd come from Liverpool as a child to New York's fabled Hell's Kitchen, where he developed from a banty rooster nicknamed "the Killer" into a dapper, sophisticated elder statesman of racketeers.

Despite the Harlem location, Madden ran the Cotton Club strictly for white patrons—Negroes were allowed solely on stage and/or in service capacities—in the manner of a posh downtown club, only showcasing exotic uptown talent. Cover charge was three dollars, beer a buck a bottle, the food prices (including neighborhood favorites like Southern fried chicken and Kansas City–style barbecue ribs) in line with the better Broadway clubs.

That the Cotton Club's late show began after-hours—when the late shows of other clubs were over—attracted entertainers, making it an "in" spot for the likes of Eddie Cantor, Jimmy Durante and Milton Berle. On a big stage—invoking the antebellum South via white plantation-style columns and a slave-cabin backdrop—cavorted a chorus line of gorgeous "high-yallar" gals (light-skinned black beauties, "Tall, Tan and Terrific!"); all under twenty-one, these girls were among the best singers and dancers in New York, and the show they gave was as wild as it was scantily clad. Both Cab Calloway and Duke Ellington had reigned over Cotton Club house bands through the years, and Ethel Waters and Lena Horne made their mark there.

The new club on Broadway opened in the fall of '36, and Calloway, Ellington and such other "colored" stars as Louis Armstrong, Steppin' Fetchit and Dorothy Dandridge (with her sisters) made it the hottest nightspot in Manhattan, pulling in thirty thousand dollars a week (despite the Depression), a new dance called the Boogie Woogie creating a sensation. The stage shows featured choreography, music, costumes and sets challenging Broadway's best.

Was it any wonder young Orson Welles was a frequent patron?

CHAPTER THREE

Cotton Clubbed

That human whirling dervish, Cab Calloway—wide eyes and wider smile turned skyward—was blazing through "Minnie the Moocher," in tailored tails, forelock flopping, working that conductor's baton as if nonchalantly yet energetically battling an invisible swordsman. Not merely his orchestra but the entire crowd—Walter Gibson and Orson Welles included—echoed the charismatic bandleader's "Hi-de-ho" chant.

Gibson had been to the original Cotton Club a few times, once with first-wife Charlotte and then again with Jewel, and he rather preferred the thatched-roof jungle look of the lavish reinvented club over the former one's Old South, moss-draped-oak-tree atmosphere. He full well realized the cannibal stereotype was even more offensive than that of the happy cotton-pickin' slave, but a tongue-in-cheek humor took the edge off. And, unlike the former club, this one welcomed Negro patrons—though relegated them to the rear.

Gibson felt under-dressed in his brown suit with a striped red-and-yellow tie, and he'd worn his vest, to seem at least a little respectable. He'd never guessed, leaving on this work trip, that he'd be going nightclubbing with Orson Welles, who in a black suit with black bow tie, black cape and black fedora didn't seem to have thrown off his Shadow persona, even if he had stepped down from the role on the radio.

Hell, Gibson hadn't even imagined he'd be sitting, clapping and yelling, "Hi de ho!" a mere few hours ago, back at the hotel. . . .

After the early-morning meeting at the Mercury Theatre yesterday, Gibson had returned to the St. Regis and caught a few more hours of sleep. Though his family had been fairly well off, particularly before the Depression, Gibson found the St. Regis almost off-puttingly posh. The eighteen-story Fifth Avenue hotel, facing Central Park, had been built in 1904 by John Jacob Astor for himself and his rich pals; Astor hadn't had much time to enjoy it, before going down with the *Titanic,* leaving behind this lavish relic of the Gilded Age.

But in hard times like these, you could feel guilty lounging around in a world of fine furnishings, marble floors and mahogany panelling with its gold-leaf-garnished molding. Bellboys didn't attend you—butlers did!

And Gibson didn't imagine any other pulp writer had ever before sat pounding away at a portable Corona at the antique writing desk in this high-ceilinged room with its silk wallpaper, Waterford chandelier and marble floor. He doubted the $75 he'd be receiving from Street and Smith for this short story ("Old Crime Week") would pay for even a night in this mink-lined flophouse.

By two P.M., having worked through what would have been lunch if it had occurred to him, he'd about hit the halfway point with the story. It featured his character Norgil—a composite of Harry Blackstone, Joseph Dunniger and several other real-life magicians—who appeared in short stories (as opposed to his novel-length Shadow yarns) in the pulp magazine, *Crime Busters.*

Pausing to take a drag on his umpteenth Camel of the

day, he was just thinking how—with Welles's interest in magic—Norgil might make an even better character than the Shadow for the boy genius when the phone on the mahogany nightstand trilled.

The voice in his ear was that familiar resonant baritone: "Walter, I didn't bring you here to loaf!"

Gibson, his fingertips red from typing, said, "I'm sure you didn't, Orson. Any suggestions?"

"I suggest you come up to my suite—toot sweet! I have a rehearsal at the theater at seven . . . so time is, as they say, a'wastin'!"

Soon Gibson, portable Corona in hand, stepped from the elevator onto the eighteenth floor, where   after calling ahead to check on Gibson's pedigree—the butler stationed there walked him to Mr. Welles's suite.

The door, which was unlocked, was opened for Gibson by said butler, and when Gibson entered, he was greeted by Welles, or rather Welles's voice, which boomed from the bedroom.

"Have you had lunch, Walter? Or for that matter, breakfast?"

"No!" Gibson called out.

The suite made Gibson's own St. Regis room seem like a bungalow at the Bide-a-Wee Motel in Peoria, Illinois. In addition to the requisite fifteen-foot ceiling with chandelier, the living room was ornately appointed in the Beaux Arts manner, with a decorative fireplace, an Oriental carpet and Louis XV furniture.

"I'm just calling down for room service!" Welles's voice informed his guest. Like the Shadow in full hypnotic mode, Welles thus far remained invisible.

Pausing to set down the typewriter to get out his Camels, Gibson suddenly put the pack of smokes away, deciding not to light up—not in here.

The expensive chairs and the two swooping sofas were stacked with spools of film, laying in careless coils, and on an end table pulled out into the middle of the room had been deposited what looked like a movie projector—sort of. The thing had two big spools (heavy with film) and an oversize viewfinder. Bits and pieces and fragments of film were scattered to either side of the machine, whose presence amid these antiques seemed vaguely futuristic, even alien.

Welles called: "*Walter!* What would you like?"

"Something light! Fish, maybe?"

"Fine! . . . Come in, come in. . . ."

Through French doors, Gibson found Welles in a bedroom dominated by a four-poster bed, on the unmade edge of which the wunderkind sat, using a white-and-gold nightstand phone that was as magnificent as the bed itself. With the command and detail of a battlefield general, Welles was giving an elaborate order for food—were further guests expected?—as he sat in a white terrycloth robe with a ST. R crest, his feet slippered in black.

Gibson stood with his portable typewriter fig-leafed before him.

After hanging up, Welles got to his feet and beamed at Gibson, shaking his hand heartily, warmly, his eyes locked on the writer's.

"Finally, we're going to get some work done, ay?" he said, as if the world had been conspiring against the pair.

A table near a bay window looking out on Fifth Avenue through sheer drapes was littered with scripts in black binders, which Welles cleared with an arm, sending them clattering to the floor, or anyway Oriental carpet. Welles gestured for Gibson to sit, which he did, and Welles sat opposite, leaning on his elbows, steepling his fingers.

"You've been very patient with me, Walter."

Gibson shrugged. "Entering your world is something of an adventure for me. I live a fairly sedentary life, you know."

"I do know, Walter—despite the whirlwind you've witnessed, much of my time is spent hunkered either over a typewriter myself—or a script with a rewrite pen. The first place a production has to be mounted, after all, is in the mind."

Nodding, Gibson asked, "If I might . . . and I don't mean to be rude or anything . . . but why would you invite me to the city to work on a project, when you have a Broadway production about to open, and a radio show to put on?"

Welles folded his arms, leaning back; the small but full-lipped mouth took on a scampish little smile. "Walter, my dear friend . . . I put on a radio show every week. And the Mercury is a full-time repertory company—we go from one play right into another, often presenting several plays simultaneously."

"So if you waited for a lull . . ."

The big man gave a tiny shrug. "No such animal in my life of late—and I believe that breed known as the Hollywood producer has the capacity to maintain his interest, his enthusiasm, about as long as a baby does a butterfly."

"I'm not sure I follow."

Welles leaned forward conspiratorially, eyebrows lifted. "I have designed *Danton's Death*—this new play, you saw some of it?"

"Yes."

"I have designed it dramatically—no, melodramatically, in a fashion that I think will demonstrate to the brothers Warner, and the minions they've dispatched to scout me, that I have the visual sense required to make films."

Gibson nodded. "The striking sets, the movement, the sort of . . . 'cutting' between scenes, it's all meant to show you off as a potential filmmaker?"

The kiss of a mouth twitched approval. "Precisely. I expect several key Warner Bros. executives to attend early performances of *Danton's Death*—and I want to be ready with a film project for them, to strike while the iron is hot, as they say."

"Is that the reason for all of the celluloid scattered about?"

Gibson asked, gesturing with a thumb toward the French doors. "And that gizmo?"

"What? . . . Oh, the Moviola! That's an editing machine. I'm still playing with the film we shot for *Too Much Johnson,* the farce we're planning to mount. We had a bad experience trying it out in summer stock, but I'm still hopeful."

"Ah. You mentioned that on the phone."

"Yes, I wanted to combine theater with film—present two lengthy portions of the show as a movie. It's delightful stuff—Joe Cotten's a natural on screen, funny as hell. But I ran into a wall."

"How so?"

"Well, I didn't realize that what I was up to required any special . . . dispensation. But it turns out MGM had film rights to the play, and they insist on charging us an arm and a leg for me to use my stuff." Welles shrugged again, a larger more fatalistic one.

Gibson wondered how this skilled if young producer could have used the bad judgment to just do what he wanted, without checking into permissions. But Gibson immediately answered his own question: Welles was a child, a fun, bright, enthusiastic one . . . also spoiled. Like all spoiled children, he wasn't much on asking permission. . . .

"I can tell you, though, Walter, playing with this film, seeing how you can tell a story through pictures, little jigsaw-puzzle pieces, well, I get a real charge out of it."

"So this Warners interest means a lot to you."

"It does. It does indeed. I have so many ideas about making films—Walter, I can barely contain myself."

"Such as?"

"You've seen the German films? *Caligari,* for instance? Fritz Lang's *Metropolis*?"

"Sure. Judging by their crime pictures, I think the guys at Warners Bros. have, too."

"Precisely! But they haven't taken it far enough." Welles sat forward, his eyes alive and twinkling, his palms open and outstretched, like Jolson on his knees. "I want to make radio . . . for the *screen*."

Gibson winced in thought. "You mean, do more heightened, sophisticated sound work?"

Welles waved a dismissive hand. "Well, that, too, but . . . Walter, do the images you produce in your own mind, when you listen to a radio show—do the motion pictures you see in your local movie house match up to that?"

"To my own imagination? Hell no!"

"Ha! Precisely. It was better back in the silent days, when the cameras weren't so bulky—think of the images von Stroheim achieved, and Griffith, and even DeMille. It was as if you were witnessing your own dreams coming to life . . . and that's what I intend to make happen again, but even more so. Low angles, high angles, lighting effects, backgrounds as carefully art-directed as one of my Mercury stage productions."

"And you think the Shadow would lend itself to this?"

A small smile twitched. "Well . . . if I may be frank . . ."

Gibson grinned. "You're buying lunch, aren't you?"

"Well, Housey's checkbook is. . . . My goal would be to do on screen the kinds of things I'm attempting on stage. Nobody's seriously tried to do Shakespeare, for example, since Mickey Rooney was Puck in that MGM fiasco."

"I liked that movie."

"You have to strip these classics down, reimagine them, for the masses. I did *Hamlet* in an hour on the radio!"

And left out the 'To Be Or Not To Be' speech, Gibson thought, but said nothing.

"I intend to do Conrad's *Heart of Darkness* . . . *Lear* . . . *The Life of Christ*!"

"If you have these . . ." The writer almost said "pretensions," but substituted: ". . . goals—why the Shadow?"

Welles expression seem to melt into a mask of chagrin. "I've insulted you . . ."

"No. No!"

". . . Please don't think I undervalue your contribution to either my career or the medium of radio."

"I didn't think—"

"I am no snob." Then, in a tone so arch it undercut everything he said, Welles continued: "In fact, I am so resolutely middlebrow as to want to bring the highbrow down to my meager level."

"Some would call the Shadow lowbrow."

"Not Orson Welles. I kept myself alive, in Spain, back in '33, plying *your* trade—writing pulp detective yarns! And you know of my love for magic—for the carnival-like thrill of prestidigitation, for velvet cloaks, for rabbits in hats, for aces of spades that appear in pockets! No, I love melodrama, and your hawk-nosed avenger . . . I'm working on my own false nose already, wait until you see me with a snoot worthy of this face! . . . Your creation is ideal for the cinema of dreams-come-to-life, my radio for not just the ears, but the eyes!"

Breakfast arrived, a small army of butlers bringing such a banquet that Gibson had first wondered who Welles might have invited to join them.

But it was *all* for them, a finnan haddie with baby red shrimps in a cream sauce for Gibson, an enormous serving of lobster Newburg for his host, plus appetizers including frog legs, scallops and oysters, with fresh-baked dinner rolls and a side salad with garlic dressing. No dessert had been ordered ("I can have them bring you something, Walter, just say the word! . . . But I'm dieting . . .") and Gibson requested none.

Talk during the meal departed from work, and was intermittent—Welles approaching the feast fairly single-mindedly—with the chief subject "War of the Worlds." He seemed both annoyed and amused that his friend Houseman, whom he loved, was such a "stick in the mud" and "stuffed shirt" where his prank was concerned. What did Walter think?

"Well," Gibson said, stuffed to the gills, "if the news

bulletins are convincing, and frequent, and maintain a believable time line . . . you may fool some of the people . . ."

"But not for all of the time! As the piece becomes more
ridiculous, which it inherently is, they'll know we've just
sneaked up behind them and said, 'Boo'!"

Welles called for the butlers to come clear the table, and
soon—as they sat across from each other, the remains of
the meal between them like the aftermath of a battlefield—
a knock came to the door.

Frowning, Welles—who was sipping his coffee—said,
"What's wrong with this hotel? They know I don't want to
be bothered with answering the door! They know to come
and take this garbage away without asking permission!"

Gibson was already on his feet, putting his napkin on
the table. "I'll get it. . . ."

"Would you mind?"

But when Gibson opened the door, the butlers were
not there: instead, a slender, very lovely—and unhappy-
looking—young woman faced him. Blonde, blue-eyed and
rather patrician in manner, in a sable jacket with matching
cap and a dark green dress with matching heels, she eyed
Gibson with undisguised suspicion.

"Are you a new slave?"

"Excuse me?"

She brushed past Gibson, saying, "Maybe not—he
prefers little men, weasels like Vakhtangov, and you appear
to be standing on two legs, not four."

Gibson closed the door, swallowed, and tried to think of
something to say.

She wheeled toward the writer, raised an eyebrow.
The blue eyes were streaked red. For all her aloof poise,
she could not hide that she'd been weeping.

"I am Virginia Welles," she said. "*Mrs.* Welles. Is the
great man in?"

"His wife?"

"Not his mother—though it is a fine line, I grant you."

Still in his white terry robe, Welles appeared at the French doors, with a curious frown quickly turning to a displeased one.

"Virginia . . . dear. You know I'm working. . . ."

"I'm delighted to see you, too, darling. Your daughter sends her best."

"I doubt that. She can't speak yet."

"How would you know?"

Embarrassed, Welles looked past his wife to say, "Dear, this is Walter Gibson—he created the Shadow. We're developing a film project."

She again turned her head toward Gibson. Thin, pretty lips managed a thin, pretty smile. "Mr. Gibson," she said with a tiny nod. "Forgive the melodramatics."

"Not at all," Gibson said, and risked a grin. "My stock in trade."

The smile disappeared. "I need a few words with my . . . better half. Would you excuse us for a while, Mr. Gibson?"

"Certainly."

Welles held the door open for her, rolling his eyes at Gibson behind Mrs. Welles's back, as she slipped inside. The French doors shut, the conversation grew to a confrontation quickly, her voice shrill, his booming—a marital dispute of epic proportions.

Gibson did his best not to eavesdrop, but it was hard not to hear the accusations of the husband's infidelity; among the most memorable phrases flung by the wife were "that little ballerina bitch," "you two-timing self-inflated bag of hot air," "that gold-digging little dancer," "you self-important, psychopathic philanderer," and "that simpering receptionist sitting on her brains all day."

This had been going on for perhaps ten minutes when a phone rang in the bedroom, and Mrs. Welles allowed her husband a brief intermission to answer it. About a minute later, Welles again stuck his head out between French doors.

"Walter? Would you mind going down to the bar, to

keep Housey company for a few minutes? He has some revisions for the radio show to share with me, and I'll be down shortly—Mrs. Welles and I are nearly finished."

The latter seemed obvious.

In less than five minutes, Walter Gibson was sharing a booth with John Houseman in the St. Regis's famed King Cole Bar, opposite Maxfield Parrish's equally famous mural behind the bar, its faces smirking enigmatically their way.

"Cheers," Houseman said, lifting his Bloody Mary to clink with Gibson's.

The Mercury producer had insisted that they order this particular drink, because it had been invented here, albeit under the sobriquet "Red Snapper."

"Orson claims to have coined the new phrase," Houseman said. "After Mary Tudor, of course."

"Did he?"

"Very unlikely. But I would be remiss not to warn you, Walter, that Orson's tendency to take all the credit for himself is not his best trait . . . though it may well be the defining one."

Gibson shrugged. "I'm a writer for hire. My publishers even own the 'Maxwell Grant' pen name. If Orson needs to feel he's 'created' our project, I'll get over it . . . if the check doesn't bounce."

A tiny smile formed. Again Houseman wore his uniform of checked jacket and bow tie, this one a light blue. "Not everyone feels as generously inclined as you, Walter. I know that Howard . . . Howard Koch, our writer?"

"Yes. We met yesterday."

"That's right, that's right. . . . At any rate, Howard has been rather bitter about Orson's refusal to credit him on the air with scripts. They've had . . . words."

"Seems Orson has 'words' with lots of people."

"He does indeed. Since childhood he's been assured by all concerned that he is a genius; it's never occurred to him to doubt that opinion."

"Well, he is a kind of genius."

"Yes he is. And he has a great heart. But he does on occasion abuse those he loves. You like him?"

"Actually, I do. I get a real kick out of the guy. Real change of pace for me—usually, I have to create monsters to hang out with them."

Houseman chuckled. "He *is* a kind of monster at that, albeit a benign one. I take it Virginia dropped by?"

"Yes. Thanks for the reprieve for yours truly. I was getting pretty damn uncomfortable."

"A happy accident. . . . The poor girl. She's as brilliant as she is lovely, you know; comes from a fine family. He treats her dismally."

"Doesn't he love her?"

"I think he did. He may still." Houseman had another sip of Bloody Mary, and his eyebrows flicked up and down. "But it's his . . . appetites. They are—as you may have noted yourself—large."

"You have the British knack for understatement, Jack."

"Thank you, Walter. But I'm not British."

Gibson didn't pursue that, saying, "Hell, I'm on my second wife. None of us are perfect. But with a rich, pretty, talented helpmate like that—well, it's a shame."

"That he couldn't make do? I should say. But of late he's developed a penchant for dancers."

"Really?"

"I believe it's the long legs."

"His wife has long legs."

Houseman twitched half a smile. "Most men cheat on their wives with physical replicas of those self-same wives. At least that's been my observation. Right now Orson is seeing two dancers, one of them very famous."

"No kidding?"

"Yes. The famous one—Vera Zorina, but do be discreet, my boy—has an equally famous fiancé . . . George Balanchine."

"Well, of course—I've heard of them both. . . ."

"Balanchine has threatened Orson's life. But then, if Orson is to be believed at least, so has the other dancer's steady beau."

"You doubt the latter?"

Houseman sipped his Bloody Mary. "I do. I happened to witness Balanchine's threat—at the Stork Club—but the other dancer, an exotic dancer from Austria, who has been a featured performer in a variety of nightclubs, reportedly has a gangster boyfriend."

"This is starting to sound like I wrote it."

"Actually, I think Orson wrote it. I do believe he's seeing this young woman, and I know that the clubs she performs in are owned by this shady individual   a fellow named Madden, I believe . . ."

Gibson's eyes popped. "Owney Madden! He's one of the top gangsters!"

"So I'm given to understand. Orson insists that this young lady has been romantically aligned with this Madden, and that he's been threatened physically by thugs at the ganglord's bidding."

"Why are you skeptical?"

With a sigh, the producer said, "I am skeptical because Orson has twice now used this as an excuse for his arriving *hours* late to theater rehearsals—his tardiness due to the necessity of avoiding killers dispatched to take revenge upon him by this renowned gangster."

"So—it's just baloney, in your opinion."

"Thinly sliced, expertly stacked in a sandwich that Orson insisted on feeding all of us—twice." Houseman sighed. "That's the real irritation—not only is he late, but when he comes in to give his excuse, he gets caught up in the yarn he's inventing, and everyone gathers around . . . myself included, goddamnit . . . and we all get caught up in his powers of storytelling."

Gibson laughed. "He's one of a kind, all right. But couldn't the gangster story be true?"

"Certainly it could. Orson has an apparent self-destructive need to throw himself in the path of danger—to associate with recklessness and risk."

"Now *you're* sounding melodramatic, Jack."

"Perhaps I am. But we must always remember that what we have here is, essentially, a middle-class midwestern boy, steeped in art, music and literature, who craves the respect of sophisticated men. No matter how much he rages, he is gentle at heart—his storms tear up the countryside, but they do pass quickly."

Showman that he was, Welles apparently knew this was his cue, because—in a cream-color suit and loose yellow bow tie—he ambled into the bar, lighted up like Christmas upon seeing them both, and deposited himself in the booth, putting Gibson in the middle.

Welles greeted them both warmly—as if he hadn't seen Gibson for hours (as opposed to minutes) and as if he hadn't been cruelly dismissive of Houseman the night before. He waved a waiter over, ordered himself a Bloody Mary, took credit for naming it, then listened patiently as Houseman brought him up to speed. This morning's rehearsal had gone well, and Paul Stewart was assembling an effective gallery of sound effects; then Houseman read him script changes that the CBS censors had insisted upon for "War of the Worlds."

"Thanks to your news bulletin approach," Houseman said, "a script that earlier in the week was deemed by all concerned too 'unbelievable' has now been found, by the network, much *too* believable."

Welles took a gulp of his Bloody Mary, which had just arrived. "What are the vultures requesting?"

"They request nothing. They demand that we remove our real place-names."

"What!"

Houseman patted the air, gently. "Not geographic names—Grovers Mill is fine, as of course is New York and various New Jersey environs. Howard has made some good suggestions to fictionalize these place names just enough to satisfy the Columbia Broadcasting System, but—"

"Not enough to alert the listener to what we're up to. Good. Examples, please."

Houseman looked at a sheet of paper tucked into the front of his script. "Langley Field, for example, is now 'Langham.' Columbia Broadcasting Building is now simply 'Broadcasting Building.' United States Weather Bureau is 'Government Weather Bureau.'"

"Good, good," Welles said, hands tented now, eyes almost glowing.

"New Jersey National Guard is now 'State Militia.' Princeton University Observatory is now 'Princeton Observatory.'"

"Fine, fine."

Houseman closed the script cover, ominously. "There is one that you won't like, I'm afraid."

"Don't shield me, Housey."

"They won't let us use Roosevelt as a character."

Welles sat up, alarmed and dismayed. "But that's *vital*—a message from the president in a moment of national crisis!"

"They'll allow another official—they're suggesting 'Secretary of the Interior.' This one appears to be non-negotiable."

Welles was thinking. "I may have a way around that . . ."

Houseman's eyes hardened. "Orson—you know that I don't approve of this approach . . ."

"I seem to recall something to that effect."

". . . but we have to keep CBS happy. Because if this backfires in any way, we dare not take all of the responsibility on our own shoulders."

Welles drew in a deep breath. Finally he expelled it, and said ambiguously, "I won't compromise the Mercury."

Houseman frowned. "Artistically? Or financially?"

Welles leaned forward and patted Houseman's hand. "I won't let you down, Jack." Then he turned to Gibson and

said, "We only have a few hours left, before my rehearsal
at the theater. Let's get to work!"

They left a somewhat dejected-looking Houseman, who
was ordering another Bloody Mary, to return to Welles's
suite.

For the next several hours, however, the subject of their
collaborative Shadow film got sidetracked. Welles, on a
passing mention of Hallowe'en in reference to their "War
of the Worlds" prank, came to recall that Houdini had died
on that day; this launched the showman into a lengthy dis-
cussion of magic.

Since this was Gibson's own favorite subject, he found
himself unable to resist the off-the-track journey.

"You know," Welles said, seated in a chair next to his
bed, getting a shave from a hotel barber, "as a child, I received magic lessons from Houdini."

Gibson had pulled up a chair, his position similar to that
of an interviewer. "Really? I saw him for the first time
when I was seventeen—he asked me up on stage to exam-
ine his Chinese Water Torture Cell!"

"Wonderful! Details, man! Details!"

And Gibson provided details of the various times he'd
seen Houdini, and of his own relationship with the famous
magician, starting with a meeting at Houdini's brownstone
in New York in 1920, having to do with the Society of
American Magicians (of which Houdini was president at
the time). The friendship developed over the years, with
Gibson a frequent backstage guest at Houdini shows.
(Perhaps significantly, Welles offered no details of his
childhood magic lessons from the magician.)

Later, as Welles received a manicure from a lovely girl in
nurse's whites, Gibson demonstrated several tricks Houdini
had taught him, including "Instanto," which involved swiftly
cutting the cards and then identifying the cut-to card before
turning it.

Welles was particularly intrigued to learn that Houdini

had seen Gibson perform, and had wanted the young magician to teach him a certain trick.

"The Hindu wand trick," Gibson told the rapt Welles, who was now getting a pedicure from the same girl in white. "Houdini wanted to buy the routine, but I presented it to him as a gift . . . only, he died before doing it."

"I'd love to see it!"

"It's an apparatus I don't have with me—two wands with tassels that get cut but magically remain attached."

"You must show me!"

"Next time we're together, I'll bring it."

"If I like it, could I use it? Could I buy it?"

"Well . . . certainly, Orson. I'd be glad to give it to you, as a friend and fellow magician."

Welles's eyes floated skyward. "Imagine—to have a trick Houdini sought to perform, but never got the chance. . . ."

"Are you anticipating doing an act, professionally, Orson?"

The boy-man nodded vigorously. "I'm hoping to mount an elaborate vaudeville show, someday soon."

"You do have your . . . goals. Your ambitions."

"I came to this party to have a good time." The eyes twinkled, cheeks dimpled. "Didn't you, Walter?"

A good time, certainly; but Gibson had also "come to the party" to work . . . and no more work was accomplished. The afternoon—between magic talk and Orson's grooming—flew.

Just past six-thirty, darkness gathering at the windows, Welles showed Gibson to the door of the suite. "We'll have breakfast tomorrow, and then go over to the studio together. You'll get to see whether or not this 'War of the Worlds' can really fly."

Feeling like the portable typewriter in his hand was purely decorative, Gibson asked, "What about our project?"

A hand settled on the writer's shoulder, and his host said warmly, "A big part of what we're doing this weekend,

Walter, is getting to know one other. Establishing a bond. If you can stay over through Monday—"

"I could. I can."

Welles patted Gibson's shoulder, and took a step back, opening the door wider onto the waiting hall. "Well, we'll squeeze in some work tomorrow, but Monday is yours, until rehearsal time. And we'll be rehearsing well into the morning again, tonight . . . you're welcome to drop by the Mercury and kibitz, of course."

"Actually, I'm working on a story. I'll be in my room, should you need me."

"Highly unlikely. Why don't you go out and enjoy yourself? The nightclub scene is incredible, these days."

"I might."

In his room, Gibson—not bothering with supper, after the huge lunch—continued punching the keys writing "Old Crime Week." By midnight he was finished, and he lay on his bed in his high-ceilinged room, studying the chandelier, wondering if it was too late to follow Welles's advice and go out to a club for a drink, a show and a late bite. . . .

Again, Welles was right on cue.

The phone rang and the showman had an invitation for his writer friend. "Walter, the damn elevator has broken down again . . ."

"Elevator?" . . .

"In the tower on stage! For *Danton's Death*! . . . Rehearsal is over, for tonight, while we turn the damn thing over to the mechanics."

"Ah."

"So—let's get together. Have you ever been to the Cotton Club?"

"Not the new one."

"This one lacks the primitive charm of the Harlem original, but there's a twelve-thirty show with Cab Calloway. Are you up for it?"

"Sure!"

"My ride will pick you up in five minutes."

"A cab?"

"An ambulance."

So, sitting in back of a screaming ambulance, next to an unused gurney, Gibson rode from the St. Regis to the Mercury, where Welles was picked up. Together, siren wailing, they took the short ride to Times Square and the Cotton Club.

Their table was off to one side, but with a fine view of the stage, and after Calloway had concluded, Welles ordered a "light" late supper: a plate of fried chicken for Gibson, and two plates of the same for Welles. Welles, still on a diet, had only a single helping of mashed potatoes and gravy, and a mere four biscuits.

The remains of this latest repast had been cleared away when Gibson risked a personal question.

"If you don't mind my asking," he said, "why aren't you gun-shy about coming to this place?"

"Why should I be?"

"Well . . . Jack mentioned that you've been seeing a dancer who Owney Madden considers his private property. . . ."

Welles sipped a glass of beer. "That's possibly true."

"Aren't you afraid you might run in to the guy? I mean, he's no kid, but his nickname *is* 'the Killer.' Which he earned because, well . . . he's a killer."

"That is the rumor."

"I don't think it's a rumor. He did time for it."

With grandiose patience, Welles said, "Walter, since Mr. Madden got out of 'stir,' as his crowd calls it—on his most recent sojourn of several years—he's been doing his best to stay out of Winchell's newspaper column."

"You mean—he owns the joint, but doesn't hang around here."

"That's right. His cronies may pass along my having frequented his establishment, which I'm sure will give Mr. Madden a few moments of . . . irritation. Just as I'm enjoying a few moments of amusement, contemplating as much."

"But you don't think he'll do anything about it."

"What can he do? I'm a public figure. He lays a hand on me, threatens me in any way, and, poof . . . he's back in, yes, 'stir.' Anyway, I haven't been seeing Tilly in some time. Weeks. I have other interests now."

"Like your wife, you mean?"

Welles's head tilted to one side; he sighed, but smiled as he did. "Do my excesses offend you, Walter?"

"I shouldn't have said that. My apologies."

"No, no, I understand. But I ask *you* to understand—I married too young. Before I'd sown my fair share of wild oats. And my nature is simply not monogamous. I've explained this to Virginia, and she must either learn to accept me, as I am, or we will, sadly, have to go our separate ways."

Welles was intent on walking back to the Mercury, to check on the status of the stage repairs, and asked Gibson to keep him company. Glad for the chance to walk off the big meal, Gibson quickly accepted.

Now approaching two A.M., Broadway was still alive but just starting to wind down a bit. As he strolled alongside the big man in the flowing black cape and slouch hat, Gibson contemplated how successful Welles (that baby nose hidden by a false hawk beak, anyway) might truly be at bringing the Shadow to life on screen.

Of course, the Shadow persona was actually secondary: the suave, sophisticated, man-about-town millionaire who was the Shadow's secret identity—Lamont Cranston—Welles embodied perfectly, not only physically, but in life.

As they passed a particularly dark alley, a pair of hands reached out and plucked Gibson from Welles's side, yanking the writer into the darkness. Two other large figures emerged from the shadows and thrust Welles into the alley as well.

Suddenly the two men had their backs to a brick wall and a trio of burly thugs in overcoats and battered hats—two fedoras and a porkpie—stood before them like a tribunal as imagined by Damon Runyon.

The trio was swathed in shadow, but one thing stood out clearly: the .45 automatic in the hand of the largest of them, the fleshy one in the middle, wearing the porkpie hat.

Welles, indignant, said, "What do you want with us? You want our money? You can have it! Then go, and go to hell."

Gibson said nothing; he was trembling—scared out of his wits.

The man with the gun said, "We don't want your money. We want your undivided attention—get it?"

"I've got it," Welles said, sneering.

"Think you're pretty cute, lording it up at the boss's own place. Well, you lay off that little dancer, or the next time we talk, this rod'll do the talking."

"Cheap patter," Welles said, "from cheap hoods. . . ."

"Orson," Gibson said. "Let it go . . ."

The guy with the gun said to the thug at his right, "Give him something to remember us by, Louie . . ."

Louie raised a fist, but Welles stepped forward and slammed his own fist into the man's belly. As Louie crumpled, the man with the gun took a step forward and Welles knocked the gun from his grasp, slapping the man's hand as if knocking a toy from a child's hand.

The sound of it, spinning away on the cement into the blackness, gave Gibson courage. He shoved the third hood, the one who'd grabbed him in the first place, and then the entire trio of oversized goons were tripping over themselves, as Welles pushed Louie into the fellow with the porkpie.

Then Welles ran from the alley, calling, "Taxi!"

Gibson, right behind him, sharp footsteps on the pavement echoing, followed the flapping cape of Lamont Cranston as the hailed taxi screeched to a stop, and the actor and the writer scrambled into the backseat.

"St. Regis, please," Welles said, regally casual, but breathing hard.

"Damn!" Gibson said, looking back toward the mouth

of the alley—no sign of the hoods. They'd apparently disappeared into the dark, as Welles and Gibson made their escape.

Again, a hand settled on the writer's shoulder. "Are you all right, Walter?"

"I may need a change of underwear." He gave his host a hard look. "That was a little *reckless*, wasn't it?"

Welles snorted. "I wasn't going to let those overgrown Dead End Kids get away with that nonsense."

"The leader had a gun!"

The cab driver's eyes in the rearview mirror were on them. Welles said, "He wouldn't have fired, not so close to Broadway, not with a dozen cops around. They were just trying to scare us."

Gibson blew out air. "Well, where I'm concerned, it worked like a charm."

When the taxi pulled up at the St. Regis, a doorman approaching, Welles said, "Get some rest—I'm heading back to the Mercury. We'll have breakfast in my room, around ten, then go over to CBS together around noon. Agreeable?"

But Welles did not wait for an answer, and the taxi glided away, the moon face smiling at him, a cheerfully demented, if slightly overweight elf.

In his room, between the Egyptian-cotton sheets, Gibson lay exhausted but exhilarated—and it took him a good hour to go to sleep.

It wasn't that he was disturbed, and certainly his fear had passed: but story ideas were humming through his mind. Soon he had an image of himself at the antique writing desk, starting another story, not realizing he was only dreaming. . . .

SUNDAY

October 30, 1938

Walter Gibson's famous creation was not the only Shadow cast by radio in 1938—the shadow of war also served to keep listeners on edge, and in a far more disturbing fashion. . . .

For several months prior to The Mercury Theatre on the Air's *broadcast of a certain H.G. Wells science-fiction yarn, listeners had been alerted to the troublesome state of the world, homes all across the nation taken hostage by talking boxes in their living rooms, kitchens, bedrooms and automobiles. The same gizmo that was sharing household hints and fudge recipes, cowboy adventures and comedy shows, weather reports and advertisements for corn plasters, popular tunes and classical music, was also bombarding America with the latest disasters, subjecting them to an endless parade of ominous international events. At no other time since the beginning of broadcasting had the collective audience been held in such a rapt, fearful grip, with listeners quite accustomed to their favorite programs being interrupted for news updates . . . and the news was never good. . . .*

In his September address to the annual Nazi party congress in Nuremberg, German dictator Adolf Hitler demanded autonomy over an area on the Czech border known as Sudetenland. It seemed over three million "Sudeten Germans," as the Führer called them, were "tortured souls" who could not "obtain rights and help themselves," so the Nazis had to do it for them. (The translation Americans heard was provided by the dean of radio commentators, H.V. Kaltenborn, who just months before had been chosen by Orson Welles to narrate the Mercury radio broadcast of "Julius Caesar," to add "a dimension of realism and immediacy.") On October 3, Germany made its triumphant drive into the town of Asch, and a week later, Hitler's troops occupied the Sudetenland.

Hearing of such an ill-boding event firsthand was already old hat to American radio listeners. Hitler's conquests became a kind of serial for grown-ups, the Czech crisis playing over out three tense weeks—listeners hearing firsthand the march step of Nazi boots, the accusations and the threats, the rumblings of war that included the Far Eastern menace of the Japanese. At the height of the European crisis, about a month before the "War of the Worlds" broadcast, a presentation of "Sherlock Holmes" by The Mercury Theatre on the Air had been interrupted by a news bulletin, irritating (but also making an impression on) Orson Welles.

Most Americans felt the inevitability of involvement of the U.S.A. in a world conflict in which its allies were either threatened or already embroiled: as the Germans marched into Austria, the English people were issued gas masks, and all of Europe noted with alarm Hitler calling up to active duty one million weekend soldiers from the German army reserve.

Radio statistics indicated that the medium's audience had never been larger; what the numbers didn't spell out was that these masses of listeners had never been more worried. Days before the "War of the Worlds" broadcast,

Leni Riefenstahl—German filmmaker and rumored mistress of the Führer—was in Manhattan promoting her documentary about the 1936 Olympics, finding critical acceptance and public hostility. Meanwhile in Rome, the voice of fascism—the newspaper Il Tevere—*ordered the boycott of the films of Charlie Chaplin, the Marx Brothers and the Ritz Brothers, the humor of these Jewish filmmakers condemned as "not Aryan."*

And the looming war was not the sole source of American jitters—earlier in 1938, a hurricane had hit the East Coast with devastating power; and, the year previous, the first disaster ever to be broadcast live exposed thousands to the explosion of the Hindenburg. *When the German zeppelin caught fire at its mooring in Lakehurst, New Jersey, the announcer had been in the midst of describing the huge craft's grandeur, only to witness . . . and report in "on the spot" fashion . . . the bursting flames and the dying people and all the ensuing chaos. His sobs—even his retching—had gone out over the air waves, "live". . . .*

Just four days before the "War of the Worlds" broadcast, CBS's prestigious (if little-listened-to) Columbia Workshop *aired a verse play by Archibald MacLeish: "Air Raid." Orson Welles listened to the production on a break rehearsing* Danton's Death, *because he had loaned his friend and Mercury regular, Ray Collins, to the production to be its narrator, a mock announcer reporting an air raid from a European tenement rooftop—the whine of attacking planes could be heard, the explosions of their dropped bombs, the sounds of a confused populace running for shelter, machine-gun fire, the screams of victims, including a young boy. . . .*

Though written in verse, and clearly a play, the approach invoked a live news report. Welles heard this realistic radio drama a few hours before he made his suggestions to Howard Koch, John Houseman and Paul Stewart, about revising the script for "War of the Worlds" into a collage of broadcasts interrupted by news bulletins.

As one of the participants in the "War of the Worlds" broadcast would reflect many years later, "The American people had been hanging on their radios, getting most of their news no longer from the press, but over the air. A new technique of 'on-the-spot' reporting had been developed and eagerly accepted by an anxious and news-hungry world. The Mercury Theatre on the Air, *by faithfully copying every detail of the new technique—including its imperfections— found an already enervated audience ready to accept its wildest fantasies. . . ."*

CHAPTER FOUR

Shanghaied Lady

Though he'd had a good (if dream-troubled) night's sleep—
his breakfast with Orson at the director's suite had not been
till tcn A.M.—Walter Gibson felt logy, almost groggy, in the
aftermath of the Welles morning repast. Enough orange
juice, coffee, eggs, sausage, hash brown potatoes with
melted cheese, and assorted muffins and sweet rolls had
been delivered by St. Regis butlers to attend the gastric
needs of your average lumberjack camp.

Perhaps in an ill-advised effort to keep up with his host,
Gibson ate around a Paul Bunyan's worth. Welles ate easily
two Bunyan's plus one Babe the Blue Ox's worth to boot,
conversation scant, the food commanding the boy-man's
full attention. What conversation had preceded and followed the feast touched little on the Shadow project, con-
centrating instead on their mutual fascination with magic.
Welles inquired how Gibson had developed that interest.

"Just before my tenth birthday," Gibson said, sitting
back, the meal finished, having to work to think, his body
and all the blood in it occupied with a major digestive task,

"I attended the birthday party of a friend—typical kind of kid celebration, you know. . . ."

Welles, also sitting back, hands folded on his belly (he was again wearing the bathrobe with the hotel crest), said, "I don't remember attending any birthday parties as a child."

"Pin-the-tail-on-the-donkey, games of tag, plenty of cake and ice cream . . ."

Welles—who loved being on either end of a story, and listened with keen, obvious interest—lighted up one of his pool-cue cigars.

Gibson was saying, "The parents of my young friend, a girl, knew that my birthday was coming up fast, as well, and perhaps out of deference to me, they came up with a special game: each child was presented with a long ribbon that disappeared out of the parlor into the house—a two-story house, Victorian in style. Some ribbons slithered like snakes around the furnishings, to go up and down the stairs, others led out the front and back doors. . . ."

"Walter," Welles said, sighing smoke, "you paint a vivid picture—as always."

"Thank you. Anyway, each child followed the ribbon through the house . . . and we all were led to a present of our very own!"

"Ah!"

"Mine led up the stairs and into a guest bedroom, where under the bed I discovered my prize . . ." Gibson leaned forward, milking it. ". . . a box of magic tricks."

Welles eyes widened, as if his guest had reported discovering Blackbeard's hidden treasure.

"It was German-made, with all the standard tricks of the day—I suppose, objectively speaking, it was nothing special. But it changed my life. It was as if that ribbon had led me to my future."

Welles, smiling with delight, eyes sparkling, said, "No wonder we're kindred spirits! My godfather gave me a professional magician's box of stage tricks—I was five! And it was my godfather, my guardian—Dr. Bernstein—who took me backstage to meet Houdini, when I was six!"

Finally, Gibson thought, *the Houdini story. Would it be true?*

"I apparently impressed the great man with my childish enthusiasm—I blurted out virtually everything I knew about magic in a matter of a minute or two—and that was how I came to be taught a simple but effective trick with a red handkerchief, presenting me with everything I needed to pull it off myself—the vanishing coin trick?"

"I know it well."

Placing a handkerchief over the left hand, the magician pokes a pocket in the cloth, so that the coin can be dropped there; then the magician shakes the handkerchief . . . and the coin has vanished! (This was achieved by having a rubber band around the fingers and thumb of the left hand, which closed the "pocket" the coin was pushed into, so that the coin remained caught and hidden when the handkerchief was shaken out.)

Welles leaned forward, one eye narrowed. "I was always a quick study, so I followed Houdini to his dressing room like a stray puppy. He glanced around at me, not knowing whether to be irritated or amused. 'Look, sir!' I said . . . and I performed the trick for him!"

Gibson chuckled and clapped, once.

Welles lifted his eyebrows. "Well . . . let us say that the great Harry Houdini was less than overwhelmed by my childish legerdemain. He gave me a stern scolding: never, ever was a trick to be performed until it had been practiced a thousand times!"

"Not bad advice."

"*Splendid* advice . . . but there's more. I practiced and practiced the vanishing coin trick, and a few months later, when Houdini returned with his stage act, we again went backstage, before the show . . . this time it was with my father accompanying me, on a rare visit home . . . and were welcomed warmly. Houdini remembered my obnoxious, precocious little self. I was about to demonstrate my improved stagecraft when a certain Carl Brema arrived—"

Gibson grinned. "Of course—the manufacturer of magic tricks."

"Yes. Brema had a vanishing lamp trick he'd just perfected. He demonstrated it for Houdini, who beamed and said, 'Wonderful, Carl—I'll put it in the show *tonight*!'"

Welles's roar of laughter was worthy of Henry the Eighth, and Gibson—despite the overeating-inspired discomfort—joined in heartily.

Now Gibson believed Welles had really met Houdini— the story sounded just like the man. . . .

"*There's* a coincidence," Gibson said, "that further cements our destiny together."

"What's that?"

"The trick of mine I mentioned the other day—the Hindu wand trick Houdini requested from me, but died before he could use it . . . ?"

"Yes?"

"It was Carl Brema who executed my design—who built the wands for Houdini to use."

"But never did."

"No."

His expression intense, Welles sat forward. "Walter, I must have that trick. When I take out my magic act on the road, that trick *must* be included!"

"You haven't even seen it yet, Orson . . ."

"If it's good enough for Houdini and Gibson, it's good enough for Welles. Name your price!"

Gibson raised his palms in surrender. "I already told you, Orson, it's yours—and I wouldn't take a dime for it. The experience of this weekend is payment enough."

Welles glowed, the fat cigar in his teeth at a rakish angle. He lifted a coffee cup for a toast; Gibson clinked cups with him.

"To us," Welles said. "To our collaboration. . . ."

Soon—looking every bit the magician with his Shadowesque cloak, slouch hat, black suit, bow tie and walking stick, Welles escorted Gibson to the elevators. As they waited, Welles blurted, "Walter—do you *really* believe in magic?"

"As an art?"

"As a science . . . even a religion. What we do with stagecraft—whether it's the Mercury transforming some musty classic into a vital contemporary experience, or sawing a woman in half who then gets up and walks around—is tap onto the public's fascination with the unknown, the occult. Fakers we may be, but what we touch in people is genuine."

Gibson was nodding. "I do believe in some force, something greater than the human mind."

"I ponder that frequently." Welles watched the dial on the floor indicator above the elevator doors; their ride was on its way. "Of course, our friend Houdini spent much time debunking psychics. . . ."

"He did indeed—but that was all part of a search to find *real* evidence of psychic phenomenon."

A bell dinged and in a moment they were stepping onto a car otherwise empty but for a young elevator attendant.

On the way down, Welles said to his companion, "Would you care for anecdotal evidence, to support the existence of genuine magic?"

"Certainly."

"You know of our so-called 'voodoo' *Macbeth* . . . ?"

"I do. I regret not seeing it."

Welles smiled wistfully. "It was a wonderful production. . . . Nothing is likely to top it in my experience. . . ." Then he shifted gears. "Did you know that only one New York critic wrote an unfavorable review?"

"I recall the show was a huge success, well-received."

Nodding, Welles said, "Yes, but Percy Hammond was

dismissive, and hurt the feelings of our Lady Macbeth. We had a number of real Haitians in the show, you know . . ."

"I didn't."

"In fact, we even had a sort of company witch doctor, who decided to treat the critic in question to a particularly virulent curse."

Gibson chuckled. "You're not saying the voodoo bit took hold, are you?"

With an altar boy's smile, Welles said, "I leave that for you to decide, Walter—but the facts are these: Percy Hammond's review appeared on Tuesday, he fell sick on Thursday and was dead by Sunday."

A bell announced the lobby, and the young elevator operator opened the door for them, but made no announcement, looking agape as the tall man in the cape and his companion stepped off.

No ambulance was needed today—they took a cab.

Leaning back in the backseat, arms folded, traffic gliding by his window, Welles said, "You know for all the fuss we're making about this show, tonight—we have one of the worst Crossley ratings around. Why do we try so hard?"

"For the satisfaction?"

With a shrug, Welles said, "I suppose. The blessing of having a low-rated program is that we don't have to please the lowest common denominator among listeners. Still, one craves a wider audience. . . ."

Gibson was aware that *The Mercury Theatre on the Air* was a "sustaining" program—unsponsored, supported only by the network itself (*The Shadow*'s longtime sponsor was Blue Coal). No one wanted to advertise on a program opposite something as popular as Charlie McCarthy and Edgar Bergen. But CBS had earned a reputation as a prestige network because these low-rated shows were considered artistic and creative oases in a medium ruled by sponsors who asked only, "Will it play in Peoria?"

By half past noon, Gibson was following Welles off

another elevator, this time onto the twentieth floor of the Columbia Broadcasting Building, as the uniformed attendant held the door open for them both.

"Thank you, Leo my boy," Welles said to the attendant.

Leo—a diminutive "boy" of perhaps fifty-five—beamed as if God had heard his prayer. "Thank *you,* Mr. Welles!"

They had barely stepped into the lobby when Welles's shrimp of an assistant, Alland a.k.a. Vakhtangov, was suddenly just *there* . . . as if he'd materialized, to lift the cloak from Welles's shoulders, remove his suitcoat exposing the black suspenders on the white shirt, take charge of his hat and walking stick, and then disappear somewhere. This all happened so quickly, Gibson couldn't even manage a, "Huh?"

Then Welles moved quickly across the lobby, only to stop so short Gibson almost bumped into him. The great man had paused at the receptionist's desk, where a uniformed CBS security guard sat leaning back, reading the Sunday funnies. He was about thirty, brown eyes, brown hair, average build, the textbook definition of nondescript.

"You are not Miss Donovan," Welles said, arching an eyebrow.

The security guard peered over the front page—DICK TRACY—and revealed an oval unimpressed face, eyes half-lidded, a typical blank cop mask.

"Shrewd deduction," the guard said, his wiseguy tone indicating he did not share the elevator attendant's awe of the young genius. "But then, hey—the Shadow knows, right?"

With a snorty laugh, he returned to his funnies.

Welles gripped the guard by his blue shirtfront and dragged him halfway across the desk; the funnies spilled from his hands and his cap fell off.

"When I have a yen for a smart remark," Welles said, his nose a quarter of inch from the guard's startled face, "I won't ask an imbecile like you."

Then Welles thrust the man from his grip, and the guard

bounced a bit in the swivel chair. Frightened, the guard plucked his cap from the floor, put it back on, smoothed his shirt front with his palms and said, indignantly, "You can't treat me like that! I don't care who you are! You may be a big shot, but I'm . . . I'm like a *police*man!"

Welles, coolly, signed in. "You are indeed 'like' a policeman—in every way except the following: you carry no gun, your authority is minimal, you do not work for the city, and are not in fact a policeman. . . . Where is Miss Donovan?"

The guard swallowed and said, "I dunno. She was supposed to be working today. I think she was here earlier, actually."

"Continue."

"I got a call from one of you Mercury guys saying come fill in on her desk. We can't have just anyone walking in and out of here, y'know."

Welles was frowning. For some reason he had lifted the reception book into his hands, standing there like a preacher in a wedding ceremony, wondering whether this union was worth sanctioning.

Slowly, Welles said, "Are you quite sure? What's your name?"

The guard blinked. "My name?"

"It's not a trick question. Your first name will do. We can save the harder part for later, if necessary."

"Bill. My name is Bill. Williams."

"A redundant name for a redundant individual."

"What does that mean?"

Welles turned the reception book toward him, pointing to a specific name. "Bill, were you here when this person signed in?"

"Who? . . . Oh. No. 'Virginia Welles.' What's that, your wife?"

"She hasn't signed out again, I see."

"No. But then, this desk was unattended for a while."

"How long, Mr. Williams?"

"Couldn't say. From whenever somebody noticed Miss Donovan left her post, and thought to call for a sub."

"Yes." Welles gestured with an open hand, as if paying honor to the man. "And you do qualify as a 'sub,' Mr. Williams. I will concede that."

Mr. Williams smiled, warming to Welles. "Thanks."

Welles returned to the book. "And what about this individual?"

" 'Buh . . . buh . . . ' "

"Balanchine. Were you at this post when this man signed in?"

"No."

"I note *he* did not sign out, either."

"That's right. But like I said, this desk was unattended for a while. Who knows who left? Who knows who got in?"

Welles nodded to the man, twitching a smile. "Not the Shadow, Mr. Williams." He tossed the book on the desk with a clunk. "Would you do me a kindness, despite my poor show of temper?"

"Well, sure. I was . . . I was outa line, Mr. Welles. They don't pay me to be a smart-ass."

"How could one put a price on it? . . . I'll be in Studio One, for the most part, but may well be anywhere on this floor, in the various studios and offices, until after we've broadcast this evening." Welles leaned across the desk and asked, in a conspiratorial fashion, "If either of these individuals sign out, would you send someone to let me know?"

"Sure!"

"But in that case, call for another one of your troops— don't leave your post unattended."

"I'll do what I can—but there's just a handful us on duty on a Sunday, Mr. Welles."

"I understand. All I ask, Mr. Williams, is your best effort." And he gave the guard a half-bow.

Mr. Williams blinked and half-bowed back.

Gibson had never seen anything quite like Welles's performance—from receiving an insult, answering it with a physical threat, to winning over his adversary, charming him into another acolyte—only Orson Welles could have pulled off *that* magic trick.

Falling in alongside Welles, Gibson said, "Isn't Balanchine that ballerina's boyfriend? Guy who threatened you?"

They were walking down the hall, toward Studio One.

"He is indeed."

Welles opened the door to the sound-proofing vestibule of the studio, and Gibson followed.

"Does, uh, your wife often drop by the studio?"

"Not unless she's acting in a given week's production."

"She isn't in this show, is she?"

Welles glanced back with an arched eyebrow. "No. She is not."

Inside the studio, the spectacled owlish conductor, Benny Herrmann—like so many of the men, in suspenders and shirtsleeves—was again at the piano, a small conductor's podium nearby (in addition to the large one intended for Welles); musicians, a larger contingent than at Thursday's rehearsal, were taking their places—Gibson quickly counted twenty-seven—warming up with scales and such. Actors were milling in the carpeted microphone area, a script in one hand, ear in the other.

In a reporter-ish fedora, the mustached gigolo-ish Frank Readick was the first to approach Welles, nodding hello to Gibson, then saying with an excited edge, "I've been at it just like you said."

"And what is your opinion?"

"*Great* idea! Great idea, Orson. . . . This'll knock their damn socks off."

Then Readick wandered off to join the other rehearsing-to-themselves actors, adding to the general din.

Gibson asked, "Mind my asking what that was about?"

Welles flashed a smile. "Not at all—I simply advised Mr. Readick to dig out from the news library the transcriptions of the Hindenburg crash at Lakehurst, New Jersey."

"Why?"

"To use as a model! Remember how the reporter began to weep, as he reported the scores of people dying before his eyes? Well, our reporter should have that same response to the Martian death ray."

Mournful-looking Paul Stewart—in a brown sport coat with a green tie loose at his neck—approached and, without a greeting, jerked a thumb over his shoulder and said, "I've got Ora waiting. We've got the sound gimmicks pretty well licked."

Stewart, who seemed low-key by nature, had a touch of pride in his voice.

Gibson accompanied Welles over to the sound-effects station, where the middle-aged housewifely Ora waited with quiet but obvious anticipation. Again she wore a floral dress, with pearls as a Sunday touch. Her male assistant was on hand again, but Ora and Paul Stewart led the way in demonstrating to Welles the various acts of audio magic they'd assembled.

Using the two Victrola turntables, Ora and her assistant played crowd sounds, a cannon roar and a moody New York Harbor aural collage, after which Stewart said, "That's the last survivors, putting out to sea."

"Wonderful," Welles said, eyes dancing. "What about the Martian cylinder opening?"

This was not prerecorded: Ora demonstrated the effect, which consisted of slowly unscrewing the lid off a large empty jam jar.

"Nice natural resonance," Welles said with a nod. "But we could use an echo effect—might I suggest—"

"We're ahead of ya," Stewart said. "We've already run a wire to the men's room."

Welles noticed Gibson's confusion, and he told his

guest, "A john is a great natural echo chamber—we used it for the sewers of Paris in 'Les Miserables.' That, of course, was typecasting, whereas tonight the twentieth floor men's room will display its versatility. . . . Terrific work, everyone. Ora, as usual, you are simply the best."

She beamed, and Gibson suddenly realized the sound "man" was naturally pretty, once her expression of intense concentration took a break.

"I'm an old hand at science fiction, Mr. Welles," she said, in a musical alto. "We used an air-conditioner vent on *Buck Rogers* for a rocket engine!"

Welles let loose of a short explosive laugh, then said, "Well, then, I'm sure you have contrived something incredibly grotesque for the sound these creatures make."

Her expression fell. "Well, I did—it was actually my own voice, filtered and slowed down and . . . I could play it for you, but—"

"Do—please do."

Stewart and Ora exchanged nervous glances.

Resting a hand on Welles's arm, Stewart said quietly, "Orson, the network won't let us use it."

Welles's forehead tightened. "Since when does the network preview our sound effects?"

The dark eyebrows raised and lowered. "Since," Stewart sighed, "they read Howard's script, and found it too believable and too frightening. . . . Dave Taylor was in yesterday and had me play everything for him."

With a stern edge, Welles commanded of Ora, "Let me hear it!"

She swallowed, nodded, and found the platter and placed it on the turntable; dropped the needle.

"Ullia . . . ullia . . . ullia . . . ullia!"

Gibson found the sound excitingly creepy, and said so.

"I agree," Welles said. "Lovely work, Ora . . . Paul, where *is* Dave Taylor?"

"I think he's in the sub-control booth, waiting to hear the rehearsal. . . ."

Within moments, leaving Stewart behind, Welles had stormed into the control booth to face a tall, reed-slender gentleman in an immaculate gray pin-striped suit that Gibson would've bet his next Shadow check was a Brooks Brothers. The moment Welles had entered the first and smaller of the interconnected control booths, this individual—seated at the desk from which Gibson had watched Thursday's rehearsal—had calmly risen to a full six-two.

The man stood with folded arms and hooded eyes, smiling very gently, as Welles railed on about censorship and interference. The well-groomed scarecrow faced the bear of a man, arms hurled in the air, snorting his rage.

This went on for a good two minutes, concluding with, "David, the sounds those creatures make are *vital* to the performance, and if you insist on cutting them, I reserve the right to have my understudy take my role."

The executive—his name, Gibson later learned, was Davidson Taylor—replied gently, in a voice touched with a cultured Southern accent.

"Orson, I remain your biggest fan. I have been your creative cheerleader from the very beginning, as you well know. And I think you and Howard Koch and Paul have done a remarkable job on what began as one of our weakest Mercury offerings."

Somewhat placated, Welles said, "Thank you," but his chin was up, defensively.

"But the network people above me feel you've stepped over the line here—we have another list of name changes for these real places, and there can be no compromise where that tasteless creature sound effect is concerned. It's out."

Welles reddened. "You're willing to go on the air without me?"

With a sorrowful shrug, Taylor said, "Most reluctantly, yes."

Welles put his face in Taylor's, though the exec did not flinch. "I'll be god*damned* if I'll let the CBS bureaucrats run me off my own goddamned show! *I* will be performing tonight—directing and performing, as usual. *Is . . . that . . . understood?*"

Taylor nodded solemnly. "Yes, Orson."

"Good." Welles exited, head high, as if he had just won the argument. Gibson saw Taylor smile to himself and resume his seat at the desk, where a clipboard waited.

As Welles and Gibson returned to the studio floor, Herrmann was directing his fine musicians in a rendition of "Stardust" the likes of which the world had not heard before: tempo shifted as emotions swelled. Gibson found it quite remarkable, and glanced toward Welles to say something complimentary when he noticed the babyish face was contorting to a scowl.

"Benny!" Orson howled. "Benny! *Mis*ter *Her*muhn!"

The orchestra skidded to a stop, and the owlish man turned on his podium and showed Welles a bite-of-grapefruit expression.

"And what's wrong *this* time?" Herrmann demanded, as he left the musicians behind to clomp over and confront the director. He planted himself two inches from Welles, fists on his hips. "That piece-of-shit song has never before been played so beautifully!"

Welles's voice softened. "My dear Benny—you are entirely right."

With a sigh of triumph, Herrmann nodded, and began to return to his post; but before he could, a long-fingered white hand dropped on his shoulder and clutched.

In the conductor's ear, Welles whispered, "It's not meant to be a symphony, Benny—it's *dance* music. Mundane, unimaginative, and quite run of the mill."

Herrmann whirled, and gestured to himself, as if

wounded, the baton like a weapon, ready. "You ask this of me? To be run of the mill? You, who always speak of excellence?"

Paul Stewart came over and joined the fray. "Orson's right, Benny—it's supposed to be some lousy two-bit dance band playing in a second-rate hotel ballroom. Gotta be like this . . ."

And Stewart began to snap his fingers, to demonstrate the steady uninspiring tempo.

Herrmann's close-set eyes widened, an effect magnified by the thick lenses of his glasses. He thrust the baton at Stewart, and glared at Welles. "Then one of *you* bastards conduct it!"

Stewart smirked humorlessly at Welles, who nodded in a deferential fashion.

Baton in hand, Paul Stewart walked to the small podium next to Herrmann's piano, and looked out at the musicians and gave them the downbeat. The musicians understood immediately what was required, and a steady, substandard rendition of "Stardust" followed.

Herrmann watched agape. Welles, arms folded, hid a smile behind a hand. Several measures in, Stewart stopped, stepped down and returned the baton to the conductor.

"Now *that's* how to do it!" Stewart said.

Herrmann, crestfallen, turned to Welles, who said, "We are telling a story, Benny. You are an actor in that story. You must play the leader of a mediocre danceband."

Herrmann swallowed his dignity and returned to the small podium and tried again. Perfect—perfectly mediocre.

When Herrmann dejectedly returned, he said to Welles and Stewart, standing side by side, "Is that bad enough to suit you?"

Stewart nodded and said, "Exactly right."

Welles said, "For a musical genius like you, Benny, and I know this is a sacrifice."

Herrmann pouted. "They were trying to make me look

bad," he said, apparently meaning the musicians allowing Paul Stewart to show him up. "I've known it all along . . . all along. . . ."

Welles frowned. "Known what, Benny?"

Herrmann sneaked a dark look at his players, then turned and softly said, "There's a strong fascist element in the woodwinds. . . ."

Again Orson hid a smile behind his hand, as he seemed to nod gravely, saying, "We all have much to contend with."

What followed was a stop-and-start rehearsal, paying no attention to the radio-driven demands of the clock. Welles was fine-tuning the broadcast, and he was up and down off his podium, helping actors with lines, conferring with Ora about sound effects, cajoling Herrmann to continue to do second-rate renditions of "Stardust" and "La Cumparasita."

Seated not in the control room but in a chair near the sound-effects station, Gibson watched Orson Welles whip into shape what had been a decidedly lackluster production. Welles alternated between charm and martyrdom, the latter state expressed through periodic ravings and rantings about the treachery, ignorance, sloth, indifference, incompetence and "downright sabotage!" that surrounded him.

Herrmann smashed three batons. Welles tossed his script in the air half a dozen times, and several actors did the same, albeit with less frequence. Doors slammed. Lines were rewritten on the fly in a frenzy of revision, Koch frequently emerging from the control booth for a quick line rewrite.

Miss Holliday showed up from the Mercury Theatre around two o'clock, with arms filled with bulging paperbags from which milkshakes and sandwiches were dispensed and gobbled, as if the passengers and crew of the *Titanic* were trying to get in one final meal just as the ship was going down.

By about three, as the show began really taking shape, a palpable sense of excitement pervaded the studio—as one of the participants would later say, it was like "a strange fever . . . part childish mischief, part professional zeal."

Two more run-throughs were conducted by Welles—and "conducted" *was* the word—with little or no thought to timing, occasional bathroom and/or smoking breaks, and little one-on-one sessions between Welles and this or that actor or with Herrmann or Ora.

By six-fifteen the maestro of melodrama was ready to conduct the so-called "dress rehearsal," though of course costumes for a radio show were not an issue. The timing of the piece, however, was, and at his post in the control booth, Paul Stewart was hunkered over his script with stopwatch in hand.

Jack Houseman, visible in the main control room window next to Howard Koch, waited until the end of the dress rehearsal had been reached—it was twenty-some past seven, with the broadcast looming at eight—before seeking Welles out on the studio floor.

Welles, lighting up a cigar, had met Gibson midway—they were actually in the MICROPHONE AREA—after finally reaching the end of the script. Gibson was telling his host how much he felt the piece had been improved, through the heightened realism of the news bulletins, when a grave-faced Houseman stepped up.

"Orson—surely you don't intend to stretch out those musical interludes in such a fashion. The show is terribly slow in its opening third!"

"But it builds, Jack—it builds."

Houseman's eyes tightened. "Teasing through tedium? . . . I know what you're up to—you're hoping to take advantage of the naïveté of some listeners, to fool them into thinking a real broadcast is being interrupted."

The boyish face turned more boyish, thanks to Welles's scampish smile. "Housey, please—you'd think I was crying 'fire' in a crowded theater!"

"It may well prove to be the radio equivalent thereof. If

you would not indulge yourself in these drawn-out musical passages, and the . . . pauses, the silences . . . and all of these real-sounding places, official-sounding institutions . . ."

"CBS is satisfied with our changes. I instituted all of Dave's last-minute ones, too."

"Such as removing Franklin Roosevelt, and substituting the 'Secretary of Interior'? You know goddamned well you're directing Kenny Delmar to do his FDR impression!"

The smile turned downright devilish. He whispered, "It's dead-on, isn't it, Housey? Talented boy, our Kenny."

"Orson, I'm warning you—you may get that lesson you've been asking for. . . ."

"Oh, Housey—I'm going to need more than *one* lesson, don't you think?"

Houseman sighed. "I've made my point of view known—nothing more I can do. But for your knowledge, I have Paul's stopwatch tally. We're way over."

Welles cocked his head. "Where are we, Jack? How much cutting do we need to do?"

"You're a good seven minutes long. If you're not willing to trim back those endless musical interludes, I'd say the last section—the narrative bit about the professor wandering in the city—that can and must be pruned."

Welles put a hand on Houseman's shoulder. "Well, let's get to work, then. You have your copy of the script handy?"

Houseman nodded. "It's in the control booth. And I've annotated it. I'll get it."

He went off to do that, and Welles said, "Jack's a great editor. You up for helping out, Walter?"

"Of course."

With the exception of a theater on the ground floor, the studios (Gibson learned in passing) were confined to the twentieth and twenty-first floors. Another large one, the identical twin of Studio One, was on the twenty-first, directly above them; right now the highly regarded Norman

Corwin was rehearsing a drama that would go on at nine
P.M., after the Mercury Theatre.

Welles led Houseman and Gibson down the hallway,
away from the lobby and Studio One, deep into the building.

Walking alongside Houseman, the writer asked, "Are
we heading to your offices?"

Without looking at Gibson, Houseman said dryly, "You
were in our offices on Thursday. At the theater."

"You have no office space here at CBS?"

"Of course not. They only have four or five floors of
them. Why should they spare us any? . . . We tend to use
Studio Seven, a small studio that isn't terribly well-
equipped and hence not in much use . . . as a makeshift office. Or that is, we use the control room in that fashion."

Welles, without glancing back, added, "Such as now,
when we need to do some rewriting, away from the cast and
techs. And to give Paul some breathing room to give the actors some last-minute tips."

Gibson asked, "Why isn't Howard Koch going along, if
this a writing session?"

They had arrived at the end of the hall, which ended at
Studio Eight, a hallway cutting to the left. Next to them at
right were two doors, practically side by side, labelled:
Studio Seven (left door) and Control Room (right one).

Welles opened the latter door, reached a hand over to
flick on the light switch, and with a gracious after-you-
gesture, said, "Because this isn't so much a writing session
as a cutting one—and I hate it when writers bleed."

The joke wasn't a particularly good one, but Gibson
might have forced a chuckle if his eyes hadn't been filled
with something that turned the witticism into an uninten-
tional lapse into poor taste.

This control room—not nearly as elaborately outfitted
with electronics, and absent the adjacent smaller sub-
control room—nonetheless had a large horizontal window

looking out on a studio that was perhaps a tenth the size of Studio One.

The lights in the studio were off, but (sharing the control-room illumination) revealed itself bare of anything but a table and a chair, a few microphones on stands, and a few more chairs against a wall. Nothing very exceptional, really, except for the woman seated at the table.

Or rather, slumped there, like a schoolgirl napping at her desk.

Gibson didn't recognize her at first—she was pale and her eyes were closed and her strawberry-blonde hair was askew, concealing a good portion of her face. But then it came to him: they had located the missing Miss Donovan, absent without an excuse from her receptionist post.

Only now she had an excuse, and a damned good one: her throat was slit and blood had pooled all over the table-top, some of it dripping down the sides; and from their slightly elevated position in the control booth, the hunting knife . . . with the signature ORSON WELLES on its hilt . . . could be seen, swimming in red.

CHAPTER FIVE

Now You See It

Within the control booth, the three men pressed against the glass, like children at a department store window; but unlike those dreamy-eyed kids, this trio of adults stared aghast, at a nightmare.

"The poor child," Houseman said. Then he rushed from the room.

Gibson followed, and saw Houseman at the studio door, reaching for the knob. He clutched the producer's arm and said, "What about fingerprints?"

"What if the girl is still *alive*?" Houseman's normally unflappable expression was replaced by one of wide-eyed horror.

"With her throat cut? With all that blood . . . ?"

"Are you a doctor, man?" Houseman snapped, and he clutched the knob, and twisted.

The door did not open.

"Locked!" Houseman blurted. He touched a hand to his forehead as if checking for a fever. "The goddamned thing is locked. . . ."

Gibson took the few steps back to see what had become of Welles. Through the open doorway of the control booth, Welles could be seen, moon face as white as its namesake, the long tapering fingers touching his lips, those normally rather Chinese-looking eyes now as wide as a Cotton Club dancer doing stereotypical shtick.

Gibson stood in the doorway. "Orson—are you all right?"

Welles's body remained facing the window, but his head swivelled and the huge eyes under raised eyebrows stared unblinkingly at the writer.

Very softly, Welles said, "I am decidedly not all right. That poor young woman—that sweet young woman . . . 'For in that sleep of death, what dreams may come?' "

Gibson thought if Welles was going to quote Shakespeare, it ought to be that line from *Macbeth* about how surprising it was, how much blood there'd been.

"Orson—join us in the hallway."

He drew a deep breath, nodded gravely, but did not otherwise move, remaining as frozen as Lot's wife.

In the hall, Gibson faced Houseman. "I believe she's past help."

Houseman had found his usual calm demeanor, if a troubled version thereof. "It would be difficult to break the thing down—all of these studios have heavy, soundproofed doors."

Gibson pointed toward the small room from which Welles had yet to emerge. "What about that window?"

"Again," Houseman said, shrugging fatalistically, "it's heavy glass, perhaps unbreakable—part of the necessary soundproofing between control room and studio. Poor thing . . . poor thing. . . ."

"Her name was Donovan."

Houseman's eyes tightened, in surprise. "That's right— how did you know her, Walter?"

"I was here for the Thursday run-through. We spoke. She was friendly, efficient . . . an intelligent girl."

"Yes." Houseman seemed to taste his next two words: "But ambitious."

Sensing something judgmental, Gibson asked, "By that you mean, she wanted to make it in show business?"

The producer nodded slowly, a priest pronouncing a benediction. "She'd performed in the front of our Mercury microphone, in minor roles." Another tasting of words followed: "Thanks to Orson."

"She was . . . ?"

"One of his little conquests, yes. He has assembled quite a 'cast' of nubiles—actresses, dancers, ballerinas."

Remembering, Gibson said, "A certain renowned ballet master signed Miss Donovan's reception book, today."

Frowning, Houseman said, "What? Are you sure? I haven't seen the man anywhere around. Balanchine, you say?"

"Yes. And Virginia Welles signed in, too."

Houseman shook his head. "Well, I haven't seen her."

Gibson nodded toward the locked door. "Well, Miss Donovan did—as I say, they both signed her book, but did *not* sign out. . . ."

Gibson quickly explained about the security guard who'd taken over Miss Donovan's post.

Houseman stood motionless, like figure in a wax museum; when he spoke, his lips moved so slightly, the statue effect remained in place: "I do not have the pulp sensibilities of yourself, Mr. Gibson, nor of my gifted young partner. But in seeing . . . I suppose the term is, 'the scene of the crime' . . . it would seem clear that either Orson himself performed a particularly senseless, sloppy crime of passion upon that child, or—"

"Or someone framed him for it."

Houseman's mouth twitched a smirk. "Using a weapon literally signed by the designated 'killer.' "

Gibson's eyes narrowed. "Jack, that murder weapon does limit the suspects."

"How, pray tell?"

The writer thumped the producer's chest gently with a forefinger. "It has to be someone who has access to your office at the Mercury Theatre—who could lift that grisly memento off its nails from its place of honor on your wall."

The lipless smile that formed on Houseman's face was like a cut in his flesh. "How much difficulty did *you* have, Walter, entering the Mercury unheeded at an odd time?"

"Well . . ." Gibson thought back to the slumbering Miss Holliday in the box office window. ". . . none, really."

"Precisely. And there is no lock on the door of our eagle's-nest office. Actors, crew, reporters, total strangers, come in and out of the Mercury at all hours."

"But who would know about that *knife*?"

Houseman's brow tightened slightly. "Well, certainly Virginia has been there, often enough, and likely saw it. And Mr. Balanchine, for that matter."

"What was Balanchine doing there?"

Houseman's eyebrows rose but his voice did not. "Threatening Orson's life."

"How about Owney Madden? Did he ever come around?"

Houseman blinked and grunted a single laugh. "The gangster? Why ever would he be in our office?"

Gibson raised an eyebrow. "How about that dancer Orson and Owney . . . shared? Was *she* ever in that office?"

"I believe . . . several times."

"That gives her knowledge of the knife that she could have passed along to Madden, however innocently."

Houseman shook his head, confused. "Walter, why does this gangster come to your mind? Did *he* sign in at Miss Donovan's station, as well?"

"No—but wasn't he cuckolded, in a manner of speaking, by Orson?"

Houseman drew in a breath; his eyes were alive with thought. "If having your way with another man's mistress could fall under that description . . . yes."

Gibson pointed toward the locked door. "I'm not saying Madden did it himself—but one of his people could have, and that social class knows all about framing people, and they aren't squeamish about a little blood, either."

"Again, Walter—why do you suspect Madden, when we know that both Balanchine and Virginia Welles were in the building? Perhaps one, or both, still are!"

Gibson told Houseman of the incident in the alley last night, outside the Cotton Club.

Finally, Welles came shambling out of the control booth, his expression mournful. *No tears, however,* Gibson noted.

The three men stood in a tight circle.

Houseman faced his partner and said, "Is this true, Orson? Were you accosted last night by ruffians?"

Blinking, Welles said, "What? . . . Oh. That. Yes. Yes, of course. Walter and I, uh, went to the Cotton Club, which perhaps was ill-advised, considering Mr. Madden's temper. . . ."

Houseman thrust a finger toward the door—the gesture had an accusatory aura, even though the digit did not point at Welles himself. " 'Ill-advised' indeed, if what happened to Miss Donovan is the handiwork of Madden's minions."

Welles swallowed. His tone was strangely apologetic. "You know of course, I did not—"

Houseman waved that off. "That goes without saying."

Gibson said, "You did have opportunity, Orson."

The grief in Welles's face turned to outrage, the white flesh to scarlet. "What are you saying, man?"

Patting the air, Gibson said, "Not that you did this—I don't believe for an instant that that's the case. But looking at it, objectively . . . you could have done this early this morning, before you and I breakfasted—"

"No," Houseman said. "That blood is still glistening."

Welles closed his eyes, shivered.

"Still shimmering wet," Houseman continued. "This could not have happened long ago, elsewise it would have congealed, dried to a black patina, not that terrible red river."

Welles glared at Houseman. "A little less poetry, Jack, and a little more help! Please!"

Softly Houseman said, "My apologies. But I think we're all agreed that this young lady is beyond anyone's help, now, save the Almighty."

Welles swallowed.

Gibson nodded.

With a heave of a sigh, Houseman said, "Walter, however, is correct, Orson: you did have the opportunity."

"Nonsense, Housey! I was in that studio all afternoon!"

Houseman waggled a finger. "No. Not 'in'—in and *out* of that studio, yes."

Welles shook his head. "No. No, I was—"

Gibson said, "Orson, you left for at least two lengthy bathroom breaks. You also exited to get a sound-effect gizmo for Ora, at one point."

Eyes closed as if in prayer, Welles nodded. "Yes. Yes, goddamnit, you're right. And I stepped into the hall two other times, to smoke and think away from the chaos. I *did* have opportunity."

"*And* means," Houseman said. "You certainly had access to the weapon."

Welles threw his hands in the air. "But would I be so idiotic as to contrive a crime and leave my very signature?"

"It might be argued," Houseman said, chin up, "that you had brought the knife here to present Miss Donovan with a keepsake of your relationship, which I understand reached a somewhat acrimonious apex, just days ago."

Welles swallowed thickly. "We did—break up, so to speak. I told her that . . . well, it's none of your business, either of you, what I told her."

"Perhaps not," Houseman said, "but it will be the business of the police."

"The police," Welles echoed numbly, as if the existence of the law enforcement entity had only just now occurred to him.

Houseman continued, his voice emotionless: "And as for what you said to Miss Donovan, you were quarreling in the hallway outside Studio One, most vocally, certainly publicly, and any number of people heard you—myself included. Any number saw her run away in tears, shattered by your rejection, by your accusations of her 'craven gold-digging,' if I correctly recall your colorful turn of phrase."

Softly Welles said, "You do."

Houseman shrugged. "I also recall that, in the early stages of the dalliance, Miss Donovan had made a special point of praising your performance in 'Julius Caesar,' which makes the seemingly unlikely gift of that signed blade at least marginally plausible."

"I was going to present her that knife," Welles said with acid sarcasm, "as a going-away present? Absurd. Utterly absurd."

Houseman granted him a nod. "I would tend to agree. But juries have believed less likely tales."

Welles turned pale again. "Juries . . ."

Gibson had been adding it all up. "So you had motive . . . for a crime of passion, at least . . . means . . . and opportunity. A circumstantial case could easily be built against you, Orson. Surely you see that."

The big boy-man turned from one friend to another, desperation in his eyes. "I swear to you, John. Walter—*I did not do this evil thing.*"

The words were spoken with the rounded eloquence of Welles at his oratorical best.

Houseman held up a hand, traffic-cop fashion. "I assure you, Orson, that we both believe you. But you need to gather your thoughts, and be prepared for the official inquisition that is likely to follow."

"Oy," Welles said.

Gibson said, "We'd better stop jawing, and call the police."

Houseman held up the traffic-cop palm again, thought for a few moments, then said with authority, "We do have a security force here, however meager, and I would suggest we bring one of those in-house representatives of the law to this room and let him see what we have seen. It would be his place to make that fateful phone call."

"Quit it, Housey," Welles snapped.

"Quit what?"

"All that arch phraseology. This is not some script you've cobbled together for me from 'Treasure Island.' A murder has been committed, and what you both seem to overlook is that the murderer is very likely still in this building."

Houseman's head tilted, his eyes became slits. "Are you saying—we're in danger?"

Welles gestured to himself with one hand and with the other from Houseman to Gibson. "Aren't we? Someone's obviously after *me*!"

"The evidence of our eyes indicates," Houseman said calmly, "the killer was after Miss Donovan. Surely you're not suggesting a madman is among us . . ."

"Who else," Welles snorted, "could have done such a thing?"

". . . and that a homicidal maniac is running through the halls of the Columbia Broadcasting Building looking for . . . for more *victims*? Orson, it's unbelievable."

Welles thrust a thumb toward the studio door. "Why don't you ask Miss Donovan how believable it seems to her about now?"

This time a Gibson palm stopped traffic, and the writer said, "Orson, we may have a murderer among us, yes . . . but if you were framed for this crime, then the likelihood of a second murder is slight."

Houseman was nodding. "But I second the notion that the murderer may well be among us—that studio is filled with your fellow artisans, Orson, many of whom you have humiliated and attacked."

Welles seemed taken aback by this remark. "Well, I hardly think that's fair! I also lavish love on the sons of bitches!"

Houseman shot a small knowing look Gibson's way.

Gibson asked, "May I make a suggestion?"

"Certainly," Houseman said.

"Please," Orson said.

"Well, can I assume there's a janitor on duty, from whom we can get the key to this studio?"

"Of course," Houseman said.

"One of us should fetch him, or at least his keys."

"Agreed," Welles said. "And I could get Mr. Williams." Houseman blinked. "Who?"

Gibson said, "The security person I told you about, Jack—the one who took over Miss Donovan's desk."

"Ah," Houseman said. "By all means, Orson, fetch Mr. Williams."

"Good—you fellas have your assigned tasks, and . . ." Gibson gestured to the locked door. ". . . I'll stand guard on the crime scene."

"Probably wise," Houseman said.

"Why?" Welles asked darkly. "Are we expecting the corpse to make a break for it?"

Holding up two fingers, Gibson said, "Two reasons for me to take this post—first, I don't have any other task. John, you're getting the keys; Orson, you're bringing the house law. Second, we don't need anyone else coming along and stumbling on to this horrible thing, before we can be seen to have acted responsibly."

Houseman half-bowed. "I concur. Well reasoned."

Putting a hand on the writer's shoulder, Welles said, "I do appreciate this, Walter. I appreciate your belief in me—after all, we've only known each other a short time. . . ."

Gibson found a grin. "Which means I'm not a suspect, 'cause I'm on the short list of those you have not as yet alienated."

Welles looked hurt for an instant, then came up with a dry chuckle. "Nonetheless—Lamont Cranston thanks you, sincerely."

The big boy-genius started down the hall, making his way toward the studio; then he paused and looked back to say, "And do be careful, Walter! Remember the old saw, 'The murderer always returns to the scene of the crime.'"

"Just a cliché," Gibson said.

"All clichés," Welles called, before disappearing around the corner, "have a kernel of truth."

Then Gibson was alone with Houseman in the hall. The latter said, "I agree with Orson. Do be careful."

"I'll keep my back to the wall—literally. Are we making a mistake not going into the main studio, and telling everyone there's been a . . . a murder?"

"What, and start a panic? No, my friend, we'll operate on the assumption that the invasion from Mars goes on as scheduled."

Gibson grunted a sort of laugh. "Do you really think the show will go on?"

Houseman thought about that for a moment. "Oddly, I do. That's another cliché with truth in it: 'The show must go on.' I can rather imagine the police standing by while Orson and his cast complete the show, and then our poor gifted changeling being dragged off to the pokey. Radio has a strange power over people—police included."

Gibson half-smiled. "You do look at all of this with a . . . jaundiced eye, don't you, Jack?"

Houseman's gaze lifted; it was as if he were searching some far-off horizon. "I love that talented young man. He may well be the genius showman of our generation. And his heart is, largely, a good one. But he is also a spoiled brat, who has treated everyone around him wretchedly . . . at least, from time to time. So I am not surprised by this, not really."

Gibson reared back. "You're not surprised by the murder of Miss Donovan?"

Houseman was already shaking his head. "You misunderstand—I am shocked and dismayed by this loss. She was a sweet child, and demonstrated considerable talent, as well." The producer looked down his nose at the writer, literally if not figuratively. "No, I refer to Orson's poor judgment and his . . . the word you used, correctly, was I believe 'alienation' . . . of those who respect and follow and even worship him. That he has been . . . to again invoke melodrama, but meaning no disrespect to the unfortunate deceased . . . *'framed'* for murder is, in the sense that Orson has paved the way for such a thing, not a surprise."

Houseman gave Gibson a head-bob of farewell, and walked down the hall, in his measured manner, going the opposite way from Welles.

Gibson leaned his back against the wall, facing and staring at the door behind which a young woman lay, slaughtered like a beast. Shaking his head, he lighted up a Camel, folded his arms, and contemplated the realities of crime and murder—which he had occasionally encountered in his reporter days—and the odd fact that storytellers like himself could find this unpleasant source material so useful in entertaining a mass audience.

Faced with a real murder, the creator of the Shadow felt a twinge of guilty embarrassment for trivializing such dire, somber matters in his yarns. And yet what better subject for a story than life and death, crime and punishment? Perhaps the saddest reality was that in real life, no Shadowesque avenger existed to right such a wrong.

Welles was the first to return. Because of the puppy-like manner in which security guard Williams tagged after

Welles, the guard did not seem to Gibson to be aware that he was approaching a murder scene, or indeed anything of significance. It was as if Welles had reported spotting a mouse running down the hall.

Gibson's reading proved correct, when Welles—chagrin in his eyes—said to the writer, "I told Mr. Williams we have a problem, and that I thought a man of his perspicacity was called for."

"Riiight," Gibson said.

Welles and Williams had barely arrived when Houseman came bustling up the hall, alone, but with a key in hand.

"The janitor shared this passkey with me," Houseman said. "Should do the trick . . ."

The producer stood before the door, and drew a deep breath, perhaps gathering courage to unlock so ominous a passageway. Then he inserted the key, a click was heard, and Houseman gently pushed the door open, and all three men stepped inside, to find . . .

. . . the room was empty.

Oh, the table was there, all right; but no young woman. And no blood.

Houseman whirled on Gibson, saying, "You pledged you would stand guard!"

Gibson extended his hands, palms up. "I did—I swear I did! No one went in or out."

The security guard, looking about as bright as a potted plant, asked, "What was it you wanted me to see, anyway, Mr. Welles?"

Welles turned to Williams and patted him on the shoulder of his powder-blue uniform. A little too pleasantly, Welles said, "Bill, I made a small wager with Mr. Houseman here that I could go summon you on a crisis and that you could get here before our esteemed producer could acquire the key from the janitor. Leaving at the same time, you understand."

Gibson and Houseman exchanged glances; neither man had ever heard such incoherent inanity in all their lives.

But Bill the security guard just grinned in a horsey fashion and said, "So I won you some money, huh, Mr. Welles?"

"Yes, Bill," Welles said, walking him to the door, an arm around the man, "and I mean to share the wealth with you."

"Ha! Just like Huey Long, right, Mr. Welles?"

"Just like him, Bill—like the man says, 'Every man a king.'"

The guard was in the hall now, Welles in the doorway, turning toward Gibson to say, "Walter—do you have a five spot for this gentleman?"

Gibson dug out his wallet and handed a five-dollar bill to Bill, who grinned in his Seabiscuit way, and trotted off, chuckling as if he'd really put one over.

His expression grave, Welles shut the door.

The three were now alone in the small studio.

To Gibson, Welles said, "No one in, or out?"

"No! That fiver's going on the expense account, by the way."

Houseman, who'd been prowling the room, was over in the lefthand corner. "This connecting door to Studio Eight—it's locked, too."

Impatiently, Welles said, "Well, hell, Housey—you have the janitor's passkey!"

Absentmindedly, Houseman looked at the key, still in his hand, and said, "Ah, yes, of course," and unlocked the door.

The adjacent studio, whose own control-booth window was across the room, was even emptier than Studio Seven—not even a table, much less a corpse. Various microphone stands and stools and various junk lined and littered the walls, indicating the room saw more storage than production, these days.

Dazed, the trio returned to the studio where they'd seen the dead girl.

"Maybe she did get up and walk out," Welles said hollowly.

Gibson was having a look at the table and chair. "There *was* blood here! Look, you can see the faint smearing on this tabletop—somebody used a cloth or towel or something, and sopped and wiped it up. . . ."

The others came over, had a look and confirmed the writer's opinion.

Gibson, however, was already crouched on the floor, kneeling, Sherlock Holmes–style. "And blood drops—starts on the chair and dribbles onto the floor. The killer missed these."

Welles, hands on his knees, bent down. "By God, you're right—it's a *trail* . . . "

Houseman saw it, too. "Leading away . . . toward that door to the other studio. . . ."

The blood drops had been sopped into the soundproof-friendly carpet and led into the adjacent Studio Eight, where the droplets continued to the side of the room and a coat tree (empty), next to which lay a stack of tarps, from some recently finished painting job.

The trail drizzled to the tarps, then started up again, ending at the doorway to the hall.

Gibson, hand on his chin, said, "I'm sure I'm merely saying what you're all thinking, but it needs to be spoken . . ."

"Do," Houseman said.

"Please," Welles said.

Gibson went to the door that connected the studios and reenacted it from there: "The murderer heard us entering the control booth, and scooted next door, to Studio Eight. But he . . . or she . . . couldn't slip into the corridor, to make a getaway, because, Jack—you and I went back out into the hall almost immediately. So the killer waited, hearing us speaking . . . and we spoke quite a while, truth be told."

"We did not," Houseman dryly said, "spring into action, no."

Gibson continued: "When the killer heard your voice in the hall, Orson, he, or she, knew the control booth with its window was free of observers. So the killer returned, sopped up the blood with something . . . what I don't know . . . and dragged the corpse into the adjacent studio. The killer wrapped up the body in a tarp, ready to transport it, and—"

"No," Welles said, raising a finger. "I believe the killer waited until hearing John and me go to get the security man . . . and a key . . . and, realizing that you were outside standing watch, Walter, the killer had to stay trapped in these adjacent studios, otherwise risk a confrontation."

Gibson was nodding. "I think you're right, Orson. But the killer must have figured out that when help—and a key—*did* arrive, we would all rush into Studio Seven!"

Picking it up, Welles said, "That is when the killer cleaned up the table, moved the body, wrapped it for transport, and . . . when he . . ."

"Or she," Houseman said.

"—heard help arrive, and all of us enter Studio Seven— prompting the killer with tarp-wrapped cargo in tow to quickly exit Studio Eight and make it away, down the hall."

"A killer who by now," Gibson said, "thanks to our blathering, is well away from here."

"But probably still in the building," Welles said.

"Well . . ." Gibson thought about that. ". . . *possibly* still in the building. Certainly, Orson, you were right in that assumption you made earlier, and I was wrong to pooh-pooh it."

"But what now?" Houseman said, hands wide-spread. "We have no murder, because we have no body."

"We have blood droplets," Gibson said, pointing floor-ward, "and a table with what I believe to be smeared traces of cleaned-up blood."

In full tragedian mode, Welles asked, "Would you have me call the police?"

Gibson shrugged. "Yes. Sure. Of course."

Houseman seemed puzzled. "What do we have to show them?"

"The traces I mentioned," Gibson said. "And our report of what we saw."

"Including," Welles said aghast, "a murder weapon with my *name* attached?"

Gibson shrugged again, more elaborately. "What else is there to do?"

Welles, quietly, reasonably, and conspiratorially, said, "We go on with the show. We have our broadcast in . . ." He checked his wristwatch. ". . . less than fifteen minutes. If we call the authorities now, I may well be tied up with them, and we'll let CBS down."

"I would think," Gibson said, edgily, "that the welfare of Miss Donovan is rather more important than that of the Columbia Broadcasting System."

Welles looked properly abashed, but nonetheless said, "While I understand that sentiment, the truth is, Miss Donovan in no way benefits from our scuttling the broadcast."

"If we call the police now," Gibson said, "the chance of the killer's apprehension is greater . . . much greater. The first several hours of a murder investigation are key—"

"But," Welles said, lifting a lecturing forefinger, "our killer is either in the building, or not in the building . . . would you agree?"

Gibson frowned. "Well, aren't those the only two options?"

"Indeed. But if the killer is gone, the killer is gone, and bringing the police here sooner doesn't catch him . . . or her . . . any the sooner. But if the killer is in the building, perhaps one of our own broadcast family, then we may have the opportunity to nab him, or her, ourselves."

"Our*selves*?" Houseman said, eyes popping. In other circumstances, this reaction from the low-key producer would have amused Gibson; right now, it merely seemed grotesque.

"Think about it," Welles said. "The killer knows that we are aware a murder has been committed. If we go about our business as if nothing has happened—and, again, if the killer is one of our own—he or she may well tip their hand . . . express in some fashion surprise, behave nervously, or even blurt something incriminating."

"Possibly," Gibson granted.

"Also," Welles said, "while I undertake to go on with my broadcast-business-as-usual, you, Walter . . . if I am not imposing . . . could make a few discreet inquiries around the building."

"I'm not sure I follow."

Welles made an expansive gesture. "Well, on Sunday this building is something of a skeleton operation . . . so to speak. The offices, whether clerks or executives, are shut down—really, only the seventeenth floor, which is the news department, and the twentieth and twenty-first floors, where the studios are, are in use."

Gibson asked, "What about the eighteenth and nineteenth floors?"

"Strictly offices. Some are assigned permanently, others are for general use."

Lifting his eyebrows, Gibson said, "Plenty of places for a killer to hide."

"Yes, but I'm not suggesting you search a twenty-two-floor office building."

"Thank you so much. What *are* you suggesting, Orson?"

"Seek out the other security people, the actors and crew on the floor above us . . . working on Norman Corwin's show, for instance . . . and say that Mr. Welles wondered if any of them have seen his wife, Virginia, today. Then ask the same thing about George Balanchine. In addition, ask if they saw Dolores Donovan at all today, away from her desk—and who she might have been speaking with."

Finally Gibson was starting to buy in. "And whether or not any suspicious characters are around? Madden's boys?"

Welles thought about that. "Maybe limit that query to the security guards. They'd note a presence like that, and you could say 'Mr. Welles has had some death threats' or some such."

Fumbling for a fresh Camel, Gibson said, "So let's say I agree to gather this info, Orson. Then what?"

"Right after the broadcast, you let Jack and me know what, if anything, you've discovered. Then . . . by all means . . . we call the authorities."

"How do we explain waiting more than an hour to report a murder?"

With a gesture reminiscent of a ringmaster introducing an elephant act, Welles said, "We tell the truth—that we saw what appeared to be the dead body of our receptionist. That we found the door to be locked, and went after the key, and fetched our security guard . . . but found the studio empty."

"What about the evidence traces we discovered?"

"That," Welles said, raising a forefinger, "would be best discreetly left unremarked upon. The police are quite capable, I'm sure, of discovering clues for themselves."

"What do we say to the cops," Gibson said, "when they ask us what we thought when the corpse disappeared?"

"We say," Welles said, with a pixie smile, and a mock-innocent tone, "that we simply didn't know *what* to think . . . that we got quite naturally caught up in the pressures and deadlines of putting on our weekly broadcast, but that after the show, we determined we needed to inform them of what we'd seen."

Sighing, Gibson asked, "Isn't Howard Koch a lawyer? Maybe he could advise us as to whether we'd be breaking any laws, waiting to make that call—"

"I would suggest not," Houseman said. He was clearly on Welles's side in this. "Howard is indeed an attorney, which means he's an officer of the court. He would be legally required to make that call, immediately."

Gibson was shaking his head, not in a "no" fashion,

rather indicating his uncertainty. "The odds of us . . . of *me* . . . solving this thing in the next hour is, well, it isn't much, Orson."

Welles looked somber now; that flash of a pixie smile had been only a mild interruption in his desperate state. "It isn't much, Walter—but it's all I have. I've been framed for murder, dear boy. And the only Shadow that can help me now is a shadow of doubt cast over my guilt . . . which I am counting on *you* to conjure."

CHAPTER SIX

War of the Welles

At 7:56 P.M., E.S.T., Miss Holliday was wandering through Studio One with a wastebasket in hand, a Joannie Appleseed in reverse, bending to pluck the litter of the long day, chiefly waxy sandwich paper and empty cardboard coffee cups. It wouldn't do for anyone to step on such refuse and make an uncalled-for impromptu sound effect.

As she completed her task and disappeared with her small infectious smile through a doorway, Orson Welles—his shirtsleeves rolled up—stepped up onto his platform-style podium. To his left was Bernard Herrmann at his smaller podium (piano nearby) and his twenty-seven-piece orchestra. To Welles's right was the horizontal picture window of the control booth, behind which were numerous anxious faces, belonging to CBS exec Davidson Taylor (in the sub-control room's separate adjacent pane), Howard Koch, Paul Stewart, and John Houseman; next to Houseman, engineer John Dietz in his headphones, attending his console, lacked the anxiety of the others, seeming instead coolly focused and professional. Assembled before Welles were his actors, some on their feet, at microphones, script in hand, awaiting their cues within the rectangle of carpet, others at the two tables where they sat waiting for their own time to come.

A few moments before, Welles had casually asked if any one had seen his wife Virginia around today, or even this morning. No one had, or at least so they professed. Then, as a seeming afterthought, he said, "Say, somebody said George Balanchine was hanging around, earlier—anyone see him?" No, they said.

Now Welles was at his conductor's post, a microphone stand with its large CBS head on a skinny chrome neck squeezed between him and his music stand. His Andy Gump-ish assistant Alland (aka Vakhtangov)—in a fedora and suspenders—was one of the actors this evening, but right now was attending to his charge. He handed up to Welles a large bottle of pineapple juice, which the director chugged—part throat remedy, part superstition—then passed the empty bottle back.

Alland walked over to set the bottle on one of the actor tables—already cluttered with Sunday newspapers and magazines, as well as scripts—and returned to the carpeted square.

Welles cleared his throat, clamped on his earphones, loosened his tie, made rubbery motions with his mouth, limbering up his face. High on the wall behind Welles— where everyone but himself had a good view of it—was a round gray clock with white hands; alongside this circle a rectangular extension held two bold white-letter warnings, the upper one of which was lighted up now: STAND BY. Hands lifted in a conductor's manner, echoing nearby Herrmann who stood poised before his musicians, Welles waited, poised to begin. Then—though he couldn't see the second white warning flash on—he somehow heeded the words perfectly: ON THE AIR, and . . .

. . . cued his announcer, Dan Seymour, who rather

liltingly, even lightly intoned: "The Columbia Broadcasting System and its affiliated stations present Orson Welles and *The Mercury Theatre on the Air* in 'The War of the Worlds' by H.G. Wells."

The other Welles threw Herrmann his cue and the maestro led his musicians in twenty seconds of the *Mercury Theatre* theme: "Tchaikovsky's Piano Concerto No. 1 in B Flat Minor."

Then Seymour, hand to his ear in time-honored announcer fashion, said, "Ladies and gentlemen, the director of the Mercury Theatre, and the star of these broadcasts—Orson Welles."

Not missing a beat, Welles spoke into the microphone in a fashion both intimate and important: "We know now that in the early years of the twentieth century, this world was being watched closely by intelligences greater than man's, and yet as mortal as his own. We know now that—as human beings busied themselves about their various concerns—they were scrutinized and studied, perhaps almost as narrowly as a man with a microscope might scrutinize the transient creatures that swarm and multiply in a drop of water. . . ."

Welles paused.

"With infinite complacence," he continued, "people went to and fro over the earth about their little affairs—serene in the assurance of their dominion over this small, spinning fragment of solar driftwood which, by chance or design, man has inherited out of the dark mystery of time and space."

Another dramatic beat, then Welles pressed on: "Yet across an immense ethereal gulf, minds that are to our minds as ours are to the beasts in the jungle . . . intellects vast, cool and unsympathetic . . . regarded this earth with envious eyes, and slowly and surely drew their plans against us."

After the slightest breath, Welles changed his tone from vaguely portentous to briskly matter of fact: "In the thirty-ninth year of the twentieth century came the great disillusionment. Near the end of October, business was better, war scare was over, more men were back at work, sales were picking up. On this particular evening, October thirtieth, the Crosley service estimated that thirty-two million people were listening in on radios. . . ."

A starry night seemingly like any other had settled over Grovers Mill, a bump in the New Jersey roadside consisting of little more than a gas station, general store, feed store and mill pond. Eight miles east of Trenton, the state capital, fifty miles southwest of New York, this was the epitome of sleepy small-town America, described by one wag as "nestling in a time warp of refinement and genteel country living." To find a hamlet more typically American than this, you'd have to go to the backlot of MGM.

On a small farm just a few miles east of Grovers Mill, family members had gathered around the tall walnut cabinet of the household radio in a living room that also held a wood-burning stove and a spinet piano, as well as doily-pinned furnishings reflecting the tastes of the woman of the house, who had passed away less than a year ago.

Les Chapman, twelve, his younger brother Leroy, ten, and their eight-year-old sister Susie were spending Sunday evening with their grandfather, Andrew, a widower of sixty-two who ran his small farm pretty much by himself, though his son Luke helped out some—Luke worked in the feed store at Grovers Mill. Luke and Alice, the parents of these children, usually spent Sunday night here at Grandfather Chapman's, where the extended family listened to the radio together, Charlie McCarthy a particular favorite. But Alice was down with a bad cold and Luke was tending to her, so the kids had gone off to spend the evening with Grandfather.

Les, Leroy, and Susie were bathed in the glow of the radio's yellow dial, transported by this magical box to mental landscapes of their own creation—a journey they took regularly, to various outposts. Every one of the kids had his or her favorite show—Les loved *Jack Armstrong,* which aired every afternoon for fifteen exciting minutes ("Wave the flag for Hudson High, boys!") and, right after that, Susie's favorite came on, *Little Orphan Annie* ("Who's the little chatterbox, the one with all those curly locks?"). But even Susie admitted that however much she loved Orphan Annie, she couldn't make herself swallow their sponsor's product, Ovaltine. Or as Susie put it, "Oval tar!"

Leroy's favorite had been on earlier, this afternoon— *The Shadow* ("Who knows what evil lurks in the hearts of men? The Shadow knows!"). But Leroy didn't think it was as good as it used to be. They had a new Shadow now, and Leroy just couldn't get used to him.

Right now all three kids were laughing as Charlie McCarthy made a dummy out of Edgar Bergen. Attracted by their laughter, Grandpa came in from the kitchen, where he'd been cleaning up after the sandwiches and milk and cookies he'd served (the kids had washed, and put away, the dishes).

"I'll moooow ya down," Charlie McCarthy was saying, in his wiseguy kid voice; the catchphrase was one that never failed to create peals of laughter from listeners, and the Chapmans were no exception.

Grandpa, settling into his comfortable chair, chuckled, too, even if he didn't quite seem to know why.

In Studio One, a standard weather report had been faded up to start mid-sentence, after Welles's opening. Kenny Delmar, with his black-rimmed glasses and curly hair, was wrapping it up: "This weather report comes to you from the Government Weather Bureau. . . . We now take you to the Meridian Room in the Hotel Park Plaza in downtown New York, where you will be entertained by the music of Ramon Raquello and his orchestra."

Bernard Herrmann directed his world-class musicians in

a sluggish version of "La Cumparasita" that was so down-right mediocre, it had everyone smiling.

Everyone but Herrmann.

Ben Gross and his wife Kathleen were sharing a quiet little dinner with a few friends in an apartment in Tudor City. The salad had barely been served when the host asked, "How about turning on Charlie McCarthy?"

Gross, the radio columnist of the *New York Daily News,* liked Charlie McCarthy as well as the next guy; but he was a bigger fan of Orson Welles and his *Mercury Theatre on the Air.* He'd been making a point, lately, of catching Welles's Sunday night broadcasts, which the critic consid-ered the best experimental dramatic productions currently on the air.

So he found himself saying, "Okay, but do you mind if we first hear what Orson Welles is up to?"

"I thought you weren't working tonight, Ben," their hostess said, as she filled his coffee cup.

"Well, you know—no rest for the wicked. But if anybody does anything worth me *writing* about tonight, it's probably going to be Welles."

Gross could almost not believe his own words. When he'd dropped by CBS a few days ago, he'd run into one of the actors on the show, Ray Collins, an avuncular sweetheart of a guy.

When Gross had asked about this week's Mercury offer-ing, Ray had said, "Just between us, Ben—it's lousy. Orson couldn't get a script of 'Lorna Doone' up and running, so he's falling back on that old H.G. Wells chestnut, *War of the Worlds.*"

"*That* museum piece?" Gross had said.

"Yeah. We're trying to blow the dust off." Collins had a wry smile that was like a wrinkle in his face; the guy was only in his forties but he seemed like he'd been born sixty. "Good Sunday-funnies fantasy, but for radio?"

"I'd think Orson would leave that kind of thing to the kiddie shows, like *Buck Rogers*."

Collins shrugged, then said, "Well, he has dressed it up some. And this *is* Hallowe'en weekend. It's better than it was at a first read-through, anyway."

"Should I give a listen?"

"Aw, I wouldn't bother, if I were you. Probably bore you to death."

Now here, a few days later, Gross was imposing on his hosts to give up their favorite comedy show, at least for a few minutes (and everybody knew the best part of the Charlie McCarthy/Edgar Bergen hour was the opening monologue), to let him check up on what a Mercury insider himself said was Welles at his lousiest.

Still, you never knew with that boy-genius. Welles coasting along was better than most people at full throttle; and if Mr. Mercury Theatre displayed some ingenuity in dressing up that familiar fantasy, who knew? Might be worth a line or two in his column for the late edition.

So everybody ate their salads as the show began, conventionally enough, with the standard intro and theme and a sonorous opening by Welles.

Then it took a strange turn.

"*Ladies and gentlemen,*" an announcer was saying, "*we interrupt our program of dance music to bring you a special bulletin from the Intercontinental Radio News—at twenty minutes before eight, central time, Professor Farrell of the Mount Jennings Observatory, Chicago, Illinois, reports observing several explosions of incandescent gas . . .*"

The hostess asked, "Is that the program, or . . . ?"

The announcer was saying, ". . . *occurring at regular intervals on the planet Mars.*"

The host smiled and said, "It's just the show—it's Mars they're talking about. 'War of the Worlds,' remember?"

Somebody else said, "No such thing as the 'Intercontinental Radio News' service."

Then everyone was smiling and laughing, feeling nicely superior, as the announcer continued: *"The spectroscope indicates the gas to be hydrogen and moving toward the earth with enormous velocity. Professor Pierson of the observatory at Princeton confirms Farrell's observation, and describes the phenomenon as, quote, like a jet of blue flame shot from a gun, unquote. . . . We now return you to the music of Ramón Raquello, playing for you in the Meridian Room of the Park Plaza Hotel, situated in downtown New York."*

The tango limped back on.

And stayed on.

"Heard enough?" the host asked.

Kathleen whispered to her husband: "Dear . . . this is boring. Don't you think?"

Gross swallowed a bite of tomato drenched in Italian dressing, which was tart enough to make it seem like he was making a face when he said, "Please—just a few more minutes. . . . You know, Doris, this dressing is delicious. Just great."

The others at the table smiled at him.

But they didn't seem to mean it any more than Gross had meant his salad-dressing compliment.

James Roberts, Jr., twenty, was behind the wheel of a Buick coupe purchased for him by his father, James Roberts, Sr., business executive. Wearing a rust-colored sweater and dark brown tie on a yellow shirt, the young man was slender, well-groomed, with neatly cut and combed brown hair, an attractive college man but for his rather close-set blue eyes that gave an impression of less than stellar intelligence, an impression which James Jr. seldom gave cause for reconsideration.

Riding with him was his friend Bobby, another junior at Princeton University. They were on their way back to their frat house, having visited Bobby's girlfriend, Betty, for the weekend in Manhattan.

Blond, round-faced Bobby, lighting up a Philip Morris cigarette, asked, "What did you think of Betty's sister?"

"Cute," James said, hands on the wheel. No one called him "Jimmy" just as—oddly—no one called Bobby "Robert."

"Cute, huh? Then why didn't you make a move?"

"A little young. Naïve."

"Nice chassis on her, though, for a sixteen-year-old, don't ya think?"

"Yeah. Oh yeah." James thought it might be somehow impolite or even gauche to mention that the sister had an even better build than Bobby's Betty, who was kind of broad in the beam and flat in the chest, for James's tastes.

"Sometimes," Bobby said with a knowing wink, "naïve ain't such a bad thing."

The two laughed.

The night was bright, with a moon and stars, and the countryside had an unreal aspect, bathed in ivory—a very pretty blue-gray, though a gentle fog was starting to roll in, not a hazard, merely a touch of unreality. Funny how the cold concrete of Manhattan could disappear into the idyllic countryside of New Jersey in a seeming flash.

"Mind if I switch on the radio?" Bobby asked.

"Not at all," James said.

Dance music was on.

Pretty soon a news bulletin interrupted "Stardust," and Bobby turned it up.

New York State Troopers Carmine and Chuck had spent an uneventful, even sleepy afternoon on the job. They'd even kept the top down on their '37 Ford Phaeton, to better enjoy the beautiful fall day, and keep a good wide view of the landscape, including the ribbon of cement that was their responsibility. The majority of state-trooper strength, this Sunday, had been on the road, dispatched to deal with heavy weekend traffic as the upstate resorts emptied their clientele back into the city.

And on Hallowe'en eve, the usual run of adolescent pranks could be assumed, though nothing yet. Maybe the teenage ghosts and goblins would wait till tomorrow night to spring with their stuff.

Carmine and Chuck's job was to keep traffic moving, and to handle any accidents or other mishaps. But after several hours of not-much-of-anything, they headed in to make a stop at HQ. This was necessary because the troopers had yet to score the newfangled radio communications gear some big city forces were getting, and rural police did not have call boxes to make checking in a snap.

So for updates and new assignments, periodic stops at HQ were a must.

In the teletype room, the trooper on duty—Rusty, a burly, boyish guy whose curly red hair had given him his moniker—looked up as Carmine and Chuck swaggered in. Rusty's trademark was a corncob pipe that he puffed harder, the more excited he got about a subject.

"Any wants?" Carmine asked.

"Any lookouts?" Chuck asked.

"A few stolen cars. Here's the list." Rusty handed it over. Puffing away like Popeye, he gestured to the portable radio at the desk from which the trooper monitored the teletype machine; dance music was playing. "The regular programs have been interrupted a couple times—some kinda, I dunno, lunar disturbance out in South Jersey."

Carmine frowned. "What kind of what?"

Rusty shrugged. "Do I look like a scientist? I just hope it ain't a earthquake, 'cause I got my folks over there in South Jersey, and they ain't young."

"Well," Carmine advised from the doorway, "you keep one ear glued to that radio—we'll stop back in an hour and see if there's anything *to* this thing."

Rusty nodded. "Roger," he said, and puffed on his pipe. "Hey—it's supposed to be gettin' foggy: Watch it out there."

The two troopers nodded, gave casual forefinger salutes, and went back out into a quiet night that was about to get louder.

Walter Gibson, blissfully unaware that the Mars broadcast had already begun to stir hornets, was conducting his murder investigation.

He began by chatting with Williams, the security guard, describing Virginia Welles to the man. It turned out Williams knew who Mrs. Welles was but, today or tonight, he hadn't seen "hide nor hair" of her. Then Gibson passed along a description of Balanchine (courtesy of Houseman), as well.

At the reception desk, Williams shook his head. "I never seen that guy that I know of."

Then Gibson described, as best he could, the three thugs who had accosted Welles and himself down the street from the Mercury Theatre last night.

But Williams was no help there, either.

"And I'm pretty familiar with everybody who comes in and out of the place," the guard insisted.

His effort barely begun, Gibson already felt helpless, unsure of what to do next.

"Kind of a dull program tonight," Williams said.

"Huh?"

The guard nodded over toward a speaker positioned high on the wall, over the doorway to the Studio One hallway; the live broadcast was being piped in—dance music, right now. Gibson, who'd heard the show rehearsed half a dozen times, had been oblivious to it.

"The Mercury show," Williams was explaining. "Kinda dull—please don't tell Mr. Welles I said so!"

"I won't, Mr. Williams. I won't."

"About these people?"

"Yes?"

"Why don't you check with George? He's on the floor just above us."

"I'll do that."

"And Fred's down on seventeen—the news bureau?"

"Thanks. Any other security on duty?"

"No, sir. That's it."

As Gibson was getting on the elevator, a fake news flash kicked in.

In Studio One, Dan Seymour had just reported a request from the Government Meteorological Bureau that the nation's observatories keep a watch on "any further disturbances" on Mars. Shortly, listeners would be taken to the Princeton Observatory in New Jersey where "noted astronomer" Professor Pierson would give an expert assessment of the situation.

"We return you until then," the announcer said, "to the music of Ramón Raquello and his orchestra. . . ."

In Lambertville, New Jersey, Miss Jane Dorn, 57, and her sister Miss Eleanor Dorn, 54, returned from an evening church service to their small house, inherited by them jointly from their minister father, a Baptist.

The two women had never worked for a living, sharing a modest but secure income from investments their late father had made during a lifetime of service and sacrifice. Both were chiefly interested in their Bible studies and baking pies for themselves and church bake sales; neither had ever had a serious beau—they had also inherited their father's looks, which is to say, hawkish, pinched countenances, poor eyesight necessitating thick-lensed glasses, and odd lanky yet thick-hipped frames.

In small-town America of the thirties, the Dorn sisters of Lambertville were considered "old maids," a term not terribly pejorative then; but the sisters considered themselves Godly women doing the Lord's work—which, again, consisted primarily of Bible studies and pie baking (and eating).

The two had only grammar school educations, but considered themselves serious-minded. They both did a great deal of reading, Miss Jane partial to biographies of great men like Martin Luther and Abraham Lincoln, while Miss Eleanor was a devotee of the Brontë sisters and Jane Austen. When they decided to buy a radio console for their living room, the sisters agreed they would restrict their listening to religious and educational programming, though they had become quietly addicted to radio serials, in particular *Mary Noble, Backstage Wife* and *One Man's Family*. This penchant for soap opera was the closest thing to a vice in the shared life of the sisters.

So it was, when they returned from Sunday evening service, that Miss Jane switched the radio on to an interview-in-progress, with Professor Richard Pierson.

This seemed to fill the educational requirement they still pretended to honor (none of their "stories" were on at the moment), so the sisters settled into twin rockers and began their knitting while, without a word to each other, they both became enthralled with the scientific discourse, which was accompanied by the hypnotically compelling sound of a ticking clock.

The reporter, Carl Phillips, described the scene vividly: Professor Pierson stood on a small platform, peering through a huge microscope in a large semi-circular room, "pitch black but for an oblong split in the ceiling." Through that opening, stars could be seen. Mr. Phillips warned listeners that the interview might be interrupted at any moment, as Professor Pierson was in constant communication with astronomical centers around the world.

"Professor, would you please tell our radio audience exactly what you see as you observe Mars through your telescope?"

"Nothing unusual at the moment, Mr. Phillips. A red disk swimming in a blue sea. Transverse stripes across the disk. Quite distinct now, because Mars happens to be the point nearest the earth . . . in opposition, as we call it."

"In your opinion, what do these transverse stripes signify, Professor Pierson?"

"Not canals, I assure you, Mr. Phillips."

The sisters smiled to themselves as the professor assured the reporter that, despite "popular conjecture," the possibility of intelligent life on Mars was "a thousand to one."

Miss Jane said, "God's in His Heaven."

Miss Eleanor said, "And all's right in the world."

This exchange was a common one between the sisters; but right now, with all this talk of Mars and the heavens, it seemed particularly apt.

Walter Gibson tried George, the security guard on the twenty-first floor.

The heavyset, florid man was leaning back in his swivel chair behind the reception desk asleep and snoring, when Gibson approached and cleared his throat.

George's eyes popped open and he lurched forward. "Yes! Yes!"

Only the fact that he was investigating a murder kept Gibson from laughing.

He introduced himself and explained to the security guard that he was trying to ascertain whether or not anyone had seen Virginia Welles or George Balanchine around the building today—and if so, when? How recently?

George knew who Mrs. Welles was, but hadn't seen her; he just shook his head when Gibson shared Balanchine's description with him. The same response came when Gibson asked about the three thugs from last night.

"Like I say," George said, "I haven't seen Mrs. Welles today. I've been on this desk since Sadie, the receptionist, left at five P.M. Before that, I was in the security office on the eighteenth. I've got Sadie's phone number—you could call her."

Gibson took the number, writing it down in the notebook he carried to record plot brainstorms and to write descriptions of people and places he happened upon.

The "War of the Worlds" broadcast was piped in onto this floor, too—right now the two Shadows were in a scene together, Shadow-Number-One Frank Readick playing a reporter asking Shadow-Number-Two Orson Welles various questions about Mars.

"Professor, for the benefit of our listeners, how far is it from Mars to Earth?"

"Approximately forty million miles."

"Well, that seems a safe enough distance."

The security guard was shaking his head. "Mr. Gibson, I'm sure I haven't seen this Balanchine character, or those hoodlum types, neither."

"Why so sure, George?"

George shrugged. "First of all, I haven't seen anybody this evening who I don't recognize as one of the actors or other production personnel, on one show around here or another. And second . . ." Another shrug. ". . . I would've stopped anybody I didn't recognize. Mr. Gibson, nothing gets past me."

Gibson nodded. "Thank you, George."

George grinned and nodded.

Gibson stepped back onto the elevator, wondering how long it would be before George was asleep again.

In upstate New York, at the state troopers' HQ, Rusty was puffing away at his corncob pipe like a tugboat smokestack.

On the radio, reporter Carl Phillips was reading the listeners an urgent telegram that had just arrived for Professor Pierson at Princeton Observatory.

" 'Nine-fifteen P.M. eastern standard time. Seismograph

registered shock of almost earthquake intensity occurring within a radius of twenty miles of Princeton. Please investigate. Signed, Lloyd Gray, Chief of Astronomical Division.'"

Frowning at the word "earthquake," which echoed his earlier fears about his parents in New Jersey, Rusty turned the volume dial up on the radio, even louder.

The professor was confirming that this meteorite was of an "unusual size," and that the disturbances on Mars had no bearing on the event—it was merely coincidental.

"However," the professor was saying, *"we shall conduct a search. . . ."*

Rusty wondered if he should notify the corporal, who was at the duty desk, two floors below, particularly when the next bulletin reported "a huge, flaming object, believed to be a meteorite," falling on a farm near Grovers Mill, not far from Trenton.

The flash in the sky (the radio said) could be seen within a radius of hundreds of miles, the impact heard as far north as Elizabeth, New Jersey.

Somehow, when the reporter turned the air back over to the New York studio, where a pianist was tinkling away at "I'm Always Chasing Rainbows," Rusty was even more convinced something was wrong, *really* wrong. . . .

Thinking about his folks, the teletype trooper began to tremble; his eyes teared up, and it wasn't from the smoke his corncob pipe was producing.

He would tell the duty corporal to turn on the radio and hear for himself. Who knew? They might need to start mobilizing, to help the New Jersey troopers out, any time now.

Slight, spectacled Sheldon Judcroft, a student member of the University Press Club at Princeton, was at a desk in the student newspaper office, working on an editorial protesting the radical-right radio preachings of Father Coughlin, preferring the quiet here to the hubbub of his fraternity.

The phone rang and something amazing happened: the

city desk editor of a real newspaper, the *Philadelphia Inquirer,* was on the line.

"We have a radio report of a meteorite that has hit near Princeton," the voice said (male, urgent, yet matter-of-fact). "Place called Grovers Mill. What do you know about it?"

"Nothing—I don't even have the radio on."

"Oh. Okay."

And the phone clicked dead.

Sheldon thought about the call. He felt he'd somehow failed to measure up, faced with a real newspaper story. He turned on the radio and switched the dial until he found the report and listened.

Indeed, a meteor did seem to have struck in New Jersey, a big one that had been heard for miles around (though, oddly, Sheldon hadn't heard it himself, nor felt the impact . . . too wrapped up in the Father Coughlin piece, maybe).

Then something else amazing happened: Sheldon found himself calling Arthur Barrington, Chair of the Princeton Geology Department, at home.

After Sheldon's apologies and explanation, the Department Chair said, "I haven't heard anything about this either, son . . . but it sounds big."

"Yes it does, sir."

"Mr. Judcroft, are you by nature adventurous?"

"Of course," Sheldon squeaked. "I'm a newsman!"

"Good. I'll swing by and pick you up."

"Pick me up?"

"If ever there was a job for journalism and geology, this is it. . . . Put on something warm."

"Yes, sir!"

Sheldon hung up, and got his notebook.

And a sweater.

At 8:12 P.M., Edgar Bergen turned his microphone over to a guest artist, Nelson Eddy.

The host of *The Chase and Sanborn Hour*—thanks to the

vocal gymnastics required to keep such characters as Charlie McCarthy, Mortimer Snerd and Effie Clinker as vivid and real as himself (more so, some would say)—needed a nice break after each week's opening monologue, which he and Charlie (which is to say, Bergen himself) did alone.

So tonight, while Bergen sipped a glass of water, Eddy—singing star of radio and film—began to warble "Neapolitan Love Song."

Bergen felt confident about this booking—Eddy, half of a wildly popular screen team (the other half, of course, was Jeanette MacDonald), would surely keep listeners rapt at their radios. The singer seemed a fine preventative, if not cure, for that spreading disease of dial turning (push buttons and airplane dials made it so easy!) that especially plagued a rigidly formatted show like Bergen and McCarthy. Listeners knew just how long they could sample the wares of other stations, before returning for the next dose of humor from the ventriloquist and his dummy—unless, of course, some other show caught the dial-turner's attention and held it. . . .

Still, Bergen figured he didn't have much to worry about. In addition to Eddy, he had Madeline Carroll and Dorothy Lamour, two top actresses, and Dottie Lamour would sing several of her biggest hits.

So even in the unlikely event that Eddy lost a listener, momentarily, that listener would be back.

After all, who would want to miss out on all that excitement?

CHAPTER SEVEN

Journey into Fear

At 8:11 P.M., E.S.T., in Studio One, Bernard Herrmann's undistinctive dance-band music was interrupted by announcer Kenny Delmar, saying: "We take you now to Grovers Mill, New Jersey."

After a long, rather ominous beat, the sound of the remote location kicked in, as all of the actors, on their feet, circling about a single microphone like Indians around a campfire of war, created a convincing aural approximation of a much larger, milling crowd.

"Ladies and gentlemen," Frank Readick said into another mike, reading from his script, "this is Carl Phillips again, out at the Wilmuth farm, Grovers Mill, New Jersey. Professor Pierson and myself made the eleven miles from Princeton in ten minutes."

Ora Nichols had already dropped the needle on a disc that layered police sirens and the sound of wind into background of the "Carl Phillips" remote report.

Readick, as Phillips, was describing the scene as being like something out of a modern Arabian Nights.

"... I guess that's the thing, directly in front of me, half buried in a vast pit. Must have struck with *terrific* force. The ground is ... covered with splinters of a tree it must have struck on its way down. What I can see of the object itself doesn't look very much like a meteor ... at least not the meteors I've seen. It looks more like a huge cylinder. It has a diameter of ... of ... what would you say, Professor Pierson?"

All of that had been heard by Grandfather Chapman and his three grandchildren in the living room of the Chapman farmhouse, just outside Grovers Mill, the airplane dial having been turned to avoid a boring song by Nelson Eddy.

Even Grandfather, who wasn't keen on much that was current, knew after weeks and weeks of Charlie McCarthy just how long the family could get away with cruising rival stations, looking for something more interesting to pass a few minutes than a sissy tenor.

"Grandpa," the younger boy, Leroy, said, "*we're* Grovers Mill!"

Grandfather, sitting forward on his armchair, said, "We sure are, Leroy. Did he say Wilson farm?"

Les said, "I think he said Wil*muth*."

"City reporter musta got it wrong," Grandfather said. "They must be at the Wilson farm. . . . Turn that up, a shade."

The children all looked toward their grandfather with surprise—usually he demanded just the opposite. With caution, Les raised the volume on the glowing magic box.

"*What would you say,*" the reporter was asking the professor, "*what's the diameter of this?*"

"*About thirty yards.*"

Les and Grandfather exchanged glances. Thirty yards was a lot. Thirty yards was . . . big.

"*The metal on the sheath is, well, I've never . . . seen . . . anything . . . like it. The color is sort of . . . yellowish-white.*

Curious spectators now are pressing close to the object in spite of the efforts of the police to keep them back, uh, getting in front of my line of vision. Would you mind standing to one side, please?"

Leroy asked, "That other man? The professor?"

Somewhat impatiently, Les said to his kid brother, "What about him?"

"I think he's the Shadow."

"Leroy, be quiet."

"The old Shadow, the good Shadow."

Sharply, the grandfather said, "Le*roy*!"

Sitting up on his knees, the little boy looked at the adult with earnest eyes. "Grandpa, I think this is just a story."

"Leroy, be quiet."

"But—"

"Shush! They're interviewing Wilson. . . ."

"Grandpa!"

Grandfather, irritated by the younger boy's lack of sophistication, raised a hand, signaling him to stop. The child did—folding his arms, smirking in sullen silence.

The farmer was answering Carl Phillips' questions. *"I was listening to the radio and kinda drowsin', that professor fellow was talkin' about Mars, so I was half-dozin' and half . . ."*

"Yes, yes, Mr. Wilmuth. And then what happened?"

Les said, "He said 'Wilmuth' again, Grandpa."

Grandfather said, "Cityslickers always get it wrong."

"I was listenin' to the radio kinda halfways. . . ."

"Yes, Mr. Wilmuth, and then you saw something?"

"Not first off. I heard something."

"And what did you hear?"

"A hissing sound. Like this—" The farmer hissed for the reporter. *"Kinda like a Fourth of July rocket."*

"Yes, then what?"

"I turned my head out the window, and would have swore I was to sleep and dreamin'."

"Yes?"

"I seen that kinda greenish streak and then, zingo! Somethin' smacked the ground. Knocked me clear out of my chair!"

Leroy was staring at the side wall, turned away from the radio, as if it had betrayed him. He said, firmly for such a little boy, "That . . . is . . . just . . . a . . . *store*eee!"

Grandfather had never struck any of his grandchildren (though of course their father, also an insolent pup, had met the razor strop many a time, as a boy), and he told himself tonight would be no exception. He rose and knelt by the child and put a kindly hand on Leroy's shoulder.

"Not everything on the radio is a 'story,' my boy. You have to learn to know the difference between the news commentators and the storytellers."

"Look who's talkin'."

Grandfather felt red rise into his face. But he said nothing more, and merely returned to his armchair.

Carl Phillips was saying, *"Hundreds of cars are parked in a field in back of us, and the police are trying to rope off the roadway, leading into the farm, but it's no use. They're breaking right through. Cars' headlights throw an enormous spotlight on the pit where the object's half buried."*

With the exception of Leroy, the Chapmans sat forward. Little Susie had cuddled up next to her older brother and was holding his hand. Tight.

". . . some of the more daring souls now are venturing near the edge. Their silhouettes stand out against the metal sheen. One man wants to touch the thing—he's having an argument with a policeman. Now the policeman wins. . . . Ladies and gentlemen, there's something I haven't mentioned in all this excitement, but . . . it's becoming more distinct. Perhaps you've caught it already on your radio. Listen, please . . ."

The Chapmans leaned forward—and even Leroy turned

back toward the radio. A scraping sound, faint but distinct, crackled over the air waves.

The reporter was asking, *"Do you hear it? Curious humming sound that seems to come from inside the object. I'll move the microphone nearer. Here . . . now, we're not more than twenty-five feet away. Can you hear it now?"*

The Dorn sisters had heard all of it.

They, too, had turned up the volume (the younger sister, Miss Eleanor, doing the honors) and their knitting was dropped to their laps, unattended, as their wide eyes stared toward the radio.

Ironically, neither woman had much interest in the news, normally—they took pride in not reading much of anything in the local paper except the church news. Neither sister read current magazines; why waste their time reading trash? History, the Bible, education, religion.

Miss Jane's hands were folded. "God is in His Heaven," she said.

Having resumed her chair, Miss Eleanor said, "And all's right in the world."

But neither of them sounded terribly sure of either statement.

In the modest living room of an apartment in Brooklyn, an out-of-work housepainter named Dennis Chandler, 36, sat with his wife, Helen, listening to the radio. The childless couple had guests—Helen's younger brother Earl and his wife Amy and their five-year-old Douglas. Dennis and Helen had neither a car nor a telephone. He and his wife went to a local Methodist church about once a month. They'd gone this morning.

Like many listeners, Dennis had switched from Charlie McCarthy only to accidentally land on the station reporting the fall of a meteor. He and his wife and their guests had heard exactly the same thing that the Chapmans had, and most of what the Dorn sisters had.

Dennis, too, was excited and concerned, though not as frightened as his wife and their guests, who were sitting forward, trembling. Douglas was on his mother's lap, arms draped around her neck.

"You know, Earl," Dennis said, "we could drive out in your car to where the meteor hit. Could be something to see."

Earl, who was in his late twenties, said he wouldn't mind. "Sounds like an adventure," he said.

But then, when the radio announcer said that he and the Princeton professor had travelled eleven miles in ten minutes, Dennis sat forward in his armchair and said to his wife Helen, "That wasn't any ten minutes, was it? They were just *on*!"

Helen said, "It's hard to keep track of time, but . . . you might be right."

"It was ten minutes," Amy said. "Wasn't it, Earl?"

Earl wasn't sure.

Dennis said, "Anyway, with all these news flashes, the streets around Princeton would be packed—they couldn't get there that fast, even if it *was* ten minutes!"

Helen, frowning in thought, suggested, "Why don't you check the listings, in the paper?"

Dennis snapped his fingers. "Good idea, honey."

The husband went to the kitchen where the Sunday *Daily News* lay on a counter, waiting to wrap garbage. He shuffled through to the radio listings and found that CBS was offering *The Mercury Theatre on the Air*'s presentation of H.G. Wells's *War of the Worlds* at eight P.M.

Chuckling to himself, he returned to the tiny living room, settled back in his armchair and said to all assembled, "It's just a silly play! What knuckleheads we are—shall we switch back to Charlie McCarthy?"

"No!" Helen said. "If it could fool us like that, then it's well done. Let's keep listening!"

Everybody agreed that was a good idea, so they indeed kept listening, and really enjoyed the show, laughing heartily at times, little Douglas smilingly shrieking with safe fear.

But the Chapmans (with the notable exception of young Leroy) were legitimately terrified.

Carl Phillips's excited voice crackled out of the console:

". . . do you still think it's a meteor, Professor?"

"I don't know what to think. The, uh, metal casing is definitely extraterrestrial . . . uh, not found on this earth. Friction with the earth's atmosphere usually tears holes in a meteorite. This thing is . . . smooth and, as you can see, of cylindrical shape . . ."

Leroy said nothing.

But in his mind, hearing Professor Pierson's voice, the boy heard himself scream: "That . . . is . . . the . . . *Shadow!*"

His little sister was hugging Les, shivering with fear, and Les looked pretty scared, himself.

Normally, Leroy would've been sympathetic. He loved his siblings, though the three had the usual kid squabbles. But right now, he relished their discomfort.

"Just a minute!" the announcer yelled. *"Something's happening! Ladies and gentlemen, this is terrific! This . . . end of the thing is beginning to . . . flake off. The top is beginning to rotate like a screw, and the thing must be hollow . . ."*

And Leroy laughed out loud—a deep laugh, in imitation of his favorite radio avenger.

Grandfather stood, went over and lifted the boy up by the arm and swatted his blue-jeaned bottom.

But Leroy only smiled.

Like the Shadow, Leroy knew.

Rusty, at his desk at State Troopers' HQ in upstate New York, sat in gaping astonishment as the words tumbled out of his radio. Upstairs, against his better judgment, Rusty's no-nonsense duty corporal, Richard Stevens, had switched his radio on, too, and was listening.

And now Corporal Stevens was sitting at his desk with the same wide-eyed, open-mouthed astonishment as that dope Rusty.

Both troopers, seated before their respective radios, watched the little talking boxes as if they could see the images reporter Carl Phillips was describing, and indeed on the movie screens of their minds, they could.

And then a succession of overlapping, agitated voices jumped out:

"She's movin'!"

". . . darn thing's unscrewing!"

"Stand back, there! Keep those men back, I tell you!"

"It's red hot, they'll burn to a cinder!"

"Keep back there. Keep those idiots back!"

Then—a hollow metallic clunk.

"She's off! The top's loose!"

"Look out there! Stand back!"

That was all Rusty needed to hear.

He ran up the two floors, corncob pipe tight in his teeth, and leaned in the doorway, from which he saw the normally cool-calm-collected duty corporal standing at his desk, staring at the radio, looking like a wild man.

And then the announcer was back: *"Someone's crawling out of the hollow top, someone or . . . some thing. I can see . . . peering out of that black hole two luminous disks . . . Are they eyes? It might be a face. It might be almost anything . . ."*

The corporal looked toward Rusty and the expressions of the two men mirrored fear and astonishment, matching the outburst of awe from the crowd at the scene.

Phillips was saying, *"Something wriggling out of the shadow like a gray snake. Now it's another one, and an . . . another one, and another one. . . . They look like tentacles to me. I, I can see the thing's body now, it's large, it's large as a bear—glistens like wet leather, but that, that face, it, it. . . . Ladies and gentlemen, it's indescribable."*

Rusty crossed himself.

"I can hardly force myself to keep looking at it, it's so awful. Its eyes are black and gleam like a serpent, the mouth is a kind of V-shape with saliva dripping from its rimless lips that seem to, oh, quiver and pulsate, and the monster or whatever it is can hardly move, it seems weighed down by . . . possibly gravity or something, the thing's . . . rising up now, and the crowd falls back now, they've seen plenty. Oh, uh, this is the most extraordinary experience, ladies and gentlemen. I can't find words. . . . Well, I'll pull this microphone with me as I talk. I'll have to stop the description until I can take a new position. Hold on, will you please, I'll be right back in a minute. . . ."

Brief dead silence was followed by a gentle waterfall of tinkling piano.

"So," Rusty managed, "was I lyin'?"

"I better call ol' Flannel Mouth," the corporal said.

That nickname—whispered in select company only—referred to their much unloved lieutenant, who lived close by.

"You better call Flannel Mouth is right, Corporal Stevens—you better right away!"

The corporal frowned and gestured dismissively. "Get back to your post! See what's coming over the teletype about this thing!"

By the time a real Princeton professor—Arthur Barrington, Geology Department head, behind the wheel of his dark blue Chevrolet sedan—rolled into Grovers Mill, one might think police cars and other emergency vehicles, plus emissaries of the press (including rival radio stations), would be wall-to-wall in the tiny town.

But as student Press Club member Sheldon Judcroft,

leaning out the front seat rider's side window, reported, nothing much seemed to be cooking.

Even for a bump in the road, Grovers Mill was quiet. An old clapboard mill and a feedstore—no gas station or lunchroom or even bar—made up the entire "downtown." A scattering of houses nearby represented the village itself. There wasn't even a street lamp.

Professor Barrington, sitting up and peering out into a slightly foggy night, said, "See what the nearest town is, Sheldon."

As assigned navigator, the student had charge of the map and was using a flashlight from the glove compartment.

"Cranbury, sir," Sheldon said. "Just five miles."

The boy pointed toward a road sign.

The professor—the real professor—nodded and drove.

Back at the Columbia Broadcasting Building, Walter Gibson remained unaware of the invasion's impact on some of its listeners. He had a murder to try to solve, and an hour to do it in.

The speaker in the twentieth-floor lobby was sharing the latest fake broadcast: *"We are bringing you an eyewitness account of what's happening on the Wilmuth farm, Grovers Mill, New Jersey."*

As the program returned to gentle fingering of piano keys, Gibson pressed the button for the elevator.

"We now return you to Carl Phillips at Grovers Mill."

The elevator car arrived and the writer rode down to the seventeenth floor, where yet another security guard—Fred—had seen neither Viriginia Welles nor George Balanchine, nor the alley-thug trio. And if Fred had seen Dolores Donovan around, boy, he'd've remembered it, a dish like that.

Gibson did not bother speaking to any of the news people on Seventeen, because they were either on the air or bustling around reading teletypes and making phone calls and typing up stories, much like a newspaper office.

Anyway, he had the immediate sense that in this building, the world of news and that of entertainment, several floors up, were twains that never met.

On the elevator he asked the same questions of the elevator operator, Leo, that featherweight "boy" pushing sixty who seemed to worship Welles.

As they spoke, the elevator car stayed on the seventeenth floor. Leo didn't mind if Gibson had a Camel; in fact, Leo took the occasion to smoke a Chesterfield. Hey, it was Sunday night. Traffic was light.

Leo knew who Mrs. Welles was, didn't think he'd seen her today; but then there was another elevator (self-service, for the ambitious), and a service one, too. So that meant next to nothing.

Floundering, Gibson said, "What do did you mean, by you don't *think* you saw Mrs. Welles? . . ."

"Well . . . I, uh . . . well . . ."

Gibson figured this stall for a prompt, and showed Leo a couple of bucks to prime the pump.

But Leo was damn near offended. "I don't want your money, sir. Any friend of Mr. Welles is a friend of mine. But—there was a lady who could've been Mrs. Welles."

"Could?"

"Yeah, well—she was in a coat and a scarf and sunglasses, and she kept her back to me."

"Like she didn't want to be recognized?"

"I dunno. Maybe."

"When was this?"

"I'm not sure. Maybe an hour ago? Half hour? Forty-five minutes, maybe—I don't keep close track. I just go up and down."

"Thanks, Leo. Thanks. Listen, can you take me to see the janitor?"

"Sure. He's on eighteen, right now. Fixing the men's

room. Name's Louis. Him—he might take your money. In fact, I'd recommend offering it."

"Thanks, Leo. Take me up a floor, would you?"

"That's what they pay me for."

The seventeenth-floor news center of the Columbia Broadcasting Building did not pipe in the network's programming, so Gibson had not heard what so many others had—the Dorn sisters, for example.

The two sisters, seated in their rockers, having set their knitting aside, had with their own ears witnessed the opening foray of Armageddon.

"Ladies and gent . . . Am I on? Ladies and gentlemen, ladies and gentlemen, here I am, back of a stone wall that adjoins Mr. Wilmuth's garden. From here I get a sweep of the whole scene. I'll give you every detail as long as I can talk, and as long as I can see. . . ."

Miss Jane reached bony fingers out to Miss Eleanor and the two sisters, still seated, held hands.

They listened mesmerized as reporter Carl Phillips told of more state police, a good thirty of them, arriving to cordon off the pit, but the crowd was staying back of its own volition now.

The captain of police was conferring with Professor Pierson, the astronomer from Princeton. Then the two men separated and the professor moved to one side, studying the object, while the police captain and two of his men approached, carrying a pole with a flag of truce.

"If those creatures know what that means . . . what anything means. . . . Wait a minute, something's happening. . . ."

Miss Jane squeezed Miss Eleanor's hand and Miss Eleanor squeezed Miss Jane's hand, as a terrible hissing turned into a diabolical hum that built and built and built. . . .

"A humped shape is rising out of the pit. I can make out a small beam of light against a mirror. What's that? There's a . . . jet of flame springing from that mirror, and it

leaps right at the advancing men. It strikes them head on! Good Lord . . . they're turning into flame!"

Terrible screams seemed to shake the radio.

The screams continued as Carl Phillips soldiered on, reporting, *"Now the whole field's caught on fire, the woods, the barns, the . . . the gas tanks, tanks of automobiles, spreading everywhere, it's coming this way. About twenty yards to my right—"*

Dead silence.

The two sisters, as one, fell out of their chairs onto the floor and hugged each other, and began to pray silently, though their lips moved. Miss Jane's prayer, in the sanctuary of her mind, went as follows: "God forgive me of my sins so that I will not be commited to eternal purgatory." Miss Eleanor's prayer was of a similar nature, though it included a private confession about touching herself in a sinful way (some years before) (frequently, though).

Then the women froze as finally the awful silence was filled by an announcer's voice, bright and almost cheerful as he said, *"Ladies and gentlemen, due to circumstances beyond our control, we are unable to continue the broadcast from Grovers Mill. Evidently there's some difficulty with our field transmission; however, we will return to that point at the earliest opportunity."*

The two sisters left their embrace to assume proper, prayerful kneeling positions, side by side but separate.

The announcer continued, all business as usual: *"In the meantime, we have a late bulletin from San Diego, California. Professor Indellkoffer, speaking at a dinner of the California Astronomical Society, expressed the opinion that the explosions on Mars are undoubtedly nothing more than severe volcanic disturbances on the surface of the planet. . . . We continue now with our piano interlude."*

And a piano, ever so sweetly, played "Clair de Lune."

As for the Dorn sisters, they remained on the floor, as the broadcast continued: kneeling; praying; off their rockers.

No one at the informal dinner party in Tudor City was requesting radio reviewer Ben Gross's permission to switch back to *The Chase and Sanborn Hour.*

Almost all dinner conversation had ceased.

Gross watched his wife and the other dinner guests as they seemed deeply if uneasily engrossed in the melodrama, which after a leisurely start of seemingly endless musical interludes had built in pace, a veritable cascade of sensational news "bulletins."

During the frightening, effective device of cutting to dead silence, after the creatures rose from the pit, spreading fire across the landscape, no one touched their food (well-done roast beef being the main course).

But no one asked for the show to be switched off, either.

Then the announcer was back on with another realistic interruption: *"Ladies and gentlemen, I have just been handed a message that came in from Grovers Mill by telephone. Just one moment, please."*

In the most crisp, convincing manner, the voice informed listeners that some forty people lay dead in a field east of Grovers Mill, including half a dozen state troopers—bodies burned beyond recognition.

"The next voice you hear will be that of Brigadier General Montgomery Smith, commander of the state militia at Trenton, New Jersey."

A weary, somber voice took over: *"I have been requested by the governor of New Jersey to place the counties of Mercer and Middlesex as . . . as far west as Princeton, and, uh, east to Jamesburg, under martial law. No one will be permitted to enter this area except by special pass issued by state or military authorities. Four companies of state militia are proceeding from Trenton to Grovers Mill, and, uh, will aid in the evacuation of homes within the range of military operations. . . . Thank you."*

"You know," Gross said, rising from a half-consumed portion of roast beef, "I think I better be getting back to the office. Some listeners might really *believe* this. . . ."

"How on earth could they?" his hostess asked. "They announced it was by H.G. Wells—that means it's fiction!"

But his host said, "Dear, those who tuned in late didn't hear the announcement."

Gross turned to his wife. "What do you think, dear?"

"I think," Kathleen said, "that's the most realistic, scary program I ever heard—and you need to get back to the city room."

He grinned at her, said, "Thanks, honey," excused himself, and went down to hail a cab.

Grandfather Chapman called his son Luke at home.

"It's an emergency," he said. "Have you had the radio on this evening?"

"No. I was reading to Alice. She's asleep, now. . . ."

"Don't wake her."

"Dad, what is it?"

"You just get over here. Bring your shotgun."

"You make it sound like we're being invaded!"

"We are."

". . . What the hell—the Germans?"

"Just get over here."

James Roberts, Jr., and his friend Bobby, had heard every moment of the broadcast on the Buick coupe's car radio.

At first the news coverage of the fallen meteor had been exciting, and James had said, "Jeez, Bobby, CBS News is really tops, aren't they? They've got people on the spot, for every emergency!"

Bobby, who would have preferred his dance music

uninterrupted, did allow as the Columbia Broadcasting System knew its stuff.

And when Professor Pierson had first come on, James said, "I think I've heard of him—at school."

"Does sound a little familiar," Bobby said.

James and Bobby were business majors.

Then all the horror had come over the air, and both boys were concerned and even scared, particularly James, whose family lived in Trenton, New Jersey.

When the general came on and said the route to Trenton was closed, James got really worried and upset. At Newark they stopped at a drugstore, to phone and see if James's folks were okay.

Two people were working in the drugstore—a pharmacist and a cashier—and three people were there picking up various needs. James and Bobby couldn't believe these fools were going around like nothing was wrong in their lives, except maybe a headache or athlete's foot!

James stood up at the front of the store and said, "Everybody—listen to me!"

The cashier put her hands up, and Bobby said, "It's not a stickup, lady."

And James—in a clear, concise manner that, had he summoned this in speech class, would have got him far better than his C-minus—told the drugstore audience about what he and Bobby had heard on the radio.

Then James ran to the bank of phone booths, ensconced himself in one, dropped a nickel in the slot and was quickly told that all the lines were jammed and that his call couldn't go through.

When he stepped from the booth, James saw everyone in the store, including Bobby, seated at the closed soda fountain, listening to a radio on the counter. The pharmacist was on the stool beside the cashier with his arm around her; she was crying. The other patrons were wailing and moaning and praying.

Professor Pierson's voice was coming over the air, but the reception was weak: " . . . *these creatures have scientific knowledge far in advance of our own. It's my guess that in some way they are able to generate an intense heat in a chamber of practically no absolute conductivity.*"

James put a hand on Bobby's shoulder and whispered: "Can't get through to Mom and Dad. Hell, can't get through to *anybody.* . . ."

Bobby turned haunted eyes toward James. "If Trenton's blocked, then . . . then we have to go back. To Manhattan. We have to make sure Betty's all right!"

"*. . . by means of a polished parabolic mirror of unknown composition, much as the mirror of a lighthouse projects a beam of light. That is my conjecture of the origin of the heat ray. . . .*"

And so it was that James and Bobby—having done the good deed of warning those in the drugstore of the deadly invasion—raced back out into the night to rescue "the girls" (Betty's sixteen-year-old sister, naïve or not, suddenly seeming well worth saving from Martians).

State Troopers Chuck and Carmine were not listening to the radio; their Ford Phaeton didn't even have one.

So when, as they continued patrolling the highway, they noticed traffic heading north was picking up, and picking up speed, they asked, "What the hell?" to each other, a substantial number of times in a short period.

Drivers were travelling at unusually high rates of speed, and in fact the whole traffic pattern seemed erratic.

"Think it's time to do our job, buddy," Chuck said.

"Roger," Carmine said.

Time to start writing out tickets for speeding and reckless driving.

A guy in dark green Chevy sedan streaked by, and the two troopers decided to make him their first example.

Carmine, behind the wheel, turned around and took off after him.

The driver showed no signs of realizing state troopers were on his tail.

They hit their siren.

He did not slow down, and—though their Ford was putting out a solid eighty miles per hour—the troopers were hardly gaining on the guy. For almost five minutes, on a winding country road, the chase went on, and finally the Ford pulled up alongside the Chevy, and—siren screaming—as Chuck blasted on the horn, Carmine motioned sternly, then wildly, for the son of a bitch to pull over.

The driver shook his head and kept his eyes on the road.

"My God," Carmine said, over engine roar, "bastard's got his wife and kiddies in the car with him! Little boy and little girl!"

"What is wrong with this idiot?" Chuck asked.

"Can't force him off the road—might hurt those innocents. . . ."

Then other honking cut through the thunder of engines and shriek of sirens . . .

. . . and Carmine looked behind him and saw other motorists, right on the speeder's tail and the troopers' tail, too—and each others. . . .

An armada of autos, honking for the troopers to get the hell out of the way—and the troopers were going eighty-five!

The father behind the wheel of the Chevy was hunkered over like a fighter pilot, and Chuck said, "Carmine—fall in behind this s.o.b."

"What? You can't—"

"Fall in behind him, and let these maniacs pass us."

Glancing behind him, even as he rode herd on the Chevy, Carmine swallowed and said, "Shit," and let the Chevy get out in front, and pulled in behind him, slowing to sixty, while one car after another flashed by, passing not only the troopers but the madman in the Chevy.

Carmine pulled over. "What the hell? . . ."

"Something's happened. Something big."

"Has law and order completely broken down on this highway?"

Chuck nodded. "Yes."

They sat and watched as car after car flew wildly by.

"You know," Carmine said, "we maybe oughta check in with headquarters. Let's find us a phone."

At a gas station, Carmine used the phone; it took a while to get through; the HQ switchboard must've been buzzing. But finally the duty corporal came on.

Carmine began to tell the corporal about the crazy traffic conditions, but got cut off.

"They're fleeing the area, Carmine. The countryside's on fire, monsters from outer space are eating people alive, it's a goddamn Martian invasion."

"Little green men from Mars?"

"They're not green and they're not little. Get your asses back to headquarters, for further instructions."

The phone clicked dead.

And the worst part, Carmine had to now go report this to Chuck. . . .

CHAPTER EIGHT

Punkin Patch

In Studio One, Dan Seymour was at the microphone, saying, "Ladies and gentlemen, here is a bulletin from Trenton. It is a brief statement informing us that the charred body of Carl Phillips has been identified in a Trenton hospital."

At a nearby table, "Carl Phillips"—that is, Frank Readick—was sitting going over his script; like most radio actors, he had more than one part in the drama.

"Now here's another bulletin from Washington, D.C.," Seymour was saying. "The office of the director of the National Red Cross reports ten units of Red Cross emergency workers have been assigned to the headquarters of the state militia stationed outside Grovers Mill, New Jersey."

Readick felt the show was going well—it had really come together at rehearsal, and tonight the thing was like clockwork—literally: Paul Stewart seemed almost bored in the control booth window, poised at his stopwatch.

"Here's a bulletin from state police, Princeton Junction— the fires at Grovers Mill and vicinity are now under control.

Scouts report all quiet in the pit, and there is no sign of life appearing from the mouth of the cylinder. . . ."

Howard Koch had slipped out perhaps ten minutes ago. Readick could hardly blame the writer—the poor guy was bone tired, and had been worked like a dog by Welles and Jack Houseman. Let the guy rest up—tomorrow would be the start of another week of radio "war."

Still, this was going well, very well indeed.

Yes, once again, Orson had worked his magic. . . .

From Trenton Police Headquarters report, October 30, 1938: "Between 8:20 P.M. & 10 P.M. received numerous phone calls as a result of WABC broadcast this evening re: Mars attacking this country. Calls included papers, police depts including NYC and private persons. No record kept of same due to working teletype and all three extensions ringing at the same time. At least 50 calls were answered. Persons inquiring as to meteors, number of persons killed, gas attack, military being called out and fires. All were advised nothing unusual had occurred and that rumors were due to a radio dramatization of a play."

"We have received a request from the state militia at Trenton to place at their disposal our entire broadcasting facilities. In view of the gravity of the situation, and believing that radio has a responsibility to serve in the public interest at all times, we are turning over our facilities to the state militia at Trenton."

In a residential section of Trenton, a Mrs. Thomas went to answer a banging at her door to find her neighbor friend from across the way with her car packed with belongings and her seven children.

"For God's sake, Gladys, come on!" the neighbor shouted. "We have to get out of here!"

Elsewhere in Trenton, thirteen-year-old Henry Sears,

doing his homework, heard the news flashes about the invasion and went downstairs into the tavern owned by his parents. He and a dozen patrons of the bar listened to the broadcast with growing fear and, finally, a well-lubricated contingent proclaimed they were getting their guns and going to Grovers Mill, to find the Martians.

Indeed, as panic spread to pockets of the country, Trenton and its environs were the hardest hit, many residents believing the arrival of the interplanetary invaders imminent. Gas masks from the Great War were dug out of mothballs, while some wrapped their heads with wet towels, to fight the inevitable poison gas. The highways were jammed as cars streamed toward New York or Philadelphia, in hopes of staying one step ahead of the Martian forces.

The Mienerts of Manasquan Park, New Jersey—barrelling down the highway, kids, dog and canary making the trip with them—took a break for fuel and nature at a gas station; the pause also provided an opportunity to get the latest news (their car radio was on the fritz). Other motorists, who hadn't heard the broadcast, reacted as if the Mienerts were mad people; so did the gas station attendant and cashier.

A desperate Mr. Mienert, hoping for an update, called his cousin in Freehold, New Jersey, praying to get an answer, as the cousin's farm was directly in the destructive path of the invaders.

But his cousin, right there on the front lines, answered cheerfully.

Confused, Mr. Mienert asked, "Are the Martians there?"

"No," said his cousin, "but the Tuttles are, and we're about to sit down to dinner."

The Mienerts went back home.

"This is Captain Lansing of the Signal Corps, attached to the state militia, now engaged in military operations in the vicinity of Grovers Mill. Situation arising from the reported

*presence of certain individuals of unidentified nature is now
under complete control. The cylindrical object which lies in
a pit directly below our position is surrounded on all sides
by eight battalions of infantry. Without heavy field pieces,
but adequately armed with rifles and machine guns. All
cause for alarm, if such cause ever existed, is now entirely
unjustified."*

In Manhattan on East 116th Street, a restaurant hosted the
wedding reception of Rocco and Connie Cassamassina. No
one was listening to the radio in this happily preoccupied
private dining room; in fact, almost everyone was dancing
to the five-piece band, spiffy in maroon-and-gray tuxes,
playing romantic tunes of the day.

The bride and groom were not dancing right now, because Rocco—a singing waiter from Brooklyn—was sitting in with the band, doing a romantic version of "I
Married an Angel" just for Connie.

The last verse was wrapping up when some agitated late-
comers wandered in and one of them—stone sober, it would
later be recalled—snatched the mike away from Rocco and
said, "We're under attack! We're being invaded!"

The five-piece group stopped playing, in one-at-a-time
train-wreck fashion, and the guests at first laughed. But the
speaker—another waiter from Brooklyn, who many of
them knew and trusted—told in quick but vivid detail of
what he'd heard on the radio newscasts.

Murmuring confusion built to complete panic, as the
guests ran to grab their coats and flee before the outer-
space invaders could crash the party.

Connie, in tears, rushed to the stage and took the mike
to beg her friends and family to stay. "Please don't spoil
my wedding day, everyone!"

A handful remained.

Rocco was again at the microphone.

He began singing "Amazing Grace."

* * *

"The things, whatever they are, do not even venture to poke their heads above the pit. I can see their hiding place plainly in the glare of the searchlights here. With all their reported resources, these creatures can scarcely stand up against heavy machine-gun fire. Anyway, it's an interesting outing for the troops. I can make out their khaki uniforms, crossing back and forth in front of the lights. It looks almost like a real war."

At the Chapman farm, the children's father, Luke, had arrived.

Grandfather had been moving from window to window, staring into the foggy night, his old double-barrel shotgun (retrieved from a kitchen hiding place) ready to blast Martians into green goo. He'd already organized the two boys (even the skeptical Leroy) in the effort of barricading the farmhouse doors with furniture—which of course meant unbarricading the front door to let their father, carrying his own double-barrel shotgun, inside.

Leroy gave it another try, tugging on his father's sleeve. "Papa . . ."

"Yes, son?"

The boy gestured toward the glowing radio. "That isn't real—it's just a show, a story. The Shadow is on it."

His father, whose face resembled Grandfather's minus most of the wrinkles, smiled gently and knelt—leaning on the shotgun—to look the boy right in the eyes. "Son— we've had this talk, haven't we?"

"What talk?"

"About make-believe and real life. I know you love your shows. I know you love to play cowboy and soldier and spaceman. I know you love the Shadow. But you simply have to learn the difference between fantasy and reality."

"I *know* the difference. Do you?"

And the kindness left Luke's expression. He took the

boy roughly by the arm and almost threw him onto the sofa.

"You just sit there, young man!"

Leroy shrugged; his eyes were filling with tears, but he refused to let any fall.

Les sat before the radio hugging his sister, who had stopped crying and lapsed into a trembling silence. The altar of news continued issuing forth updates, none of them encouraging. Right now the Signal Corps captain was describing the battle scene at a farm that was within a few miles of the farmhouse the Chapmans currently cowered within.

"Well, we ought to see some action soon," the captain was saying. *"One of the companies is deploying on the left flank. A quick thrust and it will all be over. Now wait a minute, I see something on top of the cylinder. No, it's nothing but a shadow. Now the troops are on the edge of the Wilmuth farm, seven thousand armed men closing in on an old metal tube. A tub, rather. Wait . . . that wasn't a shadow!"*

And Leroy, over on a sofa now, arms folded, smugly smiling as he brushed away a tear with a knuckle, thought, *Oh yes it* was. . . .

Passing photographers laden with full gear, who were scurrying toward the elevator he'd just departed, Ben Gross entered a *Daily News* city room that bustled like election eve.

An assistant at the city desk called out, "Hey, Ben—what the hell's going on tonight?"

"You're asking me?"

The switchboard was ablaze, lines jammed, phones ringing like a swarm of mechanical baby birds demanding to be fed. In their cubicles, rewrite men frantically tried to get through to CBS with zero luck.

A harried switchboard girl sounded like she was doing a skit on the Jack Benny program. "No, madam . . . no, sir—we *don't* know anything about an explosion in New Jersey. . . . Men from Mars? . . . Yeah, we *know* it's on the radio, but . . . it didn't happen. . . . Nothing's going on, I tell you! . . . No madam . . . No sir . . . *there ain't no men from Mars!*"

Nearby, another city desk assistant, frazzled beyond belief, was telling an official from the police commissioner's office, "It's just a phony—a radio play!"

The assistant city desk man finally hung up, then turned to Gross and pointed an accusatory finger. "You're the one always touting this guy Welles! You either get CBS on the line, or get your tail over there and see what in God name's going on."

Gross walked into the radio room and two phones jangled; he picked up a receiver in either hand.

A female voice said, "Are they abandoning New York?"

"No, lady, it's just a play."

"Oh no it isn't!" she screamed, and hung up.

On the other wire was a guy from the Red Cross. "I hear they're broadcasting about a terrible catastrophe in New Jersey—do you know where it is, so we can get our people out there?"

"It's only Orson Welles—he's on with a fantasy, tonight."

"That can't be! My wife just called and said thousands have been killed."

Gross reassured the man that the show was just a show, hung up, and his young female assistant bounded in, looking far less attractive than usual, her hair tendrils of despair, her eyes pools of frustration.

"My God, Mr. Gross! These calls have been driving me batty!"

The radio reviewer said nothing, merely headed for the door.

His assistant nearly shrieked, "You're not going to leave me all *alone* with these . . . these *phones*, are you?"

"Yes," he said, already halfway out.

In moments he was on the street, hailing another cab.

Climbing in, Gross realized the cab's radio was tuned to WEAF.

"Put CBS on," Gross said, "would you?"

The cabbie did so.

"It's something moving . . . solid metal, kind of a shield-like affair rising up out of the cylinder. . . . Going higher and higher. What? . . . It's, it's standing on legs . . . actually rearing up on a sort of metal framework. Now it's reaching above the trees and the searchlights are on it. Hold on!"

"God almighty!" the cab driver said.

"It's just fiction," Gross said.

"Are you sure?"

"You don't see any panic-stricken people running around the streets, do you, bud?"

And as if to prove the reviewer wrong, the cab passed a movie house on Third Avenue, from which half a dozen women and children streamed, while men poured out of nearby bars, to take root on the sidewalks and stare at the sky.

On Lexington Avenue and 51st Street, a woman sat on the curb, crying and screaming, while a cop in the middle of the street stood mobbed by agitated citizens.

"Fiction or not," the cabbie said, "something the hell's goin' on!"

And yet when Gross was dropped off at the Columbia Broadcasting Building, no sign of outer or inner turmoil could be seen—the usual number of pedestrians strolled by, traffic seemed about normal.

No one would ever guess that this was the County Seat of Hysteria in the United States, right now.

In six weeks, the American Institute of Public Opinion would estimate 9,000,000 Americans had heard the "War of the Worlds" broadcast, a majority tuning in too late to catch the disclaimer opening. The Chapmans, the Dorns, James Roberts and his friend Bobby, Sheldon Judcroft and Professor Barrington, and the troopers at the HQ in upstate New York were among the estimated 1,700,000 listeners who believed they were hearing actual newscasts, including the following one:

"Ladies and gentlemen, I have a grave announcement to make. Incredible as it may seem, both the observations of science and the evidence of our eyes lead to the inescapable assumption that those strange beings who landed in the Jersey farmlands tonight are the vanguard of an invading army from the planet Mars."

State troopers Chuck and Carmine made it back to headquarters, despite a highway filled with lunatics driving north like the devil was on their tails.

But HQ was no better. Everyone was doing their best to follow Corporal Stevens's orders; previously cool in any crisis, the corporal was on edge, snapping at his men wildly.

The quartermaster sergeant had come in from home to issue the troopers rifles, machine guns and ammunition, and he, too, was caught up in it, yelling like a boot-camp drill instructor.

Then Lt. Flanders showed up. Ol' Flannel Mouth had loaded up his car with household possessions, leaving room for his wife, a blowsy middle-aged blonde who had a crucifix in one hand and a bottle of rye in the other (she would alternately kiss the cross and swig the bottle).

The lieutenant took over from the duty corporal, who had clearly been enjoying the power and disliked having it taken away from him. After Lt. Flanders gave several orders that Corporal Stevens disagreed with, the latter decided he'd had enough of the former.

"Lieutenant, I know we're all going to die," the corporal said. "And I've been waiting seven long years to tell you something."

"Well, spit it out, man! We have things to do."

They were outside the front of HQ, the troopers all around, weapons in hand, waiting for their orders.

The corporal was saying, "Nothing is more urgent than me saying this: you are a flannel-mouthed son of a bitch, no-good, rotten bastard. I have half a mind to grab you by your miserable neck and squeeze it till your tongue turns black."

That wouldn't take long, as the lieutenant was already turning purple; in the background, his wife toasted the corporal with her rye bottle, in "hear hear!" manner.

Corporal Stevens had more: "I'd be doing everybody in this troop a favor by shoving this .45 up your tail and pulling the trigger. But I just hate the thought of wasting a good bullet on your miserable carcass, when we have an enemy to fight."

The corporal folded his arms, held his chin high and waited for a response.

The purple left the lieutenant's face. He seemed to be working hard to retain his composure.

All the men had gathered around as the confrontation had built, and now Lt. Flanders said to them, "Men—this is no time to pull old chestnuts out of the fire. Let's let bygones be bygones, forgive and forget, that's what I've always said."

If so, no one assembled here remembered hearing it.

"Let us pool our energies," the lieutenant said rousingly, "and fight the common enemy that threatens us. We will make our last stand on the hill. Get to your posts. . . . You men with machine guns will concentrate your fire on the approaches to headquarters, and you men with rifles will make the last-ditch defense from high ground."

Shouts of support and even applause came from the troopers—with the notable exception of the stiff-necked corporal.

Then the lieutenant showed his true colors: as his troopers were busy setting up the defenses, he got into his car with his missus and roared off into the foggy night. Heading north.

Corporal Stevens was shaking his head. Carmine and Chuck were standing nearby, and he said to them, "I *knew* it! . . . I'll *never* regret telling off that worthless son of a bitch."

Then Rusty, corncob pipe puffing smoke signals, leaned out from a second-floor window and shouted, "Come on in, you guys! The whole thing is a phony! It was just a radio show by some joker named Orson Welles!"

Carmine smiled at Chuck and Chuck said to Stevens, " 'Never,' Corporal?"

And the troopers sheepishly shuffled back inside HQ to put their firearms away.

As the Buick hurtled at top speed, James Jr. and Bobby kept the car radio blasting.

What they heard was unsettling, to say the least.

"The battle which took place tonight at Grovers Mill has ended in one of the most startling defeats ever suffered by an army in modern times—seven thousand men armed with rifles and machine guns pitted against a single fighting machine of the invaders from Mars. One hundred and twenty known survivors . . . the rest strewn over the battle area from Grovers Mill to Plainsboro, crushed and trampled to death under the metal feet of the monster, or burned to cinders by its heat ray."

Bobby was smoking; he had his window down. James told him to roll it up.

"Why, James?"

"The Martian gas . . . I think I can smell it."

"The monster is now in control of the middle section of New Jersey and has effectively cut the state through its center. Communication lines are down from Pennsylvania to the Atlantic Ocean. Railroad tracks are torn and service from New York to Philadelphia discontinued except routing some of the trains through Allentown and Phoenixville."

James began to pray, watching the headlights cut through the foggy darkness as best they could. In his mind, he said, *If there is a God, please help us now!*

"Highways to the north, south, and west are clogged with frantic human traffic. Police and army reserves are unable to control the mad flight. By morning the fugitives will have swelled Philadelphia, Camden, and Trenton, it is estimated, to twice their normal population."

Bobby was sitting forward, frowning. "James—we were just in Trenton. We didn't see any crowds like that. . . ."

"Martial law prevails throughout New Jersey and eastern Pennsylvania."

Bobby began to twirl the radio dial, trying to find other reports.

Walter Gibson remained clueless as to the imaginary invasion having spread nationwide; but he was seeking a clue to something else by having a conversation in the eighteenth-floor men's room.

As elevator "boy" Leo had predicted, Louis didn't get talkative until Gibson offered him a couple of dollars. Louis, in a gray uniform that would have been at home in a prison, leaned against the door to a stall, plunger in hand, bell down.

"I don't know Mrs. Welles, but I didn't see no woman who looks like that in the building. I'd remember. I got an eye for the ladies."

Louis weighed around 250 pounds, was perhaps five-eight, had greasy black hair, bulging cow eyes, yellow crooked teeth, and cheeks and chin so blue with the need for a shave that it was safe to say the ladies did not have an eye for him.

Descriptions of Balanchine and the three thugs also fell on deaf ears.

Gibson, smoking his umpteenth Camel, had a stray thought. "Louis, are you the only janitor on duty?"

"One and only."

"When did you come on?"

"Around one P.M."

"You know Mr. Houseman?"

"Sure."

"You loaned him your passkey, right?"

"Sure."

Well, that was a dead end.

But Gibson pressed on: "And he returned it?"

"Sure. First thing."

Gibson asked a few more questions, then hitched a ride with Leo back to the twenty-second floor.

In the lobby, where security guard Williams remained seated at his desk, Miss Holliday—the shapely, sturdy girl was in a blue dress with white polka dots and white collar—stood waiting to catch the elevator.

"Miss Holliday—hello."

She flashed her infectious smile. "Hello, Mr. Gibson."

"Got a minute?"

"Sure. I was just heading over to the theater, to get things ready."

"Ready?"

"Yeah. . . . There's a *Danton's Death* rehearsal right after the broadcast."

"Ah. A few questions?"

"Shoot."

"Let's sit . . ."

They took two chairs in the reception area. Williams was within earshot, but it didn't seem to matter to Gibson, who asked Miss Holliday about Virginia Welles and George Balanchine, who she too had not seen around here today . . . "though I've been in and out, back and forth, 'tween here and the theater, running errands, ya know?"

But the three thugs, strangely enough, got Miss Holliday's pretty brow furrowing.

"Describe them again," she said. "In more detail."

Gibson did, best he could.

"Those sound like actors."

Gibson frowned. "Actors?"

"Yeah—spear-carrier types. Mr. Welles uses them in crowd scenes, sometimes."

"You're sure?"

She made a funny smirk. "No, I'm not sure—you don't have a picture to show me, right? But your descriptions are good—you're a writer, aren't you? And those three goon types sound like minor actors Mr. Welles uses, from time to time."

"Thank you, Miss Holliday."

"You can call me Judy."

He walked her to the elevator, his mind abuzz.

Finally he had clues—but what he'd learned from the janitor seemed to contradict the direction Judy Holliday's information indicated. . . .

Quiet as a mouse, heedful but not halted by the bold ON THE AIR sign over the door, the writer slipped into Studio One, passing through the vestibule, into the live broadcast, and padding carefully up the short flight of stairs into the control booth.

Kenny Delmar was being introduced as "the Secretary of the Interior," but the voice he did was a dead-on impression of President Franklin D. Roosevelt.

"Citizens of the nation—I shall not try to conceal the gravity of the situation that confronts the country, nor the concern of your government in protecting the lives and property of its people. However, I wish to impress upon you—private citizens and public officials, all of you, the urgent need of calm and resourceful action."

On his podium, Welles was grinning like a big gleeful baby.

Delmar continued: "Fortunately, this formidable enemy is still confined to a comparatively small area, and we may place our faith in the military forces to keep them there."

Gibson had paused in the sub-control booth, and CBS executive Dave Taylor was shaking his head, sighing—Welles had been told not to invoke the president, and (technically) he hadn't; and yet of course he had.

Delmar was wrapping up: "In the meantime, placing our faith in God, we must continue the performance of our duties, each and every one of us, so that we may confront this destructive adversary with a nation united, courageous, and consecrated to the preservation of human supremacy on this earth."

Delmar took a dramatic pause, then: "I thank you."

The bulletins continued at breakneck speed: from Langham Field, scout planes reported a trio of Martian machines visible above the trees, heading north; in Basking Ridge, New Jersey, a second cylinder had been found and the army was rushing to blow it up before it opened; in the Watchung Mountains, the 22nd Field Artillery closed in on the enemy, but poisonous black smoke dispatched by the invaders wiped out the battery.

Eight bombers were set on fire by the tripods in a flash of green. More of the lethal black smoke was leaching in from the Jersey marshes, and gas masks were of no use, the populace urged to make for open spaces.

Recommended routes of escape were shared with listeners.

When the phone rang, the Dorn sisters—kneeling before their living-room radio as if taking communion—yelped in surprise and fear.

Miss Jane rose, patted her sister's shoulder, and went to answer it, in the nearby hallway.

Her friend Mrs. Roberta Henderson, a third-grade teacher, was calling to ask about the upcoming bake sale. Could Jane and Eleanor provide their usual delicious cherry pies?

"Haven't you heard?" Miss Jane asked, frantically, amazed that her friend could be caught up in such mundane matters at a time like this.

"Heard?"

Miss Jane's words tumbled out on top of each other, uncharacteristically, as she told of the news reports of the Martian invasion.

"You can't be serious, Jane—that's the radio."

"Of course it's the radio!"

"No . . . no, I mean, it's just a play."

"A . . . play? Why, that's nonsense! It's, it's . . . news!"

"No—just a play. A clever play. Jane, you need to settle down. Is Eleanor handy?"

"She's in the living room. Praying. Roberta, surely you understand that the forces of God are overpowering us, and we are at last being given our deserved punishment for all our evil ways."

"Hmm-huh. Listen to me, Jane. Call the newspaper office. Promise me you will."

"Well . . . all right."

"Do it now."

Miss Jane said good-bye, hung up, and asked the operator to connect her with the local paper.

"We're getting a lot of calls," a male voice said. "It's just a radio show. Kind of a . . . practical joke."

"Well, it's not very funny!"

"I agree with you, lady. Have a happy Hallowe'en!"

"No thank you! It's a *pagan* celebration!"

"Ain't it though. Good night."

Miss Jane went into the living room and, as Miss Eleanor looked up at her like a child, shared what she'd learned.

Soon they were sitting in their rockers, the radio switched off.

Miss Eleanor cleared her throat and said, "I'm glad I asked for forgiveness, even if I didn't have to."

Miss Jane shared that sentiment, adding, "It was a good opportunity to atone for our sins. The end will come, and those who have freely indulged will face a horrible reckoning."

"It is the life after this life which is important," her sister added.

"I don't mind death," Miss Jane said, "but I do want to die forgiven."

The two women smiled at each other, serenely. They again began to knit. In silence.

But within themselves, they were furious—though they were not sure why. A vague sense enveloped them that they had been duped by the sinful world.

Well, the joke was on the sinners. Though the Martians hadn't come, one day sheets of God's vengeful fire would sweep over this wretched land.

And the girls had that, at least, to look forward to.

Gibson was sitting in a chair behind John Houseman, who sat between stopwatch-watcher Paul Stewart and the sound engineer. That polished scarecrow, CBS exec Davidson Taylor, stepped in, his expression grave.

"We're getting calls," Taylor told Houseman. "Switchboards are swamped downstairs—people are going crazy out there."

Houseman, who swivelled toward Taylor, asked, "Crazy in what manner?"

"If it's true, deaths and suicides and injuries of all sorts, due to panic."

"How widespread?"

"I don't know, Jack, but you have to force Orson into making an explanatory station-announcement. Right now."

Houseman, despite his misgivings about Orson's approach, took a hard line. "Not until the scheduled break."

"This isn't a request, Jack—"

"I don't care what it is. We're approaching the dramatic apex of the story, and the announcement will be made, as written, just after that. It's a matter of minutes."

Taylor shook his head. "Why do I back you people? You're insane!"

Houseman made a little facial shrug, and turned away.

Amiable Ray Collins was out there, stepping up to a microphone, saying: "I'm speaking from the roof of Broadcasting Building, New York City. The bells you hear are ringing to warn the people to evacuate the city as . . . the Martians approach. Estimated in the last two hours, three million people have moved out along the roads to the north . . ."

Gibson leaned forward and whispered to Houseman, "So you stuck up for Orson, after all?"

Houseman offered a small, dry chuckle. "That is my fate, I'm afraid."

"Jack—I know you did it."

Houseman looked at Gibson.

The writer said, "I've finished my investigation. And I know you're responsible."

"Ah. Might I request you keep that information to yourself, just for the present? If Mr. Taylor is correct, we may have a crisis on our hands, first."

"You can't be serious . . ."

"Oh but I am. And don't forget—I'm the one who signs your expense-account check." He smiled beatifically and returned his attention to the window through which Ray Collins could be seen.

The actor was saying into the mike, "No more defenses. Our army is wiped out . . . artillery, air force, everything, wiped out. This may be the . . . last broadcast. We'll stay here, to the end. . . . People are holding service here below us . . . in the cathedral."

Ora Nichols blew through a hollow tube, approximating a ghostly boat whistle.

"Now I look down the harbor. All manner of boats, over-loaded with fleeing population, pulling out from docks. Streets are all jammed. Noise in crowds like New Year's Eve in city. Wait a minute, the . . . the enemy is now in sight above the Palisades. Five—five great machines. First one is . . . crossing the river, I can see it from here, wading . . . wading the Hudson like a man wading through a brook . . ."

Around the country, listeners—the fooled and the merely entertained—heard the "last announcer" speak from the CBS building rooftop of Martian cylinders falling all over America, outside Buffalo, in Chicago and St. Louis.

Among the radio audience were Professor Barrington and the student reporter, Sheldon Judcroft, who arrived at the quaint, pre-Revolutionary War hamlet of Cranbury, New Jersey (pop. 1,278), to find half a dozen State Trooper patrol cars parked in front of the post office.

"So it *is* real," Sheldon said breathlessly.

The professor pulled over, got out and went over to talk to the troopers. Sheldon stayed behind, to monitor the news on the radio.

The announcer was saying, *"Now the first machine reaches the shore, he . . . stands watching, looking over the city. His steel, cowlish head is even with the skyscrapers. . . . He waits for the others. They rise like a line of new towers on the city's west side. . . ."*

Sheldon watched the professor talking to a trooper who was shaking his head. Then it was the professor who was shaking his head. . . .

"Now they're lifting their metal hands. This is the end now. Smoke comes out . . . black . . . smoke, drifting over the city. People in the streets see it now. They're running to-ward the East River . . . thousands of them, dropping in like rats."

The professor returned, got in the car and just sat there, wearing a stunned expression.

"Now the smoke's spreading faster, it's reached Times Square. People are trying to run away from it, but it's no use, they . . . they're falling like flies. Now the smoke's crossing Sixth Avenue . . . Fifth Avenue . . . a . . . a hundred yards away . . . it's fifty feet. . . ."

The sound of the collapsing announcer on the roof was followed by ghostly boat whistles, and then . . . silence.

"My God," Sheldon said.

"Good, isn't it?"

Sheldon blinked. Twice. "Good?"

"It's a radio show, my boy. Orson Welles and the Mercury Theatre. Only question, is—how big a fool should you make out of us when you write up the story for the school paper?"

"Oh, I don't believe it—"

"The trooper says the countryside is crawling with farmers with shotguns, looking for Martians. The fire chief has checked out half a dozen nonexistent fires, already."

"Why are these troopers here, then?"

"To calm the populace, son. To find and disarm these 'defenders' before somebody gets hurt."

They were halfway back to Princeton before the laughter started—the professor kicked it off, but the student joined in heartily. They were laughing so hard, tears coming down, they almost hit a deer, in the fog.

It was the second-most frightened they'd been that night.

All around America, newspaper offices, police departments, sheriff's offices, radio stations, as well as friends and relatives, received calls from believing listeners. The *New York Times* received 875 calls from its highly sophisticated readership. The worldly reporters of the New York *Herald Tribune* donned gas masks when they went out to cover the story. The Associated Press found it necessary to alert its member newspapers and radio stations that the invasion from Mars was not real. Electric light companies were called with demands that all power be shut down to keep Martians from having landing lights to guide them.

In Manhattan, hundreds jammed bus terminals and railroad stations seeking immediate evacuation; one woman calling a bus terminal asked a clerk to "Hurry, please—the world is coming to an end!" In Harlem, hundreds more poured into churches to pray about that very thing. Every city in New England was packed with cars bearing refugees from New York. Many people living within sight of the Hudson River reported seeing the Martians on their metal stilts, crossing.

In Pittsburgh a husband discovered his wife about to swallow pills from a bottle marked POISON because she would "rather die this way than that!" A woman in Boston reported seeing the fire in the sky. In Indianapolis, a woman ran into a church, interrupting the service to scream that the world was coming to an end—she heard it on the radio!— and hundreds of parishioners scurried into the night. In sororities and fraternities, especially on the East Coast, students lined up at phones to call and tell their parents and boy- or girlfriends good-bye. In Birmingham, Alabama, the streets were rushed en masse.

In Concrete, Washington, the coincidence of a power failure served to convince the populace that the Martians had indeed landed.

James and Robert were nearing the city when the chilling, solitary voice of a ham radio operator emerged, pitifully, from their car radio's speaker.

"Two X two L, calling CQ. . . . Two X two L calling CQ. . . . Two X two L calling CQ, New York. Isn't there anyone on the air? Isn't there anyone on the air? Isn't there— anyone? . . . Two X two L. . . ."

A horrible vacant silence followed, and James (at the wheel) glanced over at Bobby; both college boys looked bloodless white. In their minds was posed the question:

Should they head north? Did they dare enter the ravaged city, to save Betty and her sister?

Then, suddenly, another voice emerged from the speaker, a pleasant, even good-natured one, saying, *"You are listening to a CBS presentation of Orson Welles and* The Mercury Theatre on the Air *in an original dramatization of 'The War of the Worlds' by H. G. Wells. . . . The performance will continue after a brief intermission. This is the Columbia Broadcasting System."*

The college boys, drenched in perspiration, looked at each other in astonishment. They didn't seem to know whether to laugh or cry, feel relief or anger.

So they stopped at a diner and had burgers.

Leroy Chapman was laughing and laughing. His little sister was, too, somewhat hysterically.

Les was shaking his twelve-year-old fist at the radio, saying, "What a gyp!"

"I told you so! I told you so!" Leroy did a little wild Indian dance. "It was the *Shadow!* It *was* the Shadow! Who knows what evil lurks in the hearts of man—yah hah hah hah hah! Leroy does! Leroy does!"

Meanwhile, Grandfather and his son Luke and several other farmers they had stumbled into, in the woods, managing not to shoot each other, were taking aim at a Martian, which rose above them on its giant metal legs, frozen against the sky, clearly about to strike.

Grandfather and Luke and the three other farmers let loose a volley of shotgun fire, but the water tower they attacked did not even seem to notice. The tower itself, with the Grovers Mill water supply therein, was safely out of firing range.

The remaining twenty minutes of the broadcast abandoned the "news bulletin" approach as Welles, playing Professor Pierson, recounted his adventures as one of earth's lone survivors. The traditional conclusion as written by H.G. Wells was reached—the Martians defeated by "the humblest thing that God in his wisdom had put upon this earth," bacteria—and Bernard Herrmann directed his orchestra in a dramatic crescendo, finally utilizing the power of the composer/conductor.

Houseman, becoming more and more aware of the chaos they had unleashed, had sent Welles a note on the subject.

This may have influenced Welles, who—having had to cut seven minutes on the fly—somehow managed to scribble a rewrite of his closing speech, even as he performed the bulk of the final section of the show, solo.

Now, Welles on his podium—smiling but perhaps a little shaky—again spoke into his microphone.

"This is Orson Welles, ladies and gentlemen—out of character to assure you that 'The War of the Worlds' has no further significance than as the holiday offering it was intended to be—the Mercury Theatre's own radio version of dressing up in a sheet and jumping out of a bush and saying Boo!"

In the sub-control booth, Dave Taylor had his face in his hands. Gibson noted that Houseman's expression was as unreadable as an Easter Island statue's.

"Starting now," Welles was saying, "we couldn't soap *all* your windows and steal *all* your garden gates, by tomorrow night, so we did the best next thing—we annihilated the world before your very ears, and utterly destroyed the CBS building. . . . You will be relieved, I hope, to learn that we didn't *mean* it, and that both institutions are still open for business."

The cast was on its feet, smiling at Orson. They had no idea what they had turned loose on America, and only knew that a mediocre show had been transformed into something special, by their gifted leader.

Who was saying, "So good-bye everybody, and remember please, for the next day or so, the terrible lesson you learned tonight—that grinning, glowing, globular invader of your living room is an inhabitant of the punkin patch, and if your doorbell rings and nobody's there . . . that was no Martian, it's Hallowe'en."

Welles cued Herrmann for the Tchaikovsky theme, and Dan Seymour returned to his mike to make the farewell: "Tonight the Columbia Broadcasting System and its affiliated stations coast-to-coast have brought you 'The War of the Worlds,' by H. G. Wells, the seventeenth in its weekly series of dramatic broadcasts featuring Orson Welles and *The Mercury Theatre on the Air*. . . . Next week we present a dramatization of three famous short stories. . . . This is the Columbia Broadcasting System."

When the clock hit nine P.M., the OFF THE AIR sign switched on.

That was when men in blue uniforms began to stream into the studio, and the grin on Welles's face froze, like a jack-o'-lantern's.

CHAPTER NINE

Times at Midnight

Walter Gibson and Jack Houseman, along with everyone else in the control booth, watched agape in astonishment as a dozen cops, billy clubs in hand, poured into the studio, like raiders in Prohibition days rushing a speakeasy.

Welles remained on his podium, a king surprised by revolting peasants, as his actors instinctively moved away, backing up almost against the far studio wall, and the blue invaders swarmed the platform. The police said nothing, but they were breathing hard, nostrils flared, nightsticks poised.

Then a plainclothes officer in a raincoat and fedora pushed through and looked up indignantly at the confused-looking figure and demanded, "Are you Welles?"

"Guilty as charged. What is—"

Gibson was following Houseman and Paul Stewart, who were on the heels of the CBS executive, Davidson Taylor, out of the control booth and down the handful of stairs onto the studio floor. The four men knifed through the small mob of blue uniforms.

The tall, slender, patrician exec faced the plainclothes officer, who was chewing on an unlit cigar.

"I'm in charge here," Taylor said. "May I ask who you are, sir?"

"Inspector Kramer," the copper said, flashing a badge, rolling the dead cigar around. "Don't you people know you've incited a riot?"

Alland helping him on with his suitcoat, Welles came down off the podium, men in blue parting grudgingly to make way, and his expression remained confused though indignation was edging in. "Inspector, we've just finished a broadcast, of a fantasy piece. How in God's name could we—"

The inspector had the remarkable faculty to squint and bug his eyes simultaneously. "You fake an invasion, with real-sounding newscasts, and you have the nerve to ask *that*?"

"How could anyone mistake what we were doing for reality?" Welles demanded. "It was little green men from Mars! We announced several *times* it wasn't real!"

Taylor put himself between the two men like a referee, hands outstretched. When he spoke, the exec's faint, gentlemanly Southern accent seemed suddenly more prominent. "Inspector, I understand you are responding to a genuine public crisis—"

Welles frowned. "Public . . . ?"

The executive threw his star a quick hard look, then his face softened as he turned toward the stogie-chomping detective. "But this building and this studio remain private property, and I do not believe you have a warrant."

The inspector had a water-splashed-in-the-face expression; the fragment of cigar almost fell out. "Warrant! Are you kidding?"

"No. I'm not. I'm going to advise Mr. Welles and everyone else involved not to answer any more of your questions until Mr. Paley arrives."

"Who the hell is Mr. Paley?"

"The president of the network. He lives in Manhattan, and he's on his way. These are our employees, and they have legal rights, like any other American."

The inspector poked a thick finger at Welles. "Well, you keep these jokers handy, understand? Till we can talk to 'em. The citizens they terrorized have 'rights,' too!"

"Fair enough," Taylor said. "Would you mind taking your people out into the lobby, for the time being?"

The inspector frowned. "What, downstairs?"

"No—just right outside. The area by the elevators on this floor will do nicely."

The inspector twitched a scowl, but he herded his night stick troop back out again. Though space was again available for the actors to move back up, they stayed put, apparently hoping that they were bystanders and not accomplices.

Welles said, "Dave, what the hell is this?"

Taylor reached a hand into a suitcoat pocket and came back with a fat pile of notes. "This is just a sampling, Orson, of what the switchboard's been getting since you finally broke in, after forty minutes, and identified the broadcast as fiction—outrage, indignation, death threats. You may especially enjoy the most recent one—it's from the mayor of Cleveland."

"Whatever have I have done to the fine city of Cleveland?"

"Oh, nothing much—apparently just unleashed mobs into the streets, sent women and children huddling in church corners, incited violence, looting. His Honor says he's coming to pay you a visit, Orson—to punch you in the nose."

Welles looked pale, much as he had when he spotted the body of the murdered woman. "I . . . I admit I thought we might light a firecracker under a certain lunatic fringe, but I . . . I apparently seriously underestimated the size of that group. And, Dave, I never dreamed it would go all across the country!"

Arching an eyebrow, Taylor waggled a finger in Welles's face and let him know what company policy was going to be: "You never dreamed *anything* like this—on any scale—would happen. Correct?"

Welles swallowed. "Correct."

"Now, brace yourself . . ."

"There's more?"

"Some of these calls indicate there may have been deaths—something about a fatal stampede in a New Jersey union hall, a suicide, some automobile fatalities as people fled the city . . ."

"My God. Is that possible?"

"None of it's confirmed, but I mention it so that you grasp the seriousness of the matter—none of your cheek, understand? You could face criminal charges—criminal negligence, even homicide."

". . . for a radio broadcast?"

"For a hoax. A kind of fraud on the public trust."

Welles said nothing; his eyes were unblinking, his mouth a soft pucker, as if he were about to kiss someone or something—perhaps his future—good-bye.

Taylor looked around and caught Paul Stewart's mournful gaze. "Paul! Front and center, please."

Stewart came to Taylor's side, as Welles faded back:

"Paul," the executive said, "you're in charge of rounding up every script and scrap and every record. . . . Were we making a transcription?"

"Yes," Stewart said .

"Is there a rehearsal acetate?"

"Yes."

Taylor pointed a stern finger at the assistant director. "You find every piece of paper and recording involved with this broadcast, timing sheets, casting calls, the works."

"What do I do with them?"

"I don't want to know."

Stewart frowned disbelievingly. "You want them destroyed?"

"No. Just . . . make them go away. Make them go somewhere these police can't find. And, oh by the way—Ben Gross of the *Daily News* is out in the lobby, and seven or eight other newshounds are with him."

Stewart's smile was sickly. "You know what they say— any publicity is good publicity."

Taylor's eyes were hooded. "Then 'they' are insane. Paul, get to it, and don't let that material fall into enemy hands—and I don't mean the Martians. Is the author around?"

Shaking his head, Stewart said, "No, Howard was beat—he heard the start of the show, then took off to catch a cab. He's probably asleep back in his apartment by now."

"Give him a call and warn him what's up. Okay?"

"Okay."

Stewart rushed off to call Koch, and do the assigned housecleaning.

Taylor pointed to Welles, Herrmann, Houseman and Gibson, *tic tic tic tic*. "Your four—come with me."

Gibson, touching a hand to his chest, said, "I'm not part of this."

"You were in on the rewrites, and you were around for everything, as I understand. Let's keep you off the firing line with these others, all right?"

Gibson nodded.

Taylor turned to face the actors and crew, who were quietly hugging the far studio wall, looking like *Lusitania* passengers waiting for a shot at a lifeboat.

"You people—if anyone from the police asks you a question, just say you reserve the right to speak to your lawyer, first. We have a whole fleet of Perry Masons to back you up."

Ray Collins stepped forward. "We didn't do anything wrong, Dave."

"None of us did—understand? None of us did. But not a peep to a cop, and any actor who talks to a reporter, looking to get his name in the paper, I'll see to it that you never appear on CBS radio again." He gave them a Southern gentleman's smile and nod. "Thank you."

Welles was standing like a big slope-shouldered lump. Gibson found it odd to see Welles in a situation where someone else had taken charge, particularly a seemingly mild-mannered sort like Davidson Taylor.

But right now Taylor was taking Welles by the arm like a naughty child being dragged to sit in the corner, and the exec looked over his shoulder and said, "You other three— come along."

· Soon Taylor was leading Welles down the hall, Houseman, Herrmann and Gibson tagging after.

"We need to stow you four out of the way," the executive was saying. "You keep put till I come back for you—understood? If you need to use the john, that's permissible, otherwise . . . consider yourselves under house arrest."

Then Taylor came to a dead stop in front of Studio Seven.

Welles looked back desperately at Houseman, who patted the air with calming palms, as if to say, *The body was gone, remember? Nothing to worry about. . . .*

The door was locked, however, and Taylor said, "Damn! I suppose we have to go after that idiot janitor Louis to be let in it."

Gibson stepped forward. "No, Mr. Taylor. I believe Jack has a passkey."

Houseman gave the writer a look that could be fathomed only by the two of them, then said, "I do indeed," and got it out of his pocket and unlocked the door.

Herrmann—who had not been part of the evening's earlier adventures involving the outdated studio—went in first. Gibson followed, and a shaken Welles entered tentatively, Houseman stepping in after.

From the doorway, Taylor said, "Lock yourselves in."

Houseman nodded, Taylor disappeared, the door was shut and locked, and chairs from the sidelines were put into use. Herrmann pulled his up at the table, ignorant of a corpse having sat there earlier.

Welles conferred with Gibson and Houseman, away from the composer.

"Jack," Welles whispered, "when I saw those blue uniforms, I thought surely—"

Houseman held up a hand. "Let's keep this to ourselves. Benny doesn't know anything about the, uh, other matter; and neither, apparently do the gendarmes."

Welles was shaking his head, obviously trying to fight off despair. "But if they search the building, Housey, who knows what they'll find? The body dumped somewhere? That bloody knife, with my signature?"

Houseman took Welles by the arm. "You have to trust me on this, Orson. Look at me. Do you believe me when I say there is no immediate danger?"

"Well, I . . . but . . ."

Houseman glanced at Gibson. "Walter, would you reassure him, please?"

Gibson said, "I can back Jack up on this. Those cops won't stumble onto anything; they have their hands full."

From the table, Herrmann stared over at the private trio with his owlish eyes wide behind the thick lenses. "Can *anyone* join the party? Aren't I as guilty as the next guy in this conspiracy?"

Houseman managed a small strained smile and called over, "Just a bit of business to deal with, Benny! Patience, please."

Gibson said, "You'll have enough to deal with, Orson, if this panic is bad as it sounds."

Welles sighed. "Housey, are we ruined?"

"We must weather this night, Orson. You must not say a word about . . . the other affair to that inspector, or to any reporters, should we encounter them. And Dave Taylor is right—you can't grant even the most qualified admission to the prank you've pulled. If there've been deaths . . ."

Welles smiled faintly, bitterly. "Isn't one murder enough?"

Houseman squeezed his friend's arm. "You just steel yourself. No admissions, no flippant remarks. Yes?"

"Yes."

Herrmann's voice had an irritated edge as he called to them from his seat at the table, where earlier blood had pooled. "Why am I the odd man out? We're all in this thing together, right?"

The confab over, the three pulled chairs up near Herrmann, but none of them could quite bring themselves to actually sit at the murder table.

"Maybe it's in bad taste," Herrmann said, hands folded on the tabletop like a schoolboy at his desk, "but I find this exciting."

"It is poor taste," Welles said.

"Still, it *is* exciting. Can't wait to call Lucille." His wife. "Jack, do you think they'll arrest Orson?"

Houseman said, "I should hope not."

"Would they arrest me?"

"Why, Benny?" Houseman said dryly. "Would you like them to?"

Herrmann chuckled. "Well, it might be an interesting experience. Composers don't often get tossed in the clink, you know."

Welles said, "Benny, shut up."

Herrmann, blinking behind the glasses, got to his feet; his face flushed, he said, "You can't talk to me like that!"

Houseman said, "Of course he can. He does it all the time. Sit down and do, please, shut up."

Herrmann huffed and puffed, but sat himself down.

Perhaps fifteen endless minutes of silence had dragged

by, when Gibson stood and stretched. "Jack, did you leave that connecting door unlocked?"

Houseman frowned. "I believe so."

"I'll be back in a moment."

The writer got up.

Welles and Houseman both frowned at him, but Gibson said, "Don't worry about it," and a few moments later he was standing in the adjacent studio.

Something had been nagging him, and he went to the pile of painter's tarps along one side and knelt. He sorted through them, and wrapped in one on the bottom, he found a heavy towel—large, like a beach towel—caked with dark red.

Obviously, this cloth had wiped up the blood on the table and been stowed here, before an escape had been made. . . .

Gibson sniffed the bloody stain, then returned the cloth to its hiding place, grunted a single laugh, rose and reentered Studio Seven.

He'd barely reached his chair when a knock on the door was followed by Taylor's voice, "I'm back—time to go, fellows."

Houseman rose and unlocked the door and let the executive in.

"I have a cab waiting," Taylor said. "We'll use the service elevator, and we should head off the press."

Welles said, "The police told us not to leave. . . ."

"Bill Paley's out there—in his pajamas and slippers with his topcoat over them, is how fast he came—and he's told the police that we will fully cooperate over the coming days, but that the network would not stand for the browbeating of its staff in this atmosphere."

Houseman said, "Really, unless they're prepared to arrest us, we have every right to go."

The exec nodded. "So it's the reporters who are the

threat, now. Orson, they'll make you their whipping boy, given half a chance—the papers have been looking for a way to give radio a black eye, and this may be it."

Herrmann was sent back to Studio One, to leave the building with the other musicians, actors and staff. The reporters would be after bigger fish than the man who conducted that sluggish "Stardust" tonight.

Through the rabbit's warren of hallways, Davidson Taylor led Welles, Houseman and Gibson to the service elevator. What no one had counted on was Ben Gross's familiarity with the building.

The *Daily News* reporter had anticipated the backdoor route, and he—and half a dozen other reporters, who knew enough to follow Gross's lead—were waiting armed and ready with questions.

As they waited for the elevator to arrive, Gross used his lead position to get out the first query: "How many deaths have been reported to CBS? We hear thousands. . . ."

Welles said nothing, swallowing, eyes darting from unfriendly face to unfriendly face.

Another reporter shouted, "How about traffic deaths? We have reports of the Jersey and upstate New York ditches teeming with corpses."

Gibson felt a sudden surge of claustrophobia as the faces and waving pencils and the sea of fedoras with press passes stuck in the hatbands surged forward. . . .

Another voice: "What word about rioting? How about that fatal stampede in Jersey . . . ?"

Hands up in surrender, Welles said, "Please . . ."

And another: "How about suicides? Have you heard about the one on Riverside Drive?"

Taylor said, "Call my office tomorrow for a statement, gentlemen."

Gross asked, "Don't you have any statement to make tonight, to the reading public, Mr. Welles?"

"None whatsoever!"

The elevator, thankfully, was there, and they stepped aboard and shut the gate on the hungry newshound horde.

Within minutes, Taylor had ushered the trio through the alley to the cab waiting out front, and they were en route to the Mercury Theatre. After all that fuss, life seemed to be going on an usual in late-night Manhattan—cars stopping for traffic, pedestrians out strolling, no riots, no stampedes to speak of. . . .

At the theater, the company had gone ahead and started rehearsing under the direction of one of Welles's assistants—*Danton's Death* would open shortly, and life (and the show) went on, whether their director deigned to drop by or not. The company was used to their leader being absent in battle, due to this radio show or that romantic rendezvous or just a restaurant meal that had gotten out of hand.

So no otherworldly sense of drama seized the auditorium—other than the cast half-falling downstairs as they were singing "Carmagnole"—and the only sign that something special was up were the several resourceful newspaper photographers who'd figured out that this was where Orson Welles would wind up, tonight.

The cast froze in the midst of their song as Welles climbed to the stage and asked them to take a break and take seats at the front of the auditorium.

When they had, he stood with the expressionistic sets as a bold backdrop, with its blankly staring and accusatory array of masks, and told them what had happened this evening. He told the story briefly but melodramatically, and Gibson could not tell whether the contrition in his voice and manner were sincere—particularly when he seemed to be posing for the photographers below, eyes raised to heaven, arms outstretched in crucifixion mode, an early Christian saint in need of a shave . . . and as Welles's beard tended to grow in most heavily in the goatee area, a paradoxical satanic aspect cast its shadow.

On the other hand, Gibson had no doubt that all the talk

of deaths—with the threat of multiple murder charges hovering—had made both Welles and Houseman genuinely remorseful, not to mention confused and frightened.

Finally, the boy-genius smiled a little, shrugged, and said, "Well, let's just say I don't think we'll choose anything quite like 'War of the Worlds' again."

Standing next to Houseman in the aisle, Gibson had been watching the actors. He whispered to the producer, "Why is the company taking this so . . . so lightly?"

"They don't believe him," Houseman said.

"Why not?"

"He's the boy who cried wolf—this is simply the most outrageous of his many outrageous excuses for keeping them waiting."

Gibson chuckled. "Well, I can see that, actually."

Houseman turned his head, raised an eyebrow. "You can, my boy?"

"Yes—you see, Jack, those three 'thugs' that accosted us last night, outside the Cotton Club? . . . They were actors Orson hired."

"Ah. You're starting to understand how he thinks."

Gibson nodded. "Yes, I heard somebody mention that he once hired actors to play police, as a practical joke on an actor friend with outstanding warrants."

"Yes indeed."

"So he hired those actors—knowing I wouldn't recognize them—to give validity, through me, an outsider, to that wild excuse he made to you and the cast, based on a nonexistent grudge between him and Owney Madden, over some dancer."

Houseman's head tilted to one side. "Well-analyzed—though the dancer exists, she just wasn't Madden's protégée. You are proving yourself quite a Shadow-worthy detective, Mr. Gibson."

"You know why I left our little temporary prison cell

back at CBS, don't you? And slipped back into Studio Eight?"

"I can't say that I do. I was, frankly, wondering."

"I found your bloody towel. The one that was used to wipe up all that blood. I sniffed it, by the way. Sickly sweet. Karo syrup, I'd say. Standard ingredient in stage blood."

Houseman bestowed a tiny smile. "How did you become aware that I had a passkey of my own?"

"Louis the janitor told me—I almost missed it, when he said you'd returned the key 'first thing.' But then that seemed an odd way to put it, unless you had *borrowed* the key the day before, to have a duplicate made, and then returned it to Louis—'first thing.' "

Houseman bowed slightly. "And with that piece of the puzzle, there was little left to solve."

Gibson gestured with an open hand. "Your accomplice was free to clean up and slip out, while we played out our part of the charade. By the way, Leo the elevator 'boy' told me of the woman who left the building, obviously not wanting to be recognized, not long after your accomplice would have made her getaway; he thought she might be Mrs. Welles, but then of course neither Mrs. Welles nor Balanchine were ever *at* the Columbia Broadcasting Building today. You had their names written into the reception book, knowing Welles's habit to check up on who'd dropped by, natural enough with all the affairs of the heart he's been juggling—and easy enough to find a Virginia Welles signature to copy. So I was sent scurrying after suspects who hadn't even been present when the crime was committed. Classic use of the first tactic of magic—misdirection."

Onstage Welles was sensing the disbelief around him.

"What *is* this skeptical murmur?" he said. "Every word is *factual*—it's all true!"

"Tell us another one," somebody said from the audience.

Laughter and catcalls followed, even a little light sarcastic applause.

One of the press photographers in the pit called something up to Welles, and the director leaned over at stage's edge to hear what the photog had to say. Smiling, the wunderkind got to his feet.

"So you don't believe me? Come with me, my flock of doubters—follow me, boys! *And* girls. . . ."

All of them—cast members still in full *Danton's Death* French Revolution drag—marched up the aisle after their leader and out into the crisp October night, as if looking for a Bastille to sack.

Gibson walked alongside Houseman. "So you wanted to teach him a lesson—and you enlisted someone else who wanted to get back at Orson, huh?"

With a sideways glance, Houseman said, "You understand, of course, I never imagined this panic would be so extensive—I would not have put Orson through that horror show, had I known—"

"Sure." Gibson fired up a Camel as they walked, waved out the match, sent it gutterbound. "But I think you did anticipate some kind of panic, otherwise you wouldn't have tried to talk our bumptious boy out of doing the show in so overt a 'newscast' fashion."

"Granted—had I foreseen the extent of it, however, I wouldn't have found it necessary to provide him that *other* opportunity for a comeuppance. . . ."

"So where's the murder weapon?"

"Back on the Mercury office wall."

In Times Square, on southeast corner of Broadway and 42nd Street, awash in neon and with a good view of the Times Building and its lighted bulletin, the so-called Moving News sign that circled the venerable paper's building, Welles assembled his Revolutionary army.

"There," he said, and pointed, as if to a star. In a way, he was: his own.

ORSON WELLES CAUSES PANIC, the sign flashed. MARS INVASION BROADCAST FRIGHTENS NATION.

His company, believers again, emitted *ooohs* and *aaaahs,* then began to applaud. And Welles, despite all that hovered over him, began to smile, and took a small, humble bow.

A shapely figure in one of the French low-cut peasant dresses slipped an arm through Welles's. "Hi, Orson. Hope you don't mind—Jack gave me a part in the chorus."

Welles's eyes narrowed, then widened, as he realized who was standing beside him. "Dolores?"

"No hard feelings?" Dolores Donovan said, with mischievous malice, and perhaps some affection.

For a moment he looked stricken, as if the lovely blue-eyed strawberry-blonde might be an apparition; then his eyes searched for Houseman, who ambled up to his other side, Gibson following. Everyone was doused in the red of a dancing neon advertising soap flakes.

Sounding like a little boy, Welles said, "Housey—it was just a . . . ?"

" 'Hoax' is the word, I believe." Houseman touched Welles's sleeve. "And my dear Orson, I would never have subjected you this terrible practical joke, had I known—"

Welles hugged Dolores, kissed her on the mouth. Then he looked at her tenderly and said, "I'm so glad you're alive—and by God, I'm glad, too, to have an actress of your caliber in my company."

Then he turned her loose, and—giving Houseman a hard look—said, "Is this that lesson you promised?"

"It was meant to be, but—"

"But I'll need more than one, right?"

"Very possibly," Houseman granted.

And Welles slipped an arm around his friend and began to laugh and laugh and laugh, a Falstaffian roar of a laugh that seemed to relieve Houseman a great deal. But Gibson sensed some hysteria in it.

Which was only fair, after all, considering the hysteria Orson Welles had launched tonight.

The *Times* sign was announcing the time: twelve A.M. Midnight.

"It's Hallowe'en, everyone," Welles thundered. "It is finally . . . at long last, really and truly . . . Hallowe'en."

CHAPTER TEN

The Trial

Walter Gibson had been scheduled to go back on the train to Philly on Monday morning, and—though hardly a lick of work on the project for which he'd been brought to Manhattan had been accomplished—that was what he did. Most of the way he slept, because he'd lingered at the Mercury Theatre as the *Danton's Death* rehearsal got under way shortly after midnight. Around dawn, he'd exchanged casual but friendly good-byes with both Houseman and Welles, the latter assuring him they'd be getting together again soon, to "really get down to work" on the Shadow script.

The aftermath of the "invasion," then, was something Gibson witnessed secondhand. He saw the newspaper headlines—RADIO LISTENERS IN PANIC, TAKING WAR DRAMA AS FACT (the *Times*); FAKE RADIO "WAR" STIRS TERROR THROUGH U.S. (the *Daily News*); and the *Herald Tribune* wrote of "hysteria, panic and sudden conversions to religion," in the wake of the invasion from Mars.

Contacted in England, H.G. Wells himself objected to the Welles adaptation, complaining (without having actually heard the broadcast) that apparently too many liberties had been taken with his material, and that he was "deeply concerned" that his work would be used "to cause distress and alarm throughout the United States." (Later Wells and Welles would meet and the former would express a revised opinion, backing Orson all the way, and wondering why it was that Americans were so easily fooled—hadn't they ever heard of Hallowe'en?)

CBS issued an elaborate apology and announced a new policy of banning any such simulated news broadcasts, which NBC also pompously adopted. Both CBS and the Mercury Theatre denied that the broadcast had been designed as a publicity stunt to promote the upcoming opening of *Danton's Death*. The Federal Communications Commission studied the "regrettable" matter, but never took action, despite a dozen formal protests.

The talk of criminal charges fluttered away in a day—there had been no deaths, so the "murders" the press tried to scare Welles with (in the immediate aftermath of the broadcast) were as big a hoax as the broadcast itself.

And while the litigation war drums pounded for some weeks, none of the claims went anywhere, though Welles—over the protests of Davidson Taylor and William Paley—did honor a request for the price of a pair of black shoes, size 9B, whose prospective owner had used the designated funds to buy a bus ticket to escape the Martians.

Public indignation raged only briefly, though some of it was stinging, the *New York Times* scolding Welles and CBS for creating a "wave of panic in which it inundated the nation."

But somehow the entire event was best characterized by the final phone call the CBS switchboard received, around three A.M. after the broadcast, which was from a truck driver in Chicago who asked if this was the network that put on the show about the Martian invasion; when the switchboard operator confirmed as much, the listener said his wife had got so riled up over the show, she ran outside, fell down the stairs and broke her leg. A long pause, and then:

"Jeez," the listener said wistfully, "that was a *wonderful* broadcast. . . ."

Welles liked to display a cable he received from the real FDR (as opposed to Kenny Delmar), who commented on the Mars Invasion upstaging Charlie McCarthy: THIS ONLY GOES TO PROVE, MY BEAMISH BOY, THAT THE INTELLIGENT PEOPLE WERE ALL LISTENING TO THE DUMMY, AND ALL THE DUMMIES WERE LISTENING TO YOU.

Such whimsy soon came to dominate coverage of the event, and within days the public's reaction had shifted to amusement and even appreciation.

A New York *Tribune* writer, Dorothy Thompson, said it best: "Unwittingly, Mr. Orson Welles and *The Mercury Theatre on the Air* have made one of the most fascinating and important demonstrations of all time—they have proved that a few effective voices, accompanied by sound effects, can convince masses of people of a totally unreasonable, completely fantastic proposition to create a nationwide panic."

This, the writer said, indicated the "appalling dangers and enormous effectiveness of popular and theatrical demagoguery. . . . Hitler managed to scare all of Europe to its knees a month ago, but he at least had an army and an air force to back up his shrieking words. But Mr. Welles scared thousands into demoralization with nothing at all."

She went to say that Welles had thrown a "brilliant and cruel light" on education in America; that thousands of the populace had been shown to be stupid, lacking in nerve but not short of ignorance; that primeval fears lay beneath the "thinnest surface of civilized man"; and "how easy it was to start a mass delusion."

The *Nation* made a chilling point similar to Thompson's:

the real cause of the panic was "the sea of insecurity and actual ignorance over which a superficial literacy and sophistication are spread like a thin crust."

Many years later, Welles would admit, "The thing that gave me the idea for it was that we had a lot of real radio nuts on as commentators at this period—people who wanted to keep us out of European entanglements, and a fascist priest called Father Coughlin. And people believed anything they heard on the radio. So I said, 'Let's do something impossible and make them believe it.' And then tell them, show them, that it's only . . . radio."

But at a Hallowe'en Day news conference in 1938, Welles told a different story. By the time Gibson saw excerpts in a newsreel, the furor had already died down, and last week seemed ancient history.

There Welles was, a few hours after Gibson had last seen him at the theater, now on trial before a battery of reporters, looking schoolboy contrite, a little bewildered and vaguely devilish with his goatee-ish need of a shave.

He was "deeply shocked and deeply regretful," and when asked if he was aware of the panic such a broadcast might stir up, he claimed, "Definitely not."

Some found him charming in the press conference; other shifty. Some saw a "palpably shaken," repentant young man, while others considered him "hammy," and "insulting" in the transparent way he feigned surprised dismay. One report had him, on the way out, flashing Jack Houseman a wink and an OK sign.

Welles's writer, Howard Koch, who had so brilliantly executed the prank in play form, missed the fuss, at least initially. Sunday night, when he got home, he had listened to the rest of the broadcast, felt satisfied they'd all transcended the weak material, and dropped exhausted into bed. He had slept through the ringing phone, as Paul Stewart tried to alert him to the panic and the press.

Hallowe'en morning, he'd gone out to get a haircut and

heard odd, even ominous snatches of conversation on the sidewalk, pedestrians talking of "panic" and "invasion." The scriptwriter thought that perhaps the inevitable war with Hitler had finally broken out.

When he asked his barber what was going on, the hair-cutter showed him a front page with a headline blaring, NA-TION IN A PANIC FROM MARTIAN BROADCAST.

Like Welles, Koch wondered if he was finished; but a call from Hollywood soon came, and the co-organizer of the Martian Invasion would go on to one of the most distinguished careers in the history of screenwriting, including a little picture in 1942 called *Casablanca*.

Welles had not been ruined, either, though there was no saving *Danton's Death* from the director's pretensions. The production could not even ride the biggest wave of publicity the city had ever seen, and—after mostly withering reviews—closed after a mere twenty-one performances. The Mercury Theatre would not last another season.

In later years Welles liked to point out that broadcasts in other countries, patterned on his "War of the Worlds," had resulted in jail for their perpetrators and that one radio station in Spain had even been burned to the ground.

"But *I* got a contract in Hollywood," he said.

Back in 1938, Welles and the Mercury were now suddenly world-famous. Within a week of the "invasion," *The Mercury Theatre on the Air* went from being an unsponsored, "sustaining" show to acquiring Campbell Soup as a sponsor. Changes were made—popular novels joined literary warhorses as grist for the Mercury mill, and each week a famous guest star appeared. For an adaptation of Daphne DuMaurier's *Rebecca,* Bernard Herrmann composed a full score, which prefigured his many famous film scores. Much of it was used by Herrmann, in fact, for the 1943 film of *Jane Eyre,* starring and produced by Welles from a script cowritten by Houseman.

Hollywood, of course, was Welles's ultimate reward for

the Mars Invasion, and perhaps his punishment. He was greeted as a genius, then denounced for considering himself such; his talent led to *Citizen Kane,* the 1941 film that tops most "best films of all time" lists, but his arrogance in lampooning William Randolph Hearst (and the newspaper magnate's mistress Marion Davies) created enemies who threw obstacles in Welles's career path his entire life.

In 1975, in our little corner of the Palmer House bar, the white-haired, spectacled Gibson had spent almost two hours with me, sharing the secret story of his "weekend with Orson." He seemed a little tired, but I was a kid, wired up by what I'd heard, and didn't know when to stop.

"What happened to the 'Shadow' project?" I asked.

"*That* 'weed of crime' bore no evil fruit," Gibson said, invoking the famous closing lines of the Shadow radio show. "And like the Mystery Writers of America say, crime doesn't pay . . . enough."

"Well, the proposed 'Shadow' movie was with Warner Bros., right?"

"Yes, but after the Mars broadcast, every studio in Hollywood was waving contracts at Orson, and the one he took, of course, was with RKO . . . which he famously described as a 'the biggest train set a boy ever had.' "

"So he just dropped it, the Shadow movie, when—"

"No. Orson often came back to a project, again and again—some of his finished films were shot over many years, remember. Around 1945, after he'd had some setbacks, we talked again about doing the Shadow feature, and that dialogue continued sporadically over the years— hell, just a couple of years ago, I was approached about a Shadow TV pilot that Orson was behind."

"He's a little . . . heavy to play the Shadow now, isn't he?"

Gibson smiled and sipped the last of his latest glass of beer. "Well, he still dresses like the Shadow—the slouch hat, the dark clothes. . . . Sometimes I think, for all his

Shakespearean proclivities, of every role he ever played, Orson liked the Shadow best."

I let out a laugh. "It's the whole magician persona—the cape, the aura of the unexplained, the sly smile. . . ."

Our pitcher of beer was almost gone. Gibson poured me half a glass, and himself the same. We were approaching the end.

"You know," Gibson said, something bittersweet entering his voice, "Jack Houseman and Orson—one of the really great artistic teams in show business history—split up a few years after the broadcast. And I always thought Jack's prank on Orson, the murderous 'lesson' he tried to teach him, was the first crack in the wall."

"But you said Orson only laughed about it?"

Gibson nodded, eyes tight behind the lenses. "As I'm sure you know, Orson has a big booming laugh, and it covers up a lot of different emotions—it can be filled with contempt as easily as amusement."

"And you sensed that, that night?"

He didn't answer directly, saying instead, "Houseman made the Hollywood trip, too, you know—they did the radio show from out there, took the cast with them . . . Joe Cotten had never been in a movie before Kane. Herrmann took the ride, too, did the *Kane* music, beautifully. But Orson and Houseman quarreled—they say Orson threw a burning Sterno dish at Houseman, set a curtain on fire . . . this was at Chasen's."

"Only, Houseman did work on *Kane,* right?"

"He worked with Mankiewicz, out of Orson's presence. Their draft of the *Kane* script was another Houseman prank—Kane was based more on Orson himself than Hearst!"

"And Welles didn't even realize it?"

Shaking his head, laughing, Gibson said, "Of course he did! But it was his perverse, willful nature to do it anyway, and he emphasized the resemblance even more in *his* drafts. . . . He and Houseman only worked a time or two together, after that. Currently, sadly . . . they're enemies. Each the sworn nemesis of the other."

I shook my head. "Funny—here Houseman is, quarter of a century later, having his greatest success as an old man . . ."

The 1973 film *The Paper Chase* had been a big hit with Houseman portraying crusty Professor Kingsfield, which had sparked a latter-day acting career for the producer.

Gibson picked up on it. ". . . while Welles had his greatest success as a *young* man, with the Mercury Theatre and *Kane*. Odd bookends to two careers, both of which would probably've been greater if they'd remained collaborators."

We sipped beer.

I smiled at him in open admiration. "You know, for a fan like me? Boggles my mind to imagine a Shadow film written by you and directed by, and starring, Orson Welles!"

The jowly, avuncular face split in a bittersweet grin. "That would've been fun. But it's not like I don't have anything to show for it all."

"How so?"

With a magician's grace and showmanship, he removed the impressive gold ring with the fire opal, the replica of the Shadow's ring that he said he always wore.

"I received this in the mail," Gibson said, "about a month after that memorable weekend. There was no note, but the return address was the St. Regis Hotel. . . . Look at the inscription."

Inside the ring were the words: *From Lamont Cranston.*

"You know," Gibson said, "I sent Orson a package once myself, keeping an old promise. . . ."

Again Gibson stared into the past.

"During the Second World War," he said, "Orson put up a tent on Cahuenga Boulevard in L.A., and he and his

Mercury players put on *The Mercury Wonder Show,* strictly for servicemen, and for free—sawing Rita Hayworth and Marlene Dietrich in half, Agnes Moorehead playing the calliope, Joe Cotten playing stooge, lots of pretty starlets of the Dolores Donovan variety, as magician's assistants. He took his magic show to a lot of army camps, too."

I had no idea where this was going, but I remained as hypnotized by this great pulp storyteller as the victims of the Shadow.

"Hearing about this magic show prompted me to keep my promise," Gibson said. "I sent him the works on my Hindu wand routine . . . the one Houdini liked, but didn't live to use? And Orson put it in his act—the night he got it."

That seemed as good a curtain line as any, and I picked up the check. Then we walked out into the lobby, chatting, and at the elevators went our separate ways.

I talked to Gibson once more, casually, at another Bouchercon a few years later in New York, where he performed his magic act for an enthusiastic audience of mystery writers and fans. In his last years, Gibson enjoyed these fun encounters with his public (he, too, became a Bouchercon Guest of Honor), thanks to the efforts of enthusiasts like Otto Penzler, Anthony Tollin and J. Randolph Cox. The man who was "Maxwell Grant" finally had a little of the large fame he deserved.

He was still active as a freelancer writer—and practicing magician—right up to his death in 1996.

Welles left us in October of 1985, at an ancient and yet so very young seventy. He had become the quintessential maverick of moviemakers, seeking money and shooting movies in every corner of the globe, funding his films with acting jobs that were often beneath him and, most famously, as a TV commercial pitchman for wine and other products; despite the legend that, after *Citizen Kane,* he had no real career as a director, his body of work—not counting scores of acting appearances, and projects finished by others or as yet unreleased—includes thirteen films, most of which are wonderful, every one of which is of interest.

He, too, was active up to the day he died: in a manner that would have suited Gibson, the Shadow actor departed at a desk, working on a screenplay.

At his typewriter.

A Tip of the Shadow's Slouch Hat

Author's Note: the reader is advised not to peruse this bibliographic essay prior to finishing the novel.

The War of the Worlds Murder—like previous books in my so-called "disaster" series—features a real-life crime-fiction writer as the amateur detective in a fact-based mystery. This is, however, the first time I have used a writer I actually met and spoke to at length.

That does not mean that the fictionalized memoirs that open and close this novel should be viewed as a verbatim account of my real meeting with Walter Gibson. I will say only that much of it did happen . . . just not all of it. I do not possess the gift of total recall, so conversations not only with Gibson but such writer friends as Robert J. Randisi, Percy Spurlark Parker and the late Chris Steinbrunner range from approximations to outright fabrications. The encounter with a Mickey Spillane–hating Mystery Writers of America icon (who appears here under a nom de plume) certainly did occur at Bouchercon Six. To this day people talk to me about it, and I don't know whether to be proud or ashamed.

I choose not to reveal whether or not Walter Gibson told me of his adventures working with Orson Welles on a Shadow project the weekend "The War of the Worlds" was aired. Certainly none of the official accounts note his presence; however, Gibson did know Welles through magic circles—several sources confirm this—and one source (mentioned below) insists that, so to speak, Gibson cast his own Shadow, recommending the young actor for the radio role of Lamont Cranston. It's also true that Gibson wore an elaborate Shadow ring, inscribed to him by "Cranston."

My longtime research associate, George Hagenauer, is a pulp magazine enthusiast, and was typically helpful, including devising the "murder" herein, and generally aiding on the magic-oriented aspects of the story.

Leonard Maltin—to whom this book was dedicated prior to his coming to my aid here, I must add—responded to my cry for research help by connecting me with a man who was present that historic night, directing the CBS radio show that would go on right after "The War of the Worlds."

Norman Corwin was in the studio above Studio One in the Columbia Broadcasting Building on October 30, 1938, and in 2004 he was graciously willing to share with me his memories about radio in general and the CBS Building in particular. Mr. Corwin—at 94, sharper than I have ever been—was warm, friendly, funny and patient. Only fans of the Golden Age of Radio will understand what it meant for me to talk to Norman Corwin, not just a pioneer in that medium, but one of the few greats of the form—it was like writing a movie book and being helped by Alfred Hitchcock, Charlie Chaplin or John Ford. Thank you, Mr. Corwin. Thank you, Leonard.

That said, I must point out that any inaccuracies in this book are my own. A few are even intentional. Some of what Mr. Corwin told me about life and work in the Columbia

Broadcasting Building in the late 1930s did not suit my purposes as a mystery writer, and I ignored or revised the truth into fiction as needed; but while nothing that is wrong here is the fault of Mr. Corwin, or my other research associates, much that is right belongs to them.

In this vein, I will admit that the term "pulp" was not in widespread use in 1938—"character magazines" would seem to be the correct coinage for the market Walter Gibson mastered. I run into this from time to time—"art deco" is a designation that came along after the period it describes, for example—and, while I generally do my best to avoid anachronisms, I occasionally choose to use a "wrong" term (like "pulps") because in the larger context of what I'm doing, it's "right."

Also, inconsistencies between sources were frequent here; a typical example: some say the police entered Studio One before the broadcast was over and stared threateningly at Welles through the control-room glass, while other accounts indicate the police rushed in right after the broadcast ended (one even says the police showed up several hours later). In such instances, I trust either my instincts or follow the needs of my narrative.

The connection between Welles and Gibson is not directly dealt with in Thomas J. Shimeld's biography of the Shadow creator, *Walter B. Gibson and the Shadow* (2003). Still, it's hard for me to imagine writing this novel without that vital resource, and any sense of the man that might be found in these pages results as much from Shimeld's good book as my own meeting with Gibson. To date, the only other book-length work on Gibson is *Man of Magic and Mystery: A Guide to the Work of Walter B. Gibson* (1988) by J. Randolph Cox, a bibliographic work of limited but appreciated help to this novel. Other works consulted relating to Gibson include his own *The Shadow Scrapbook* (1979) (introduction by Chris Steinbrunner); *Walter Gibson's Encyclopedia of Magic & Conjuring* (1976); and *The*

Shadow Knows . . . (1977), Diana Cohen and Irene Burns Hoeflinger, a collection of radio scripts.

Anthony Tollin has contributed his expertise on the history of radio to numerous fact-filled booklets included with boxed sets of old radio shows on CD and cassette, often for the first-rate Radio Spirits. Such booklets on both the Shadow and Orson Welles were most helpful here.

The notion for this novel seemed a natural—that the sixth "disaster" novel would involve the world's most famous *fake* disaster. And I frankly thought it would be a relatively easy book to write, compared to such major events as the Pearl Harbor attack and the sinking of the *Lusitania*. What George Hagenauer later reminded me—when I was drowning in research—was that when I wrote my Black Dahlia novel, *Angel in Black* (2001), the single Orson Welles chapter took as much research as the entire rest of the book, which covered a very complicated and convoluted murder case.

This novel took much longer to write than is usually my process, because I just could not stop reading about Welles and watching his films. In terms of the latter, the late Charlie Roberts of Darker Image Video provided numerous rare items, including the American Film Institute tribute to Welles, a BBC documentary on the filmmaker, and a vintage TV play, "The Night America Trembled." I screened most of Welles's films, including *Chimes at Midnight* (1966) and *The Immortal Story* (1968), criminally unavailable in the United States, and three documentaries: Gary Graver's *Working with Orson Welles* (1995); *It's All True* (1994), narrated by my pal Miguel Ferrer; and *The Dominici Affair* (2001), which explores a famous French murder case (the latter two films attempt to assemble and complete unfinished Welles projects).

And Welles touches on "The War of the Worlds" in his wonderful free-form documentary, *F for Fake* (1973)—in which he wanders between shots in a Shadow cape and slouch hat, and all "excerpts" from the broadcast are bogus!

Books on this great American filmmaker/actor are not in short supply, and the ones I found most beneficial are *Citizen Welles* (1989), Frank Brady; *Orson Welles: The Road to Xanadu* (1997), Simon Callow; the Welles-approved *Orson Welles: A Biography* (1995), Barbara Leaming; and *Rosebud: The Story of Orson Welles* (1996), David Thomson.

But I would like to single out *This Is Orson Welles* by Welles and Peter Bogdanovich, as a wonderful collection of interviews (edited and rewritten and shaped by Welles). The revised, expanded edition of 1998 is much preferred, as the additional autobiographical introductory essay ("My Orson") by Bogdanovich is well worth the price of admission, and arguably the best glimpse into the real Welles available anywhere. No one writes about the important figures of classic Hollywood with more intelligence, candor, humor, warmth, insight and humanity than Bogdanovich.

Other Welles books consulted include: *Citizen Kane: The Fiftieth-Anniversary Album* (1990), Harlan Lebo; *The Making of Citizen Kane* (1985), Robert L. Carringer; *Orson Welles* (1971), Maurice Bessy; the controversial *Orson Welles: The Rise and Fall of an American Genius* (1985), Charles Higham; *Orson Welles: Actor and Director* (1977), Joseph McBride; *Orson Welles* (1986), John Russell Taylor; *Orson Welles Interviews* (2002), edited by Mark W. Estrin; *Orson Welles: The Stories of His Life* (2003), Peter Conrad; and *Orson Welles* (1972), Joseph McBride. Years ago I read Pauline Kael's *The Citizen Kane Book* (1971), but I find it unkind and poorly researched, and didn't bother to dip back in.

A few magazines were of use: "The Man from Mercury" in the June, 1938, *Coronet* included many photos of the theater company at work; and *Photocrime* (a 1944 one-shot from "The editors of *LOOK*") included a photo-spread mystery story starring magician Orson Welles—a George Hagenauer find.

My portrait of Welles is a "best guess" based upon all I've read and seen, but its roots are in the memoirs of his estranged ex-partner, John Houseman. Including Houseman as a character was a treat, if a challenge, as I loved Houseman's Professor Kingsfield in the film and television series, *The Paper Chase*; his autobiographical *Entertainers and the Entertained* (1986) and *Run-through* (1972) are fascinating, frank, vividly written accounts.

Many (including Welles) consider Houseman to be an enemy of Welles's reputation; and yet for all the dirty laundry aired in his memoirs, Houseman's respect and love for the artist and man are palpable. It seems to me most of Welles's films—from *Citizen Kane* (1941) to *Touch of Evil* (1958), from *Othello* (1952) to *Chimes at Midnight*—are driven by the subtext of this failed friendship. Their bittersweet platonic "affair" provided me with a solid central conflict for a novel about this event and these times.

If the portrait herein of Houseman is largely drawn from his own memoirs, the sketches of other real figures come from straight biographies: Bernard Herrmann in Steven C. Smith's *A Heart at Fire's Center* (1991); and Judy Holliday in Will Holtzman's *Judy Holliday: A Biography* (1982). Obviously, neither Herrmann nor Holliday are central figures here, but my interest in and love for the work of both made including them irresistible. Others in the Mercury Theatre world were excluded due to space limitations, or redundancy: Joseph Cotten, for example, didn't have anything to do with "The War of the Worlds," and Richard Wilson was just another of the faithful Welles "stooges" who are represented herein by William Alland.

Most of the characters in this novel are real people, and appear under their own names. Dolores Donovan is a fictional character, however, as are such minor players as the security guards at the Columbia Broadcasting Building, the "thugs" in the alley sequence, and other spear-carriers. Throughout the "War of the Worlds" section, I have centered on real people caught up in the panic, but have changed or slightly modified their names, to give me more latitude.

The experience of the New York State troopers comes from Carmine J. Motto's *In Crime's Way* (2000) and my friend Jim Doherty's excellent *Just the Facts—True Tales of Cops & Criminals* (2004); Jim pointed me toward this colorful, amusing incident. A highly respected serious study, *The Invasion from Mars: A Study in the Psychology of Panic* (1940) by Hadly Cantril, provided a factual basis for the stories of the Dorn sisters, James Roberts Jr., and several lesser players herein. The Ben Gross storyline is derived from the critic's lively autobiography, *I Looked and I Listened* (1954, revised 1970). *Ponzi Schemes, Invaders from Mars & More Extraordinary Popular Delusions and the Madness of Crowds* (1992) by Joseph Bulgatz provided not only a great overview article, but the basis for the Chapman family's experience. Into Bulgatz's description of a farm family's reaction to the broadcast, I folded in the fact (relished by Welles) that numerous kids recognized the voice of the Shadow, and hence were *not* fooled, plus the famous foray of several farmers who tilted against the windmill of a Grovers Mill water tower (an event Welles— whose unfinished film of *Don Quixote* costarred Patty McCormack, star of my *Mommy* films—no doubt also relished).

A great website—www.war-ofthe-worlds.co.uk—provided great general background, plus the story of the Princeton journalism student and the geology professor who drove to Grovers Mill on the night of the "invasion."

Two books—both containing Howard Koch's classic script for the radio play—are vital to any examination of the incident (the Cantril study also includes the Koch script). *The Panic Broadcast: Portrait of an Event* (1970) includes Koch's own memoir of the event and a many-years-later visit to Grovers Mill. *The Complete War of the Worlds*

(2001), Brian Holmsten and Alex Lubertozzi, editors, is a definitive work, lavishly illustrated, including not just Koch's script but the H.G. Wells novella and even a CD of the original broadcast in the context of an aural documentary narrated by John Callaway; it includes the historic on-air meeting of Welles (Orson) and Wells (H.G.).

For the record, the excerpts herein are transcriptions by me from the broadcast, not taken from the actual script, which does not include certain pauses, ad-libs and actor's on-the-fly "revisions." I use these excerpts not to tell the story of the play, but to give context to the national panic attack, and for the full impact of the piece, readers are urged to seek out Koch's complete, excellent script as well as the broadcast itself (and *The Complete War of the Worlds* provides both).

A rare audio-only laser disc, *Theatre of the Imagination: Radio Stories by Orson Welles & the Mercury Theatre* (1988), includes detailed liner notes and a Leonard Maltin–narrated documentary written by Frank Beacham, "The Mercury Company Remembers," with Houseman, William Alland, Richard Wilson and other Mercury Theatre veterans talking not just about Welles and the radio show, but specifically about "The War of the Worlds" (Houseman is particularly compelling). The liner notes—unsigned but presumably by Beacham, who (with longtime Welles crony Wilson) produced the laser disc—includes the following piece of information about *The Shadow* radio show: "Welles became the lead because of his friendship with Walter Gibson, a fellow magician."

Vital to this novel, Leonard Maltin's rich, rewarding *The Great American Broadcast: A Celebration of Radio's Golden Age* (1997) is an anecdotal history of the medium. The next most valuable work to this effort was a lavishly photo-illustrated children's book, *Radio Workers* (1940) by Alice V. Keliher (editor), Franz Hess, Marion LeBron, Rudolf Modley and Stuart Ayers. General radio histories consulted include *Don't Touch That Dial: Radio Programming in American Life from 1920 to 1950* (1979), J. Fred MacDonald; *On the Air: The Encyclopedia of Old-Time Radio* (1998), John Dunning; *On the Air: Pioneers of American Broadcasting* (1988), Amy Henderson; *Tune in Yesterday: The Ultimate Encyclopedia of Old-Time Radio 1925–1976* (1976), John Dunning (including an especially detailed entry on Mercury and "War of the Worlds"); and *The Encyclopedia of American Radio* (1996, 2000), Ron Lackmann.

The following aided in re-creating the nightclub scene in 1930s New York: *Intimate Nights: The Golden Age of New York Cabaret* (1991), James Gavin; *Jazz: A History of America's Music* (2000), Geoffrey C. Ward and Ken Burns; *Nightclub Nights: Art, Legend, and Style, 1920–1960* (2001), Susan Waggoner; and *The Night Club Era* (1933), Stanley Baker. In the Baker book, material on Owney Madden was particularly useful, as was *The Mafia Encyclopedia* (1987) by Carl Sifakis. Another Sifakis book, *Hoaxes and Scams: A Compendium of Deceptions, Ruses and Swindles* (1993), was also consulted.

I screened a somewhat rare TV movie, director Joseph Sargent's *The Night That Panicked America* (1975), which does an excellent job of re-creating the broadcast and its circumstances, as well as dealing with fictional but typical examples of listener reaction. The late Paul Shenar is excellent as Welles, and John Bosley, John Ritter, Meredith Baxter and other TV stalwarts of the '70s do right by material written by Nicholas Meyer, who would go on to write and direct the wonderful film *Time After Time*, in which H.G. Wells uses his time machine to chase Jack the Ripper to the future. Paul Stewart is one of the main characters and is listed as a consultant; strangely, John Houseman is not depicted.

There's no sham about the thanks I need to express to my patient editor, Natalee Rosenstein, and her associate

Esther Strauss, who were typically understanding when the research for this book made what I'd assumed would be the easiest to write of these novels very possibly the hardest. My thanks go to my always supportive wife, Barb; my son and website guru, Nate (www.maxallancollins.com); and the able Dominick Abel, friend and agent (in that order).

My approach to the "disaster" novels has always been to research the event, first, and come up with an appropriate mystery, second, so that my fiction would interweave and complement and even grow out of the facts. As I explored the Mars Invasion Panic, I start wondering if I dared make the murder itself a hoax—I ran the basic concept by Barb, Nate and George Hagenauer, and all of them thought my approach would be both amusing and appropriate. In the aftermath of the broadcast, both Welles and Houseman believed they might well face multiple murder charges for the deaths their stunt provoked (the media leading the pair to believe many had died, when in fact no one had). Sending out this message from the Punkin Patch, I can only bid my readers good-bye, and assure them that . . . I didn't mean it . . . and remain their obedient servant.

About the Author

MAX ALLAN COLLINS, a Mystery Writers of America Edgar nominee in both fiction and nonfiction categories, was hailed in 2004 by *Publishers Weekly* as "a new breed of writer." He has earned twelve Private Eye Writers of America Shamus nominations for his historical thrillers, winning twice for his Nathan Heller novels, *True Detective* (1983) and *Stolen Away* (1991). His other credits include film criticism, short fiction, songwriting, trading-card sets, and movie/TV tie-in novels, including *Air Force One* and the *New York Times*–bestselling *Saving Private Ryan*.

His graphic novel *Road to Perdition* is the basis of the Academy Award–winning DreamWorks 2002 film starring Tom Hanks, Paul Newman and Jude Law, directed by Sam Mendes. His many comics credits include the "Dick Tracy" syndicated strip (1977–1993); his own "Ms. Tree"; "Batman"; and "C.S.I.," based on the hit TV series for which he has also written video games, jigsaw puzzles, and a *USA Today*–bestselling series of novels.

As an independent filmmaker, he wrote and directed

Mommy, premiering on Lifetime in 1996, and a 1997 sequel, *Mommy's Day.* The screenwriter of *The Expert,* a 1995 HBO World Premiere, he wrote and directed the innovative made-for-DVD feature, *Real Time: Siege at Lucas Street Market* (2000). *Shades of Noir* (2004) is an anthology of his short films, including his award-winning documentary, *Mike Hammer's Mickey Spillane.*

Collins lives in Muscatine, Iowa, with his wife, writer Barbara Collins; their son Nathan is majoring in computer science and Japanese at the University of Iowa in nearby Iowa City.